SUNSET OF THE DEAD
A ZOMBIE NOVEL

SUNSET OF THE DEAD
A ZOMBIE NOVEL

ANTHONY GIANGREGORIO

MORE LIVING DEAD PRESS BOOKS TO SINK YOUR TEETH INTO!

Prologue

"Choke on 'em! Choke on 'em!" the soon-to-be-dead Captain Stephen Rhodes screamed, as blood gushed from his mouth in dark-red bubbles.

The living dead dragging his legs away to feed ignored his taunts, concentrating on the food before them.

The man had been ripped in half by the walking dead surrounding him. Not that he felt the pain after being shot multiple times by a gun-crazy zombie. Who knew the dead could shoot firearms?

In those brief seconds before his life faded into oblivion, he thought about Dr. Logan, aka Frankenstein, and wished he could kill the man one more time before Rhodes' consciousness was let loose from this world.

The zombie that had shot Rhodes—nicknamed Bub by Dr. Logan—saluted and walked away, ignoring Rhodes' screams as the dead fed on his entrails. Rhodes' eyes were wide in amazement. *Are those really my insides spilling out of where my lower half used to be?* he thought in amazement. *Fuck, but that's impossible. My insides belong inside me. Fuck, fuck, FUCK!* he screamed in his head, his body going numb, shock taking over as blood loss and severe trauma began to claim his life.

He was dragged into a room, one he wasn't familiar with, or at least one he had never entered before. Nor should he have. He was in a section of the underground Florida bunker where the scientists had worked, and he had little to no use for them.

The fucks; at least they're all dead, too! he thought. *Fuck, fuck, fuck!* his mind screamed over and over.

Of all the things a man could think of as he was about to die, that word wouldn't be among the one chosen by many people, but Rhodes wasn't *many* people. He was a tough-as-nails soldier, who had worked his way up the ladder to become a captain by sheer willpower.

Of course, he was the captain in a nonexistent military. The Army was gone, the Navy was gone, the Air Force and Marines were gone, the entire fucking government was gone.

Fucking bureaucrats, he thought. *They did this to me! They're no different than the goddamn scientists I had to baby-sit in this underground fucking shithole! Fuck, fuck, fuck. Sarah, that bitch, this is all her fault! Fuck, fuck, fuck!*

That was the last thing that went though his mind as he succumbed to death and the dead began to grab his shirt and rip into his flesh. But just as they began to tear into him, an explosion ripped through the ceiling, sending cement and dirt falling on Rhodes and the dead trying to devour him.

Rhodes knew none of this, for he was already dead, but the zombies around him knew it, not that they understood anything. The rubble crushed bodies by the dozen, and only a few corpses falling on top of Rhodes prevented the late Captain from being crushed and flattened like a pancake.

A quite coincidental chain of events had happened only seconds earlier, the result the ensuing explosion.

The walking dead sometimes attempted to do something they had done when they were alive. Call it muscle memory of some simple task done with so much repetition in life that even in death the memory remained. One zombie—now nothing but a burnt corpse—in the next hallway over, wore a construction uniform. It was still holding the electrical wires that the dead man had pulled from a junction box, while beside it another zombie had used a hammer it held to break open a gas line. The resulting mixture of electricity and gas had caused an explosion that had burned both ghouls to a crisp, and then had ripped up into the ceiling, roiled across the gap between the two hallways, to then rupture the ceiling of the room Rhodes was in.

But no human being knew this, nor would any living person ever find out. All the humans in the bunker were either dead or fleeing for their lives, and the walking dead could keep a secret.

Inside the room that had collapsed, the dust slowly began to settle, but one fluorescent light that had been on the ceiling in the far corner somehow hadn't been knocked out of commission, and still flickered sporadically as it swung back and forth on its power cord. A few low moans could be heard as some of the zombies pulled themselves free from the rubble, while others were nothing but bloody paste, hundreds of pounds of rock and concrete having crushed their bodies.

Time passed, the exact amount unknown and irrelevant, for there was no one around who either cared or understood the concept of time. Only the dead prowled the corridors of the underground bunker.

Inside the room, rubble began to shift, to roll down the small mound that had been the tomb of Capt. Stephen Rhodes. In the flickering darkness of the one fluorescent bulb, a bloody finger wearing a gold ring with a red emerald appeared, wiggling back and forth, then another finger, then a hand.

It was slow, excruciating work for whoever was buried beneath the rubble, but then again, the person that was burrowing free didn't care about pain, or fear, or discomfort any more.

Soon, an arm still wearing the green material of a soldier's uniform thrust forth, to push aside the rubble slightly and make the hole just a little larger. For an interminable amount of time yet again, that one arm pushed and worked at the hole, making it wider by centimeters, but always moving, always working, never stopping.

Finally, a shoulder appeared, then a head, and as the flickering bulb illuminated the destroyed room, the head of Capt. Rhodes pushed itself through the hole with a moan that still sounded frighteningly human.

With pieces of concrete falling down the mound, Rhodes slowly slid his other arm free of his tomb, then with both arms he began pulling himself out of the wreckage. It was as his half-a-body came free that he lost his balance and tumbled down the mound of debris to come up against a shattered desk. Rolling onto his side, and acting much like a turtle that had fallen onto its back, he managed to roll and finally get onto his stomach. His dog tags swung back and forth as he moved and the bandolier full of bullets still criss-crossed his chest.

He dragged himself across the floor and rubble to the door that was now hanging on its hinges, destroyed in the blast. The explosion had spared Rhodes the fate of being eaten, and with no zombies to feed on him, he had died and returned as one of the creatures he despised so much.

Eventually he reached the doorway, which was full of the bodies of deceased zombies. He had to climb over the bodies, and when he reached the top, he slid down the other side of the pile of corpses to fall flat on his face in the corridor.

It was almost totally silent, only the infrequent wail of a zombie marring the peace and tranquility of the underground bunker. Only the living dead remained within its cold walls. They had fed before but that had been quite a while ago, and with no prey to chase, the zombies had taken to wandering aimlessly or simply plopping down in a corridor to stare mindlessly at the wall across from them.

Rhodes began dragging himself down the corridor, one inch at a time, his hands slapping the cold floor, his intestines dragging behind him, leaving a bloody snail trail. By the time he was halfway down the hallway, he realized it was easier to simply use his arms and hands to prop himself up.

At first this was rather difficult and his hanging intestines sometimes got in the way; he fell flat on his face as his hand pressed an intestine and he tried to move forward at the same time. Still, he kept at it, that same steel determination he'd had in life still with him in death.

Soon he had the hang of it and he waddled around like a man who had been born without legs or a waist. He became good at it, too, and by the second day he was moving around the bunker as fast as any of the living dead.

Something else had stayed with him in death; ingrained into him to his very core. One word remained, though as one of the walking dead, he didn't have the articulation to totally sound it out.

But he tried. Oh, he tried very hard.

So though no one alive was inside the bunker—and the dead didn't care one way or the other if one of their brethren made noises that sounded like words—Rhodes began to chant over and over, "Fu…fu…fu… Fu…fu…fu…"

With each slap of his hand as he moved about the bunker, the sound, "Fu…" came in tandem, until it became as much a reflex to Rhodes as moving his arms.

"Fu…fu…fu…" echoed throughout the bunker, mingling with the wails of the dead now trapped within its cold walls. "Fu…fu….fu…" sounded hollowly over and over.

The word *fuck* was on the tip of Rhodes' tongue, and sooner or later he would finish sounding it out. Deep down in his dead brain, he knew this with everything that he once was and would be again.

Bub wasn't the only dead fuck who could reason a little, could work through problems, he thought in his fugue state.

"Fu...fu...fu..." he repeated over and over and over again. "Fu...fu...fu..."

Chapter 1

The sun hung high in the clear blue sky, only a few clouds to mar the majestic beauty. A few gulls soared by overhead, riding the wind skillfully, their small white bodies rising and falling with the ebbing of the wind currents.

Sarah lay on the beach on her back, staring up at the sky and the gulls. She wished she were one of them, for the gulls were the embodiment of freedom, the birds able to come and go whenever they pleased.

Glancing to her left, she saw her own *bird* sitting on the sand, the rotor blades tied down, the doors open wide. The helicopter was only there for an emergency and it was doubtful it would ever be used again. Chopper 4.0 Alpha was no doubt grounded for the remainder of its life. And why wouldn't it? The mainland was nothing but ruins, the walking dead everywhere. She knew there was nothing left for her back in Florida, or the rest of America.

A loud bark of laughter off to Sarah's right made her turn in that direction. She saw that her two companions, John and Bill McDermott, were fishing again, and as she watched, Sarah saw John reel in his line and McDermott run into the crashing surf to grab the fish John had hooked.

The two men laughed and whooped up a storm. Sarah chuckled to herself. They were men, doing what men were supposed to do; surviving off the land. They all needed to as well. The supplies from the helicopter were almost gone, and when it had finally dwindled to nothing, it would only be what the group could find on the island that would keep them alive.

Sarah gazed down past the two men at the beach itself, her mind knowing every curve and bend. For two weeks, the three of them had been living on the beach, doing nothing but fishing, sleeping and swimming. Sarah had taken to writing in a journal to pass the time, and as she sat up, she reached over into her bag and pulled out a homemade calendar.

The days of the month had been created by her using a ruler and simply drawing lines vertically and horizontally. She crossed out the square of the day in November it was, then slid the calendar back into her bag. The calendar was new, and it had begun on the day she and her two companions had arrived on the small island they now called home.

More whooping came from John and McDermott and she looked up to see John holding the fish proudly as McDermott pretended to take a picture of it with an imaginary camera. She smiled as she watched them. They were like two junior high school boys who had known each other their entire lives. The two men were close, brothers in arms, and in blood.

Sarah felt close to them, too, John slightly more than McDermott though. John was a tall black man in his late thirties with Caucasian features, a dark goatee and hair to match his skin, and a Jamaican accent. Though not muscular, he wasn't scrawny either, but rather he had a lean, runner's body, and what he had was all muscle. He talked in a low calm voice and enjoyed chatting about philosophical ideas as much as he liked to debate the validity of religion. He was the helicopter's pilot, too.

McDermott was a direct contrast to John.

Bill McDermott was Irish. A short white man in his late forties with a black beard and bushy eyebrows, he loved to drink and felt no shame at getting sloshed each night. But now, after two weeks, his supply of liquor was dangerously low and he had taken to only drinking a little. He had become cranky because of it, but both John and Sarah let the little man rant whenever he wanted to, understanding he was basically detoxing from being a drunk all the time.

McDermott had been in charge of the radio back at the bunker, but here on the small island, he had become a fisherman as did John. He looked the part, too. The arms and legs of the gray-blue coveralls McDermott wore had been cut off so he would be more comfortable in the tropical heat. John still wore his blue jeans, but they were intact. He'd decided not to modify them.

Sarah had been relegated to cook, and though she was a strong woman who had broken the shackles of male chauvinism by becoming a doctor in biology, she found it mildly amusing how she had accepted her new role on the island with little complaint.

A gust of wind blew across the beach, causing the small, make-shift tent behind her to flap loudly. She glanced at it to see if the rope holding the fabric was remaining firm, and when she saw that it was, she looked away. The tent was nothing more than a tarp tied to a couple of trees near the edge of the beach, where the trees encroached onto the sand. What lay beyond the beach was unknown to the three people, for none of them had left the beach as of yet. There had been no need.

Upon first arriving on the island, they were simply happy to be alive.

Sarah wiped sand off her legs and sat taller. She was a beautiful woman in her early thirties, with long brown hair that had lightened from so much exposure to sunlight over the past two weeks. Normally it was tied into a knot at the back of her head, but that hadn't lasted long once arriving on the island. Now it blew around her head, caressing her cheeks in the wind. It made her look even more beautiful than she already was. Sarah had been a tomboy growing up with three brothers; that was probably one of the reasons why she had been able to hold her own inside the bunker, where she had been the only woman surrounded by Army men and her fellow male scientists.

A smile creased her lips as she watched John and McDermott begin gutting the fish at the water's edge. By doing it this way, the blood and offal would be washed back into the sea. John had his pocket knife out and he began slicing into the fish's stomach, pulling out the organs within. The sight of the blood and guts made Sarah look away, and though she didn't want it to happen, images of blood and death filled her vision as she thought back to her narrow escape from the underground bunker along with John and McDermott.

The helicopter had been the key. Without it there would have been nowhere to go after escaping the bunker and no doubt she, along with the two men, would now be long dead…or worse, would have become the walking dead.

The face of her fellow scientist, Dr. Fisher, came into full focus before her mind's eye and she squeezed her eyes closed, trying to make the image evaporate. The man was dead, shot in the head by the bastard Rhodes. She briefly thought of Captain Rhodes, but only long enough to wish the man dead. She hadn't seen him die, but with so many of the living dead inside the bunker, he had to be dead. No one could have survived the onslaught of zombies that had swarmed through the bunker.

The next person to come to mind was her ex-lover Miguel Salazar. She had cut his arm off when he'd been bit by a zombie and she had been confident she'd saved his life, that he wasn't going to become infected, but then she'd lost track of him in the ensuing chaos.

Within the adjoining caves of the bunker the dead were kept like cattle, put there so that the late Dr. Logan had specimens for his experiments. But when Captain Rhodes had found out that Logan was using Rhodes' fallen soldiers for food to feed his test subjects, the normally angry captain had gone completely crazy and had forced McDermott and Sarah into the caves, while holding John at gunpoint to make him fly Rhodes and his few men to safety in the helicopter. But John had gotten the upper hand on Rhodes, and after following Sarah and McDermott into the caves, he'd found them sorely pressed by the dead.

The three of them had then battled their way through the tunnels until reaching an old missile silo, climbed to the surface via ladder, and from there had flown away to the island they were now on.

She sighed. The death and hell she'd experienced at the bunker was over, but despite it she still couldn't stop thinking about the place, and about all the lives gone and hope for the future now lost. She felt that herself and her team of scientists had been the last hope for mankind, for there had been no radio communication with another outpost in months. Now there would be no cure for the undead plague, and the living dead would rule the world until the last human was dead, to then rise up and join the rest of the decomposing corpses.

It was all too little, too late now, as the bunker was filled with the dead, and other than her, John and McDermott, she was confident that no one else had survived the invasion of hungry ghouls.

"Look at this beauty, Sarah," John called as he and McDermott approached her.

Sarah looked up, pulled from her reverie to see John holding the fish, now cleaned and ready to be cooked. There were a few gobbets of fish guts on his pants and she had to shift her gaze, the stuff reminding her of Fisher's brains when Rhodes had shot the man in the side of the head. The image of his massive revolver only inches from Fisher's skull flooded her mind, then the report of the bullet as it left the gun and entered Fisher's head just above his ear, then his brain, and finally out the opposite side of his head. Fisher had dropped like a sack of potatoes, dead before he hit the ground. But at least he wouldn't rise again, a head shot being one of the few ways to put someone down forever if they were killed.

Sarah's complexion went a shade of white as these images flooded her mind. Upon seeing this, John knelt down beside her, laying the fish on a flat stone the group used as a small table. "You all right, Sarah darling? You don't look so good," he said with concern.

She waved her left hand before her, and managed a brief smile. "I'm fine." Both she and John knew the smile was false, but he didn't say anything, only nodded and sat down beside her on the warm sand. McDermott patted John on the shoulder, nodded to Sarah, and with his hands in his pockets, decided it was time to go for a walk. He knew John and Sarah had become closer over the weeks since arriving on the island, and figured this was one of those times they needed some alone time. He wondered if the couple would ever take the leap and sleep together, as he knew for a fact it hadn't happened yet. He sighed; he wouldn't mind a female companion either, but all he had was his booze and that was just about gone.

Ah well, McDermott mused, *maybe there's some lost tribe of natives on the island and I can accidentally stumble into them, meet the daughter of the king, and become married to her. In time I'll rise to become the king as well and will rule for many years to come.*

It was a silly dream, but then what else was there to do but dream on a deserted island in the middle of the ocean? *Ah well,* he thought again as he scratched his beard, *a man can dream, can't he?*

He pulled out his trusty silver flask—a replacement for the one he'd left back in the caves—took a small sip and relished the feeling of the brandy burning his throat, then wandered further down the beach.

Chapter 2

"Come on, Sarah, tell me what's on your mind," John said as he stretched out his long legs beside her. McDermott was a ways down the beach already and well out of hearing.

"It's nothing," she said. "I was just thinking about the past. Nothing matters too much now."

He clucked like a mother hen and shook his head. His hair was longer, but not by much, and the beginning of an afro was taking shape. "Come, come, Sarah, we both know it's not nothing. Now, spill it, what's on your mind? Tell me, you'll feel better getting it off your chest. After all, it's harder to keep things inside than to let it out."

She sighed, brushed her hair from her face, and said, "I was just thinking about all the people we left back at the complex. Rickles, Steel, Miguel, Torrez, even Logan. We saw Logan get killed by Rhodes but what about the rest of them? What about Miguel? Could he still be alive? Could he be somewhere inside the complex, hiding, surrounded by the dead?"

"I suppose anything's possible," he replied as he gave it some thought. "If we could escape, there's no one saying that they couldn't either, but I highly doubt it. There were a lot of dead things inside the bunker when we took off, you know."

"I guess we'll never know." She ran a finger through the sand, drawing a complex equation without realizing it. When she figured out what she was doing, she wiped the sand clean, as if it was an etch-a-sketch. "Do you think I saved Miguel when I amputated his arm? Was it all worth it?"

John patted her leg. "Yes, I think it was. He seemed to be doing just fine before I had to leave him to see what all the hubbub was about." He was referring to when Rhodes, Steel and Torrez had arrived with Fisher, Sarah and McDermott as prisoners. "I think you did a good thing with him. You know, not many people could have done what you did back there. You're the strongest woman I've ever met."

"I just acted, I didn't think about it until it was all over. You saw me when it was; I collapsed into your arms in tears. That doesn't sound like a strong woman to me."

"Oh please, girl, you'd just cut off a man's arm with a machete, you had a right to tear up a little. You're only human. Sometimes I think you worry too much about what people think about you." He rubbed her leg gently. "You know who you are, no one else matters."

Her blue eyes began to tear up. Sarah could be herself around John, that she didn't need to put on a tough persona for him. John knew how strong she was so that allowed her to show some emotion around him, knowing he wouldn't think anything less of her because of it.

"You're still a mystery to me, you know," Sarah said as she looked into his eyes. She had leaned closer to him, so that her lips were only inches from his. A few times before this had happened, only something always seemed to pop up to break the moment. But now, with the two of them alone on the beach, it looked like it was finally going to happen. They were going to kiss.

"Ah, but that's what you love about me, Sarah darling," John said with a sly grin, and sensing what she wanted, he leaned in closer as well.

It was a perfect moment: the sun shining bright, the water crashing on the beach, the sound of gulls crying out overhead as they played with one another.

Sarah closed her eyes, knowing what was coming, but just before their lips touched for their first kiss, the moment was ruined yet again as McDermott began calling out to them from down the beach. He sounded excited, and in a world where the dead walked, an excited voice was usually not a good thing.

The mood shattered, Sarah opened her eyes, blinked, and stood up, as did John. They stood side by side. John glanced at her and smiled, as did she.

"To be continued?" he asked in his lilting voice that she found so attractive.

"Definitely."

They both turned to focus their attention on McDermott, who was running down the beach, more animated than either John or Sarah had seen him in a long time. His gun was in his hand, the .45 reflecting the sunlight like polished glass. The three companions didn't have a lot of firearms unfortunately. Their armory consisted of McDermott's .45, an M-16 rifle John had taken from one of Rhodes' men, and a few sidearms kept in the helicopter for emergencies. Extra ammunition was light as well.

"What's the rush, Billy boy?" John asked as the Irishman grew near. "We're on a tropical island, there's always time for everything, and why are you waving around your gun like that?"

"For good reason, Johnny, I can tell you that much," McDermott said when he was close enough so that he didn't have to yell. "I saw a fishing boat down the beach floating not far from shore. I called out to it but no one answered. I think it's empty."

John looked at Sarah and then back to McDermott. "Well then, we need to check it out. It may have supplies we can use," he said.

"I agree," Sarah added, gathering what gear she thought they might need. "It could have been floating for days or years and could come in handy if we needed to sail over to the mainland instead of fly. Lead on, Bill, we're right behind you."

"It's this way," McDermott said and was off, Sarah and John following quickly behind him.

"Wait, John," Sarah suddenly said and stopped walking. "What about the fish you caught and cleaned?"

"Leave it," John replied. "What could be on that boat is much more important?"

As soon as the three survivors had left their camp and were a little ways down the beach, hungry gulls swarmed in to feast on the gutted fish.

It was gone in seconds.

Chapter 3

"There it is," McDermott said, pointing out to sea, where the derelict fishing boat bobbed in the waves. It appeared caught in opposing currents, the tide trying to pull it into shore while the sea wanted to take it back out again. The result was the boat was in a small area where it didn't move more than thirty feet before returning to its original position.

"Think there's a rip tide or an undertow?" Sarah asked John curiously.

John shrugged. "Could be, but we won't know till we get out there." He glanced at McDermott. "What do you say, Billy, wanna go for a swim?"

"Of course, I'm the one who found the damn thing; you better believe I want to see what's on it."

The two men began taking off their extra clothes. John stripped down to his underwear, while McDermott only took off his .45 and handed it to Sarah. In nothing but his underwear, John's dark skin glistened under the sun, the muscles rippling beneath his skin. There wasn't an ounce of fat on him.

Sarah let her eyes play over his body, seeing the dark curly hairs on his chest, the way his stomach moved each time he breathed.

He saw Sarah looking at him and grinned.

Their eyes met and she looked away bashfully, much like a young school girl would. Neither commented, keeping their thoughts to themselves.

McDermott had ignored the silent exchange. "Last one into the water has to make the fire tonight," he said after pulling off his second shoe and jogging to the water's edge.

John watched McDermott then turned to Sarah. "You got this?" he asked, referring to her waiting on the beach for his return.

"I'll be fine. Go see what's on that boat."

He nodded, turned, then jogged off.

"Be careful!" she called after him.

"Always, Sarah darling, always."

Though McDermott had hit the water first, John quickly caught up to the older man and passed him. On land, McDermott would have thrown a few sarcastic remarks at John, but here in the water, he saved his breath for swimming.

He couldn't remember the last time he'd had to swim like this. Hell, the most water he'd seen had been in the shower, so to now swim a good distance was something he was already regretting. Plus, the water was cold, around sixty-five degrees if he'd guessed correctly.

His breath became labored and his arms felt weak. He thrust them forward as he kicked with his legs but he was already slowing. Then there was the tide, the ebb and flow of the fighting currents, which was becoming harder to deal with.

At the back of his mind, where no man wanted to look, the word *drown* was getting louder and louder as he struggled to keep going.

The boat was ahead of him, though with each rising wave it disappeared from view, only to reappear once more. It seemed infinitely far away, and as he endeavored to push forward, he knew he had made a grave mistake in attempting this task. He couldn't even call out for help, he was so tired, the air in his chest barely enough to keep him moving.

Then it happened. The first time his arms faltered and he dipped below the surface. He held his breath and pushed harder, then rose out of the water again, but as soon as he did this, he went under again.

So this is how it begins, he thought as he forced his body to pull him back up. He sucked in seawater and began coughing, which caused him to lose the last of his momentum and sink beneath the waves once more.

As his head went under, he breathed in more water and began to spasm. But then he felt someone grab him and yank him up and out of the water so that his head was above the surface.

"Come on, Billy boy," John said breathlessly, "you didn't survive that bunker to die now."

Sputtering, McDermott tried to reply but nothing came out but grunts and groans.

John swam the remaining feet to the boat while pulling McDermott along with him, and with McDermott's feeble help, he got the older man into the boat, then climbed in after him. The aft end of the hull was low in the water so that the deck was only two feet off the surface of the ocean, and with nets lining the hull they both managed to get into the boat easily.

McDermott was lying on his side as John crawled over the lip of the boat, the older man spitting out water while coughing and hacking.

"You okay, Billy?" John asked as he slumped to his knees, exhausted. He hadn't been swimming in a long time either and the exertion of swimming plus the added weight of McDermott had taken it out of him. His arms felt like rubber and his chest burned, but with each passing second he felt his energy returning.

After all, there was no rush and he had all day to explore the fishing vessel.

"I'll…" McDermott began, then coughed some more, spit water, and finished, "I'll live. Just give me a damn minute to catch my breath."

John nodded, though McDermott didn't see it. John turned to face the beach and waved to Sarah, giving her a thumbs-up. She waved back, though she couldn't make out the gesture. The boat was too far from shore and the sun was hitting her in the face. Still, she saw both men get into the boat, though she had no idea that McDermott had almost drowned.

John got to his feet, his eyes taking in what he could see of the boat. It was a fifty-footer at least, maybe bigger, though the engine size was an unknown factor or even if it worked. They had boarded the boat in the aft end, and other than a few ropes and empty lobster cages, the boat looked and felt deserted.

McDermott was feeling better already so John went to him and helped the Irishman stand. McDermott muttered a cranky thank you, then whispered something about needing a drink.

"Let's check this thing out," John said, and after making sure McDermott was with him, the two men began moving across the deck to the wheel house in the bow.

John picked up a long wooden pole with a metal hook on the end. The tool was used to help pull in the nets but it would make a decent weapon given the circumstances. It resembled a mooring hook.

There was nothing else around that would work as a weapon, so McDermott simply shrugged and waved for John to stay in the lead, as he was the only one who was armed with something to use as either defense or offense.

Taking careful steps, John began walking down the deck, McDermott following close on his heels. John felt the warm wood of the deck under his bare feet and as he moved, the wind and sun had already begun to dry him off.

The wheel house's door was open, and John poked his head inside, then pulled it back out. He half-expected a zombie to jump at him, but when nothing did and his brief glimpse of the interior showed that it was empty, he lowered the pole and waved McDermott to follow him inside.

"See if you can find any kind of log or maps, Johnny," McDermott said, moving to a small waist-high desk in the corner.

John moved around the wheel house, searching for anything of use. It was when he reached the back and peered over a storage locker that he frowned deeply. "Billy, I found something."

"A log?"

"No, Billy boy, not a log, but it still tells a tale of what happened here."

McDermott went to John's side and peered over the locker. He nodded when he saw the decomposed body, now nothing but a husk thanks to the ocean air. The term *beef jerky* came to mind as McDermott studied the corpse. There was a large hole in the back of the head and a piece of paper in the right hand. The gun that had made the hole was nowhere to be found.

John leaned over and pulled the paper free. "It just says 'I'm sorry.' "

"Sorry about what?" McDermott asked.

John only shrugged, his lean body flowing with the gesture. It was a little chilly even though he'd pretty much dried, but he was still wearing nothing but his underwear. Now he envied McDermott who had kept on his cut-off overalls.

They left the corpse where it was. There was nothing more it could tell them. The search began anew and John did turn up some maps, but the ones back at the helicopter were actually better so there wasn't much use for them.

Finally, they wrapped it up and looked at one another.

"Nothing," McDermott said. "Where to next?"

"Next we check down below. Maybe there's some food in the galley," John suggested.

"Can't be much, this boat's size and all," McDermott said.

"True, but anything is better than nothing, man, surely you know that."

They exited the wheel house, and once more with John in the lead, they went to the raised hatch that led below decks.

The pole John carried was unwieldy in such a close environment and he had to duck once he climbed down the ladder.

McDermott, being shorter than John, had no problem walking around. "Sometimes it pays not to be so bloody tall," he told John with a wide grin.

"This way," John said, reading a sign on the bulkhead that told him which way the cargo hold was.

"Lead on, brother," came the reply from McDermott. "Maybe we can find some booze to replace what I've drunk." He began to smile. "A nice scotch or whiskey would be nice. Or a Puerto Rican rum. Even an old brandy." He put his right hand to his chin in thought. "Come to think of it, I really don't care what kind it is."

The crew quarters were in disarray but so far there was no sign of a soul, neither living or dead. The two men searched the quarters but didn't find anything of use other than a few trinkets that were irrelevant. Even a flashlight would have come in handy.

John found an old Zippo lighter hidden under a mattress with a military platoon's insignia stamped on its side. Marines if he was correct. Flicking it, he was pleased to see it worked. He slid it into the waistband of his underwear.

They went deeper into the ship.

"I don't know if it's a good thing or a bad thing that we haven't found anyone but the dead captain, Johnny."

"I know what you mean, man. Ah, here we are. The ship's hold."

"Should we open it?" McDermott asked. "There might not be anything in there but rotten fish."

"Ah, Billy, but we won't know if we don't. So what do you want to do?"

McDermott frowned and rubbed his beard, then he pulled out a quarter and held it up for John to see. "I say we flip for it. Heads we open the door, tails we leave it alone and go back to the beach and forget we ever came aboard this heap."

"Sounds like a plan. You gonna flip it?"

"Sure, why not?" McDermott tossed the coin in the air, making sure it did a few turns while airborne, then he caught it in midair and slapped it onto his tan arm, the tan thanks to two weeks exposed to the harsh sun. Upon removing his hand he said, "It's heads, Johnny. Open her up."

"Okay, let's see what's in there." John leaned his wooden pole against the bulkhead and pulled the handle on the door, cracking the seal, then yanked back on it, but as soon as he did it he already regretted it. The instant the seal was broken, the overwhelming odor of rotting flesh assailed him, threatening to knock him flat on his ass. The odor was thick as pea soup and infiltrated not just his nose, but every orifice in his body; his eyes were already watering.

As John gasped and tried not to vomit, McDermott doing the same as he tried to tell John to close the damn door, both men struggled to regain their composure.

John swallowed the bile in his throat and began pushing the door closed, but just as he did it, the first of more than a dozen arms and hands thrust through the opening, forcing it open despite John leaning against the metal door to close it.

The hands were pale and peeling, some nothing but bones with bits of dried flesh still attached. There was no doubt what was on the other side of the door, and there was definitely no doubt what they wanted.

John leaned on the door with all his weight, McDermott quickly adding his frail form to the mix. Both men weren't trying to close the door, but were simply attempting to keep it from opening more than it already was.

As the cargo hold door bucked and jumped beneath his back, John truly wished the coin had come up *tails*.

Chapter 4

Sarah waited impatiently on the beach for John and McDermott to return from going belowdecks in the fishing boat. She'd seen them enter the wheel house, then exit it and go down below through a raised hatch that had been out of sight from where she stood.

She fingered McDermott's .45 pistol over and over as she stared at the boat. What if they didn't come back up? What would she do then? Would she swim out to see what had happened to them? If she did, no doubt what had befallen them would then take her. Was it the living dead? Were people waiting below and had ambushed them? All these questions flooded her mind, making her impatient for news.

She hoped nothing bad had happened to them. So how long should she wait? What if the boat broke free of its quandary and began heading out to sea? So many questions and not one answer. She was a scientist, damn it, she had been trained to find answers, but this wasn't something she'd gone to school for. Not much had happened lately when she thought about it.

Sarah had graduated at the top of her class. She had a Masters in Health Sciences and a B.A. in Medical Technology and was damn proud of it. As a scientist she found herself mostly in a man's world, and from day one she'd had to work twice as hard as any man occupying the same position as her. But she had excelled in her field, which was why she became one of the chosen few to end up in the government sanctioned bunker.

Of course, education wasn't much of a factor in surviving nowadays. Now skills like how well you could shoot a gun was at the top of the list, as well as finding water and how to dress a kill after a hunt. Knowing how to categorize DNA and type blood cells and read a patient's white blood cell count were all useless skills.

She stomped her right foot in frustration. Where the hell were they?

"Close the bloody door, John, this isn't funny!" McDermott screamed as he pushed against the cargo hold door with his back pressed tightly against it. Pale and rotting hands slapped the door only inches from his face, as the dead tried to grasp him in their cold embrace.

"What the hell do you think I'm doing?" John screamed in reply. His dark skin was coated with sweat as he fought to hold the living dead mob at bay. But despite him and McDermott doing their best to stop the pressure behind the door, he knew it was simple mathematics that was against them. Quite frankly, two men, no matter how determined, simply couldn't stop five times their body weight.

Then it happened, as John knew deep down that it would. The dead surged forward and John and McDermott were pushed back as the door flew open.

"Run, Billy, back topside!" John screamed and grabbed McDermott by his collar and practically threw the shorter man before him.

While McDermott moved through the narrow companion way, John grabbed the wooden pole from where he'd leaned it against the wall and thrust it forward like a spear.

The sharp tip impaled the first zombie out of the cargo hold in the chest. Though this didn't kill the ghoul, it did stop any more bodies from coming at John as the passageway was only wide enough for one man to walk down it. If two men were passing one another, they would have had to both put their backs to the bulkheads and to then slide by each other with only inches to spare between them.

The zombie groaned and snarled at John, its hands swiping only inches from his face. It would have been a stalemate if not for the nine other ghouls that were pressing on the back of the one John had impaled.

The zombies were hungry and one of their own wasn't going to stop the rest from getting to the fresh meat only a few feet before them. So as John held the zombie-on-a-stick at bay, the others began pushing and pulling at the ghoul to reach John.

It took only seconds, but to John it seemed to take an eternity. He could only watch in amazement as the nine zombies behind the one he held began ripping at the impaled ghoul, yanking at its arms and head and pulling back on the body as hard as they could. There was a wet sound reminiscent of damp paper being torn, then the head and arms of the impaled zombie were gone and a dark red-black liquid was squirting out of all the newly torn holes in its body. The port and starboard bulkheads became bathed in ichor as the zombie bled out. John stared in amazement, a small part of his mind wondering how in the hell the ghoul could be spewing so much of itself if its heart didn't work. He'd had a talk with Dr. Logan one day on the subject when the two men had run into each other in the large assembly room in the bunker that doubled as both the cafeteria and meeting room. Dr.

Logan had explained that he believed because of the internal pressure of decomposing gasses within a zombie, that if an appendage was severed or a large hole placed in the body, then the gases would seek that hole to escape, and also take with it the blood and fluids that resided inside the human body. John had taken what Logan said with a grain of salt, but he had also remembered what the man had said.

After all, John flew a helicopter for a living and Logan was a doctor of medicine. Surely the man knew something about human biology.

John only thought of this memory in the briefest of seconds as it flashed through his mind as he fought to hold onto the now armless and headless zombie. But then the body collapsed to the deck, as it had no head and was basically dead for good. The tip of the pole was ripped out of the ghoul's chest and John found his weapon was free again.

But that also meant that with the body on the deck, the other nine ghouls were free to attack him. Backpedaling, he moved down the passageway, then turned when his back struck the ladder.

"There you are, I thought I'd lost you," McDermott said from above. "Get up here before they get you. Here, hand me that pole."

John didn't have to be told twice, and tossed up the pole, then with the first zombie after him barely missing his bare feet as he all but flew up the ladder, only McDermott's help to get him onto the main deck was the reason the zombie didn't grab his foot and yank him back down.

John landed heavily on the main deck. But he knew he couldn't stay there long, and as he got to his feet, the first ghoul was coming up the ladder—the ladder was more of very steep stairs than an actual ladder and the zombies had no trouble navigating it, even with their limited mobility.

"Jesus, Mary and Joseph," McDermott said and crossed himself. "How many of the buggers are there?"

"Enough," John replied. He grabbed the wooden pole with the steel tip and hook from McDermott and jumped in front of the first zombie.

John knew he had the upper hand and he used the advantage now. As the first zombie climbed out of the hatch, John was there. He used the pole more like a cattle prod without the voltage and maneuvered the oblivious ghoul to the port side of the deck, then with one good shove, pushed it over the side where it dropped into the sea with a small splash.

"Ah, Johnny, a little help would be appreciated," McDermott said as he stood before the next ghoul as it came for him.

John used the zombie's fixation on McDermott and ran at it, then charged at it like he was a hockey player and the zombie the goalie. He maintained his 'check' until reaching the far side of the deck where the zombie then struck the three foot wall that made up the railing before toppling into the ocean.

"John, come back here and stop screwing around!" McDermott screamed.

John spun to see the next ghoul in line coming at McDermott, who was doing his best to stay out of the zombie's reach.

John swung the pole around and slammed it on top of the zombie's head. The curved hook used for snagging nets and the ropes used to tie lobster cages dropped onto the ocean floor, dug in deep into the ghoul's scalp, but was too short to take it down. The tip barely penetrated the skull. John yanked hard and the zombie came towards him, trying to stand upright on the swaying deck. John wrangled the ghoul to the edge of the deck and then with a mighty yank pulled the pole free. It came out of the skull with a wet squelching sound and then quite by accident, the deck bucked under a wave and the zombie was over the side.

"John, where the bloody hell do you keep getting off to?" McDermott screamed again.

John took a fraction of a second to sigh. What did McDermott think he was doing with the zombies each time he got them off McDermott? But then the Irishman called out again and John was racing across the deck, his feet slapping the wooden planks.

John continued maneuvering the zombies to the edge of the deck where he then toppled them into the ocean over and over. But that plan finally failed when one of the zombies managed to grab the wooden pole with flailing hands as it went over the side, taking John's weapon with it.

Cursing, John spun around to return to McDermott, who was dealing with the last ghoul. It was a big bastard and John had to wonder how the zombie had managed to fit through the hatch. It must have been a tight squeeze, like when Winnie the Pooh would get stuck in the tree going for honey. But the hatch was finally clear, which had to mean there were no more living dead below decks.

"John, get the bloody thing off me already!" McDermott screamed.

"I lost the damn pole, Billy."

"So give it a shove like the others."

"I can't, he's huge."

"Well do something, he's about to kill me!" McDermott's back came up against the forward bow, where port and starboard met at the front in a sharp point.

"Jump over the side," John called out but he could see McDermott had tunnel vision. The Irishman was only looking at the fat ghoul and a simple idea like jumping off the boat didn't even come to mind.

John let his gaze move around the bow of the ship. There was an old tarp in the corner, covering rope or some other bulky items, and machinery that was bolted to the deck. Then he saw the life preserver with the boat's name on it in faded black letters. An idea came to him and he ran to the preserver, took it off the hook it was on, and ran at the large ghoul. Coming up behind Fatso, he slammed the round life preserver over its head, pushing it down as hard as he could.

In theory it might have worked, the life preserver sliding down and locking the zombie's arms by its side. But this fellow was far too fat to let the preserver fit over its torso. John managed to get the preserver down an inch past Fatso's shoulders, but the ghoul still had the use of its arms.

Angry at the distraction, Fatso was about to pounce on McDermott; the overweight zombie spun around and groaned at John in what sure looked like annoyance. Then it took a step towards John.

"Shit, that didn't work the way I wanted it to at all," John said under his breath.

Chapter 5

John stood transfixed as Fatso came at him. Sure, he could have backpedaled and jumped off the boat and into the water, but that would have meant leaving McDermott behind, and he would never do that.

He still felt guilty for having to watch Rhodes force Sarah and McDermott into the zombie corral back at the bunker. It had been a miracle they had all come out of that event in one piece. If a divine entity hadn't reached down a hand to help, then he didn't know what had happened. Luck just didn't seem to be the right word for the good fortune that had brought them alive and well to the island.

John's mind raced with how he was going to deal with one of the largest ghouls he'd ever seen. John got a good look at the attire of Fatso, then thought back to the others that he'd pushed into the water.

Fatso wore waders held up with suspenders and black rubber boots on his feet. The shirt was plaid, red and black, and the arms of the ghoul were tanned from the sun, and even the pale complexion of death did little to hide this. There was a tan line above the elbows from where the shirt always rode up on the arms. So if Fatso and the others had been the crew, then the body in the wheel house was probably the captain of the vessel. Now, the note with the words 'I'm sorry,' could be explained. Evidently, the captain had locked his crew in the cargo hold when they became zombies, and then out of guilt, the captain had taken his own life. Shooting himself in the head had been an assurance that he didn't return from the dead like his crew.

All this went through John's mind instantly, like a flashbulb on an old camera going off. Fatso was still coming towards John and his brain was racing to come up with an idea that wouldn't get him killed or leave McDermott behind to deal with the massive ghoul.

But then both dilemmas were solved when McDermott appeared with a small hand axe on the left side of Fatso. Before the zombie could shift its bulk towards McDermott, the Irishman raised the axe and hacked off first the left arm and then the right one just above the elbow, before the zombie could so much as let out a moan. Both limbs fell to the deck, the fingers still twitching.

As Fatso slowly turned to try and grab McDermott—this now slightly more complicated now that the ghoul had no arms— McDermott dropped down low and began hacking at Fatso's legs.

Like a tree toppling, the large zombie went down hard, the sound of its body hitting the deck so loud that Sarah heard a soft *thud* back on the beach, though she didn't know what the noise was from.

McDermott chopped at Fatso's legs until both had been severed just above the knees, then he jumped back. McDermott stood tall, his chest thrust outward, his shoulders back, as if he was a gladiator that had won the battle. He let out a soft, "Woof," under his breath; he was proud of himself.

As Fatso lay on the deck, limbless, the head twisting back and forth, the teeth gnashing, John went over to McDermott and patted him on the arm. "That was somethin' else to see, Billy. Well done, man. I thought that big bastard had me."

"He might've too if I hadn't found this," McDermott said, holding up the gore-encrusted hand axe.

"Thanks for saving my bacon before, Johnny, those boys came out of the hatch faster than I could think how to deal with 'em." There was blood splatter on his coveralls and a few on his cheek. He wiped it away with the back of his hand when John pointed it out to him.

"I think we're even on the saving each other part, Billy." John gestured with a bare foot to the limbless zombie a few feet away. "What say we roll this bag of lard into the water and be done with him."

Treating the zombie like a cylinder, the two men rolled the zombie across the deck and then over the side. With the life preserver still on Fatso, the ghoul bobbed in the water like a buoy, the preserver keeping it afloat.

Fatso thrashed his head back and forth, clearly not liking being tossed into the water. As the seconds passed, the body was caught in the conflicting currents, and unlike the boat that was trapped in one spot, the ghoul began getting pulled out to sea.

Both men let out a deep breath, relieved it was over. Once more John turned and went to the side facing the beach and waved to Sarah, who waved back. He tried to call out to tell her that he and McDermott were going to finish searching the boat, but she couldn't hear him so he gave up.

McDermott had wandered over to the tarp lying on the deck as he watched Fatso float out to sea. He even waved to the ghoul with a smile. "Bon Voyage, you bastard," he called. "Have a nice trip."

But it was as he was waving that the tarp at his feet began to shift slightly. Something was under there.

McDermott didn't know anything was wrong until a pale hand shot out from under the tarp and cold fingers wrapped around his ankle. The hand yanked back and McDermott found himself horizontal in the air for a brief moment. He idly wondered why this was, as he'd been standing tall a fraction of a second ago. But then he was falling to the deck, the back of his head striking the sun-baked wood hard before the rest of his body followed. He blacked out for a few seconds.

This was all the time the zombie hidden under the tarp needed to come out and begin chewing on McDermott's leg. With its mouth opened wide, it prepared to take a bite.

John had just spun around to tell McDermott they needed to get back to searching when he saw the Irishman go down and the ghoul appear from under the tarp.

Acting fast, knowing his friend had moments before he was attacked, John sprinted across the deck and picked up an empty metal lobster cage. Holding the cage, he dashed to McDermott, who was still out of it, and raised the cage high over his head. The zombie's head was rearing back to sink its teeth into McDermott's leg.

John brought the cage down so that one of the corners was the first thing to hit the ghoul's skull. The metal corner of the cage connected with the head and sank deep, crushing the skull and sending brain matter in all directions.

The zombie's body went limp, and John tossed the cage to the side where it crashed loudly, rolled a few feet, and came up against a mooring rope.

"Billy, talk to me, man," John said, worried for his friend.

"Oh, my aching head. It feels like I went on a binge. What the hell happened?"

"You got careless, Billy boy, that's what happened. But you're fine now," John said in his lilting Jamaican accent.

McDermott sat up and touched the back of his head. "Shit, I got one hell of a bump here."

"You'll live, that's what matters." John helped McDermott stand up. "Take another second to get yourself together and then we need to finish searching below for food and water."

McDermott nodded and instantly regretted it. Even slight movement of his head hurt. He closed his eyes but that didn't help. The rolling of the boat in the water made his head even worse. "Let's just get this over with so we can go back to the beach and I can get a drink for real. If I'm gonna have a headache it should be from actually drinking."

John smiled but said nothing, knowing his friend's penchant for alcohol. Once more they went below decks, and after making absolutely sure there were no more zombies about, they quickly searched what they hadn't before. They came up with nothing. The galley was empty, not so much as a scrap of food, nor was there fresh water.

It explained why the captain had taken his life. Lost in the middle of the ocean with no food or water, his crew locked in the cargo hold, now the living dead, there was little hope of a happy ending. John shook his head, not agreeing with the dead captain's choice. The man had taken the easy way out. As long as there was breath there was hope.

"Nothin', absolutely nothin'," McDermott said upon finishing the search of the last room. It had taken less than five minutes from when they had returned below. The crew quarters were small and the galley even smaller, the square footage less than three feet by two feet. The fuel tank had been empty as well. "This was an absolute waste of time, Johnny."

"I know, Billy, but there was no way of knowing that till we came on board. For all we knew there could have been guns, food and booze piled high in the cargo hold instead of the dead."

McDermott opened his mouth to reply, no doubt being something sarcastic, when two brief pops could be heard from outside.

"That sounds like gunfire," McDermott said.

"Aye, it does. Come on, Sarah's in trouble." John raced for the ladder that would bring him onto the main deck. It took less than half a minute to return to the bow of the ship and when John did, his mouth fell open at the sight before him.

McDermott came up behind John and he crossed himself, while whispering, "Jesus, Mary and Joseph."

The two men could only stare helplessly, for there wasn't much they could do to help Sarah given where they were. Even if they jumped into the water and began swimming back to the beach, they would arrive too late to assist her.

Sarah fired again, the bullet going wide, and she slowed her breathing and tried to wait a little longer for her target to get closer, though she hated to do it.

John watched her hold the gun in a firing stance, and he saw her targets getting closer. He was mumbling for her to fire, to shoot the dead bastards before they were too close, but he knew it was all on her. He told himself she was more than capable of dealing with the situation, though he wished he could be by her side.

John cursed himself for being a fool as he watched the tableaux play out. How the hell was he to know that when he had pushed the zombies overboard, they would have then sunk to the bottom to begin walking to shore? They didn't breathe so it made sense, but it still wasn't something he ever would have been able to foreshadow.

Now, eight zombies were slowly stumbling out of the surf, their clothes soaked, their hair matted to their pale heads. John was glad that at least Fatso wasn't with them. But Sarah still had eight living dead coming at her, and all she had to defend herself with was McDermott's .45.

"How many bullets you got in that thing?" John asked.

McDermott shrugged. "Half a clip, maybe less. I didn't count."

"Why not, man?"

"Johnny, we're on a deserted island, I didn't see a need."

"Damn it, why is she just standing there?" John asked. "She doesn't have to kill them now. She can retreat and lead them away and you and me can swim ashore. Then we can take them down easily one by one. Three against eight isn't good odds but we shouldn't have a problem, especially if Sarah gets back to camp and grabs the rifle we brought with us." He began waving at her, trying to get her attention, repeating what he'd just said to McDermott. She didn't seem to be able to hear him and John cursed under his breath.

On the beach, Sarah slowed her breathing and fired again, this time the bullet flying true. The round struck one of the eight zombies in the forehead and it toppled over into the water to float belly down.

She could see John waving and yelling to her to do something, but what he was saying wasn't clear, his voice lost in the wind. It didn't matter anyway. She sighted on the next pale visage and fired. The bullet struck the face but ricocheted off teeth and flew off, so it wasn't a kill shot. The zombie now had a gaping hole in its face, most of its teeth shot out and its tongue destroyed; still it plodded on.

Sarah wasn't thinking as rationally as she should have. In reality there was absolutely no danger to her. The zombies were slow and if any managed to get too close to her, it wouldn't be hard for her to simply run away.

But like a teenager at the carnival trying to win that doll for his girlfriend at the target shooting game, she wasn't going to back down. She fired again at the zombie she'd wounded and this time the bullet hit home, entering the right eye and blowing out the back of the ghoul's skull. The body slipped below the waves, floating face up.

The dead were closer now, and though that was never a good thing, it did make shooting them easier. Sarah was a good shot, and had trained for hours off and on at the bunker with Miguel, who had taught her the proper stance when firing and how to clean her weapon. Until the dead walked, she'd never touched a firearm and probably wouldn't have ever had a need. But things had changed after the dead rose…a lot of things had changed. Too much actually. So much in fact that when she thought back to the person she was in college she hardly recognized that person as herself. It was like she had morphed into an entirely new human being.

Another zombie went down with an extra hole in its head and she turned and fired again, hitting another on the shoulder, then after readjusting her aim she struck the face dead center, the bullet blowing apart the nose and tunneling into the brain.

Moving her aim slightly, she found her next target and fired, the body going down with one bullet to the forehead.

There were only three left, and as she shifted her aim to fire and squeezed the trigger, the gun clicked on an empty chamber.

"Shit," she hissed and took a step backwards. The three ghouls were less than ten feet away from her, and without a gun things had just gone from bad to worse.

John and McDermott saw this and though John hadn't heard the dry click of an empty gun, he could see she wasn't firing anymore.

"Shit, Billy, she must be out of bullets, and there's still three more left." He jumped into the water, disappeared for a few seconds, then came up, his body slicing through the waves as he hurried to return to the beach.

Billy watched John swimming away from the boat, then with a sigh, he jumped in and began swimming as well. He just hoped he could make it without drowning because if he did, John wouldn't be there to save him and wouldn't know he'd drowned until McDermott's bloated corpse washed up on the beach.

Sarah was halfway up the beach, the three zombies coming for her. She knew she needed to decide what to do next or things were about to become very difficult. The empty .45 was in her back pocket. She reached down to her side and pulled the knife she had hanging from her waist, the sheath attached to her belt. It was a Bowie knife. McDermott had given it to her, telling her when you live on an island, your number one friend was a knife.

Sarah silently thanked him for giving it to her now as she raised it before her. She quickly did mental calculations of her chances of living through the next few minutes, then decided that the part of her life that thought in formulas and calculations was over; she needed to go with her gut.

Her gut said she could take down three ghouls with a knife if she was fast and didn't let them grab her. She studied each undead fisherman as the trio came at her, Sarah always backing up to keep distance between herself and her pursuers.

She picked the one on her left first. He was about her size with a thin face. Even before death the man had been lean.

With a yell to psych herself up, she ran at the zombie and jumped up, crashing into it. Her legs went around the ghoul's waist and her momentum pushed the zombie onto its back with Sarah still on it. They ended up on the sand, with Sarah straddling the zombie, her butt on its stomach. From a distance it might have looked like two lovers playing on the beach, if not for the other two ghouls hovering around them. But then perhaps they were simply voyeurs, watching the young couple make love.

Then Sarah ruined the erotic tableaux when she raised and slammed the Bowie knife into the right eye socket of the zombie. She felt the blade slide into the socket, metal scrape on bone, to then slow as it sliced into the fisherman's brain. Pulling out the blade was harder than she expected as it had become jammed in the eye socket. But one glance over her shoulder at the two zombies only a few feet away filled her with a surge of adrenaline that gave her the strength to pull the knife free. There was a sickening squelch as the blade came free.

Sarah jumped up and ran a few feet to the left, the zombies right behind her. She picked the one on her right this time. The undead fisherman was a little taller than her, with a scruffy beard encrusted with pus and other fluids that even a dip in the ocean couldn't wash out. He was missing his right hand so she hoped that would help her kill it, as it couldn't grab her as easily as a ghoul with two working hands.

She ran at the dead man, and at the last second before they would have connected, she dodged to the right—the stump of an arm coming out to try and grab her but only brushing her arm— and swerved around him so she was now behind the ghoul.

Before the zombie could spin around, she plunged the knife into the spot directly at the base of the skull, severing the dead man's spine. Like a puppet with its strings cut the ghoul collapsed to the sand.

But Sarah had spent a fraction too long on that zombie, and as she pulled the blade free, she found that the last ghoul had come up behind her and wrapped its arms around her. The smell of rotting meat mixed with sea water was nauseating, and Sarah dry heaved even as she fought to break free of the ghoul's grip. The dead fisherman opened its mouth wide, and teeth came closer to sink into Sarah's neck.

She knew there would be no getting away from this, she was about to have her throat torn out and there was nothing she could do about it.

John had reached the beach and was sprinting across the sand directly at Sarah. Just as the dead fisherman was about to bite her, he reached them both and jumped at them, his body plowing into the zombie more than Sarah, but the result was the same and all three of them, dead and human alike, went crashing to the beach in a tangle of limbs.

Sarah was a little stunned but John knew he had to be quick. Pushing free of the fisherman, he saw that he was up near the treeline where there were rocks and stray branches. His hand reached out to grab something to use as a weapon, his fingers touching on a stick no more than six inches long and a half inch wide.

It would have to do. John snatched it up with his right hand while his left hand forced the fisherman's head down into the sand. He placed the small stick over the ghoul's right eye and began to press with all the strength he had in his arm.

The stick wasn't sharp so it hesitated when it was pressed on the eyeball, but then the eye popped like a rotten egg and the stick slid into the socket. John never stopped pushing and slowly, inch by inch, the stick slid deeper into the socket and the brain behind it. When he ran out of stick, John used his thumb to push it in deeper, making sure it was in as far as possible.

The fisherman's arms and legs kicked and jerked for a few moments and then the body went still. Blood and a syrupy-mucous seeped out of the eye socket, the tip of the stick in the middle of the oozing mess.

John fell back onto the sand and lay on his back, his chest rising and falling heavily as he sucked in air. He must have broken an Olympic swimming record for his time from the boat to the beach.

McDermott crawled out of the surf, exhausted but alive. He also dropped down onto the wet sand near the water's edge, heedless of the water rolling into him.

But when one of the corpses floating in the water came too close and he felt a hand touch him, he jumped up and ran up the beach, his head looking over his shoulder more than not, to make sure he wasn't being followed. He wasn't. The corpse that had touched him was still, face down on the beach after the tide had pushed it there.

Sarah sat up, her face flush with the excitement. She went to John and kneeled down beside him. "Thank you, John, I guess I messed up," she said with a forced smile.

"Messed up? You almost got yourself killed. And for what? There was no need to deal with them things like that, Sarah. You could have outrun them and me and Billy could have dealt with them later."

"Maybe, but what if they'd gone off into the woods?" Sarah asked. "Then we'd have to worry about them all the time. This way was better. Now they're put down and we don't have to worry about them."

"Well, you still took a foolish risk," he said, seeing her reasoning though not liking it.

"John, everyday is a risk, life is a risk." She sighed. "But I do know what you mean. Maybe it could have been handled better than it was."

"You're both right to me," McDermott said. "So can we put this behind us now?"

John hesitated and then nodded, Sarah doing the same.

"Wonderful," McDermott said. "So we're all one big happy family again."

John got up and gathered his clothes. Seeing the bodies washing up on shore, he said, "We're gonna have to come back and deal with these bodies."

"Later, Johnny," McDermott said. "We've done enough for now. It's time to relax and have a drink. Maybe soak up some more of this sun."

Sarah grabbed her bag and they set off for their camp.

"Here," she said, handing McDermott his .45. "Sorry I emptied it."

"That's all right, Sarah. It was for a good cause."

As they walked away, one of the bodies stirred in the surf but it wasn't because of the rolling water. This particular zombie wasn't dead, only stunned by the bullet that had ricocheted off its skull, and slowly it began to regain itself. But it would take time for it to become fully functional again. The three survivors didn't see a thing, nor would they have thought much about the body if they had. Each time the waves rolled across the beach, the bodies were tossed and pushed a little more onto the sand.

When the three companions arrived back at their camp, they dropped down in the sand. John had put his clothes on as they walked back, though his feet were still bare. Living on the beach, there wasn't much use for shoes and they still sat in the helicopter, taken off the first day they'd arrived on the island.

"Well, guys, I have to tell you, that was the biggest waste of time I can remember in a long time," McDermott said, exasperated. "All three of us almost got killed at least once and we have nothing to show for any of it."

John held up the Zippo lighter he had slid into his underwear before jumping back into the water to reach Sarah. "Well, at least I got this," he said with a grin.

"Oh, then I guess it was all worth it," McDermott quipped back sarcastically. "Now, if we'd found some booze, that would be another story."

"Do you think there are any more still out there in the water?" Sarah asked. "If the ones from the boat could move about under water like that, what would stop more from doing the same thing? Why couldn't they just walk into the water from the mainland, cross the ocean, and pop up here one day?"

John shrugged. "Sarah darling, I wish I could tell you that would never happen, but the truth is I have no idea. Hopefully, any more of them would get lost at sea instead of coming to shore. I guess we won't know if it's possible until they show up."

"Well, we've always had one of us on guard duty every night so I guess now we have a real reason to," she said.

"Maybe, but we have one of us on watch for another reason, too," John said. "We don't know this island other than the beach, and if we drop our guard for even a second, it could be our last." He glanced at McDermott. "We don't really know if this island is deserted or not."

"Truer words have never been spoken, Johnny," McDermott said with a smile. He pointed at the barren rock they used as a table. There wasn't so much as a scrap of the gutted fish John had placed there an hour ago. "So what are we gonna do about lunch?"

Chapter 6

A few hours later, John and McDermott were napping under the makeshift tent, the exertion of the day finally catching up to them. Sarah was sitting by the fire on a three foot long log, writing in her journal.

The sky was darkening, the orange and reds of the sunset filling the sky. It was a beautiful sight, and even after two weeks of them, Sarah still admired the beauty.

But she didn't look long, and soon had her nose buried in the notebook again.

Between the crash of the waves on the beach, the crackling fire, McDermott snoring, and the wind whipping the tarp about, hearing anything else was impossible unless it was very loud. So the soft footsteps of a zombie moving along the treeline was about as silent as it could possibly be.

There was a hole in the forehead of the ghoul, but there was another one on the right side of the head as well, this being where the bullet had ricocheted off the skull and out the second hole.

It was really just dumb luck that the dead fisherman had stumbled out of the water and had picked the direction of the camp to walk. But then, it only had two choices—right or left—and so had gone left, which now brought it to the camp. With sunset coming, the water-logged figure was all but invisible against the trees.

Though Sarah might have been on watch, she wasn't doing a very good job of her duties, and had barely looked up from her notebook more than once, and that was just to admire the sunset. The dead fisherman stumbled closer, then turned so that he was heading right for her; even passing by the tarp and the sleeping men in favor of attacking Sarah first. Perhaps it was the flickering fire that was drawing it to her, or maybe the wind was blowing just right and it could smell her, but the ghoul only had eyes for Sarah.

Lying on a small blanket besides Sarah was the M-16, a full magazine in it.

The dead fisherman came at her quickly. If it had made a sound, a moan or a groan, no doubt Sarah would have heard the approach, but this zombie wasn't a talker and so remained silent.

Sarah didn't know she was in danger until a split-second before the fisherman raised its arms and brought them down on her. In that instant she sensed more than actually knew that there was something wrong.

But it was too late. The zombie grabbed her by the shoulders and pulled her off the log she was sitting on, throwing her to the sand. She toppled over and fell hard on her back. Her notebook flew up into the air to land six feet away.

She was so startled that she didn't scream, didn't utter a sound.

With the sunset behind the dead fisherman, she couldn't see the face clearly, but the smell hit her immediately and she knew she wasn't dealing with a living attacker.

That was all she had time for, as the zombie bent over, its mouth opening wide to bite her. Even in the waning light Sarah could see the yellow teeth as the zombie's face came closer. She tried to put up her hands to stop what she knew was about to happen, but the ghoul was twice as big as her and Sarah's strength seemed feeble against it.

Still she tried, her hands going up to stop the encroaching face. Her fingers slid under the zombie's chin and sank into the soft flesh of the throat, the sensation making her want to retch. It was like touching cold Playdoh. As the malleable skin sucked in her fingers, Sarah knew that if she survived this encounter, she would never forget the feeling of rotting flesh as it sloughed off the bones.

She'd experienced another moment weeks ago that would stay with her until the day she died as well. She had gone to see Dr. Logan in the bunker, and upon finding him in his laboratory, he'd discussed with her on what he believed was happening to the walking dead, such as why they remained animated though deceased. He filled her in on how he thought that the dead were the same animals as humans, simply operating less perfectly. But while he was talking, pointing to a diagram of a human brain on a chalkboard, a zombie that was strapped to a gurney a few feet away broke free of the bond holding one of its arms.

It was still secured to the gurney, but with one arm free it had tried to shift onto its side slightly, which wouldn't have been a problem but for the simple fact that Dr. Logan had disconnected every organ in the ghoul's torso, but had left them in their appropriate places as he studied the specimen. The result was that as the zombie rolled onto its side, its organs literally spilled out of it to splash onto the floor. The wet smacks as liver, spleen and intestines struck the cold cement floor had made Sarah taste bile and it was all she could do not to vomit right there and then.

The memory haunted her constantly; that was when she truly understood why Dr. Logan had received the nickname of 'Frankenstein' by the military men in the complex.

The dead fisherman made a grunting nose as he tried to bite Sarah, but she was doing a good job of keeping the gnashing teeth at bay. But then she felt her arms being pushed backwards, the face moving ever closer.

Bits of flesh fell from the face, landing on her forehead and cheeks. Though she knew she needed to call out for help, her lips remained closed. Just the thought of one of those pieces of decrepit flesh falling into her open mouth was enough to keep her silent. Sometimes, even if a person survived, they wished they hadn't.

The teeth were inches from her nose, clacking continually, the trapped air in the zombie's lungs being expelled to blow into her face. It was beyond nauseating and she had no choice but to open her mouth as vomit surged upward and into the zombie's face, then back down onto her.

As she retched, her throat burning from stomach acids, her arms went slack, and the ghoul had its opportunity to feed. Its head snapped forward, as there was now nothing stopping it from getting its prey, and Sarah knew she was about to die.

Then suddenly, as if by magic, the ghoul's head exploded into a hundred bloody chunks, brain matter splattering Sarah's face and neck. Already covered in vomit, this wasn't an issue for her.

The body on top of her went limp and Sarah used its falling weight to let it roll to the side and off her. But that was where the fire was, and the body rolled right into the flames. Immediately, the sickly-sweet odor of cooking flesh filled the air.

Though Sarah hadn't heard it, there had been the report of a gunshot just before the zombie's head exploded, and the sound had woken John and McDermott. With guns in hand, they jumped up to see Sarah lying by the fire with another body beside her. Both men ran to her.

"Sarah, what happened," John asked, his eyes searching the beach for signs of more intruders. He went to Sarah and helped her stand. "Are you hurt?"

McDermott ran for the fallen figure, and after grabbing the corpse's feet, dragged the body out of the camp fire, then tossed some sand onto it to extinguish the flames. "This guys been shot;

his head's pretty much gone, too," he said and on further inspection added, "Wait, this guy wasn't alive to begin with. I think he was one of the dead that were on the fishing boat."

"How the hell did it get here? I thought we got them all," John said, his eyes constantly searching the shadows for more attackers. But it was quiet, only the trees gently swaying in the wind.

Sarah shook her head. "I don't know. One second I was alone and the next I was being forced to the ground." She wiped her face with the bottom of her plaid shirt, and when that didn't work, she took it off and began again. She wore an armless t-shirt underneath the plaid one so she was still clothed. "I thought it was all over and then…and then its head exploded."

"We're not alone." John studied the treeline even harder, knowing someone was out there. "If anyone's still there, come out, we mean you no harm. In fact, we owe you a debt for saving Sarah."

No reply came and John frowned.

McDermott moved closer to John so he could whisper, "You really think someone's out there?"

"Has to be," John said out of the side of his mouth. "We both heard a gunshot and then that thing's head exploded, according to Sarah. Wasn't magic, Billy boy, it was someone with a gun." John turned his attention to the treeline and called out, "You can come out or at first light we can come looking for you. Either way, sooner or later we'll meet. But like I said, we mean you no harm. In fact, if we had any, I'd buy you a beer in thanks."

Only the crash of the waves on the beach could be heard. Sarah had finished cleaning herself up as best she could for now, and she joined the two men. "Anything?" she asked.

John shook his head. "Whoever's out there is shy."

Sarah took a step forward, then another so that she was closer to the treeline than the men.

"Sarah, what are you doing?" John hissed. "Get back here; we don't know if it's friend or foe out there."

Sarah glanced over her shoulder at John and McDermott. "The way I see it, whoever's out there could have shot me but they didn't, and even now if they wanted us dead they'd have had us a dozen times over. Think about it. When you came running to help me you were easy targets. No, whoever's out there means us no harm." She spoke loudly so that whoever was in the trees would hear her, too.

"You're right," a male voice said from the treeline. "I don't mean you any harm. That's why I saved you a few minutes ago."

"Then come out so we can see you," Sarah said. "Please."

Once more there was nothing but silence, as if the man was considering whether to do as Sarah asked. Sarah was about to call out again, hoping to prod her mysterious savior from hiding, when a man stepped out of the treeline about thirty yards from where the camp fire was. He held a sniper rifle in the crook of his arm. He walked slowly but confidently towards Sarah. If he was concerned that he might be attacked by John or McDermott, he sure didn't show it. On his right hip was a handgun in a plastic holster and on his left hung a hunting knife. He looked to be in his late twenties, with curly blonde hair and stubble on his cheeks. His eyes reflected the sunset and seemed to glow a bright orange, but when he got closer, Sarah saw that his eyes were blue, like hers. She did notice abstractedly that he was handsome, his physique strong with no body fat that she could see. She had a feeling she would be hard-pressed to find any if she was so inclined.

When the man was three feet from Sarah, he stopped and with a warm smile held out his right hand for her to shake. "Hello, I'm Thomas, but everyone calls me Tom."

"Hi, Tom, I'm Sar…" she began to say but he cut her off playfully.

"You're Sarah, and the two men behind you with guns aimed at me are John and Bill. I know who you all are. I've been watching you for hours."

"Then why didn't you…" she began but he cut her off again.

"Because the people I live with don't like strangers, that's why. But I had to tip my hand to save you and now you know about me, and about my people, so I guess it doesn't matter anymore. There's no more need to stay hidden." He raised his left hand casually, like he was about to swat a fly on his neck, and as if by magic, five more men stepped out of the treeline, guns drawn and leveled at Sarah, John and McDermott.

"Just do as I say and I promise you that no one will get hurt," Tom said, the smile never leaving his face.

Chapter 7

With no options opened to them, John and McDermott dropped their weapons as the five men came out of the treeline. The men retrieved the weapons and then stood back, though their guns were still leveled at John and McDermott.

Tom nodded upon seeing them relinquish their weapons. "I knew you two were sensible men," he said pleasantly. "Please trust me when I tell you that you're in absolutely no danger. This is just a precaution."

"A precaution for what?" John asked.

"Oh, this and that," Tom replied. "Meeting people for the first time can be a dicey fucking thing even before the world fell apart, but now it can be downright dangerous. When people are startled they can get itchy trigger fingers, if you know what I mean. No one wants to take any chances here."

"So what next?" McDermott asked.

"Oh, that's simple. You three will come back with me and my men to our village. Once there we're going to ask you a few questions. Nothing difficult, just where you came from and what news you might have of the outside world. Once we're satisfied at what you tell us. You'll be released to either stay with us or come back here to the beach. But I have to tell you that once the storm season comes this beach won't be a nice place to be."

"When's that?" Sarah asked.

Tom rubbed his chin as he thought about it. "Oh, I'd say another three weeks, give or take a few days."

"What do we do with the chopper?" one of the men asked Tom.

"Leave it where it is, Mark," Tom instructed. "Only John there knows how to fly it and I doubt he'd leave without his friends even if he didn't come with us."

Tom made eye contact with Sarah first, then John and McDermott. "So, people, would you please come this way? Our village is about a two hour walk from here on the other side of the island." He checked his watch. "But it's only six so we should be there by eight at the latest."

John's jaw locked tight, his eyes creasing. "Well then, man, I guess we don't have a choice in coming with you."

Tom looked back at John, his visage equally hard. "No, you don't."

The three companions' gear was quickly gathered by the five men that had come out of the trees, then everyone set off into the forest on what John saw was a small path if you knew what you were looking for. Overhead, birds called out to one another as darkness fell. The lead man in line carried a torch that he waved before him as they all followed him, the beacon easy to see.

Sarah, John and McDermott were in the middle of the line, with three men before them and Tom and two more behind them.

"I was watching the three of you since Sarah had to shoot the dead fucks that came out of the ocean," Tom explained. "I was close by when the gunshots sounded. Until then no one even knew you were here, you know, living on the beach. But once I heard those shots I went to investigate. See, I was already close by, hunting. Then I stayed in the trees and watched you guys, so I could get a feel for who you were and why you were on the island. Good thing I stayed, too, or Sarah would be dead by now…or worse, infected."

"And did you get what you needed, man?" John asked.

Tom shrugged. "Pretty much. To me you three seem like people that came here to get away from the dead fucks on the mainland, that's all. From what I saw you seem harmless enough to the people I live with."

"Then why do we have to go through these interrogations you spoke of?" McDermott asked.

"Look, maybe the word *interrogation* isn't the right word. I may have misspoke. Let's just say we need to 'debrief' you before we can let you join us."

"What makes you think we want to join you?" Sarah asked.

Tom's eyebrows went up. "You mean you don't? I just assumed…"

"Well, don't, man," John said, cutting Tom off. "We just got out of a place with too many people that thought they knew what was right for everyone else. Maybe we just want to be by ourselves."

"Well, even if you don't want to join us I don't make the fucking decisions," Tom explained. "That will be up to the professor."

"The professor? Who's that?" Sarah asked, the title of another academic intriguing her.

"Professor Langford. He's our leader. Well, not really our actual leader, but we needed someone to sort of be in charge and he got voted in. As I recall, he didn't even want the position, he just wanted to only do his research, but we all convinced him that it was for the best. He finally relented on the agreement that we try not to bother him too much. But I know he'll want to meet you three. We haven't had anyone new arrive on the island in over a year."

"That brings up a question I've been thinking about," John said. "How did you and the people you're with get here in the first place? How long have you been here?"

Tom pushed an errant branch out of his way as he walked. "Ah, John, I could tell you but I know that's one thing Professor Langford will want to do himself. He loves telling the tale of how we all wound up on this island. So I wouldn't want to spoil the surprise by telling you now. Sorry."

"No worries, man, I can wait," John replied.

They walked for almost two hours until the trees began to thin to eventually open up onto a wide glade that led to a small valley—more of a crack in the earth really—nestled between two mountain peaks.

The moon was out and the cloud cover was nonexistent, the stars twinkling overhead like a blinking blanket. Because of this, the valley was easy to see and all that it contained.

Complete with a small stream that was fed by rocks that led into the mountains, the valley was sectioned off into square plots, where lush crops could be seen.

There were the towering stalks of corn, the green carpet of lettuce and squash, and even some kind of cereal grain, the golden tops swaying in the night air. Another section had orange and lemon trees.

"Wow," was all Sarah could think to say.

"I know, right?" Tom said proudly. "I'm used to the sight, but I always love to see the faces when new arrivals see it for the first time. I've missed that I guess. We've truly grown something wonderful here, despite what's happened back on the mainland. Hell, maybe even because of it."

On the edges of the plots were small, glass buildings that had to be greenhouses, and beyond those were small buildings that looked like they were used for storage of such things like the tools to work the crops and to also store the crops in once they were harvested.

There were a few people in the fields even now, taking advantage of the cooler night air to work. Sarah studied them, but other than that they looked like typical farmers with overalls and work boots; not much more could be made out.

"Come on, this way," Tom said, using an arm to gently usher Sarah along, and by doing so, John and McDermott, too.

The group continued walking, then came upon a path that led to the valley that finally brought them to an open area where buildings lined both sides of a dirt road. The buildings had been put together with care with whatever had been around. Logs from trees were used, as well as sheet metal and scrap wood. To John it reminded him of the poorer sections of his homeland back in Jamaica.

People sat on logs and small boulders just the right size for sitting on. These had been rolled out of the mountains and the ones too big to be used in construction of buildings were then used as resting places.

As Tom led everyone onto the dirt road, the people sitting out watched with curiosity by way of torchlight. John glared at them, at the moment trusting no one, but McDermott nodded to a few villagers, smiling and waving at a few more, the latter mostly women.

At the end of the dirt road was another building—though a shack would be a better description—indiscriminate from any of the others.

"This is where you'll be sleeping tonight," Tom said to Sarah, John and McDermott. "Someone will bring you food in a bit, and water to drink and wash up. Tomorrow morning, bright and early, you can meet the professor." One of the other men opened the door to the shack, and in doing so the message was clear.

John looked at Sarah and McDermott, then stepped inside the shack, followed by Sarah. McDermott hesitated and turned to look at Tom, then said, "Might you have some sort of grain alcohol or something similar around here? It might help us to pass the night."

"Sorry, we don't have anything like that here," Tom said, smiling politely.

"Ah well, a man can dream," McDermott said and entered the shack.

Tom followed and stood in the doorway. "You folks have a good night sleep."

"Hey, tell me something, Tom," John said, sounding as if he was asking about the weather. "What if we didn't want to stay here tonight? What if we wanted to go back to the beach and fly away in my whirlybird?"

"I couldn't let that happen, especially now that you know of our existence here. Sorry, John."

"So what you're sayin' is that we're prisoners here," John said, making more of a statement than a question.

"Prisoners would be too harsh a word, John," Tom said, his smile fading slightly. "Let's just say that for now you're our guests and leave it at that."

"Ah, maybe so, man, but a cage is still a cage, no matter what you call it," John added.

Tom said nothing, then began closing the door. "Have a good-night, guys. See you in the morning. We rise early here, with the sun." The door closed and then he said through the door, "Food and water will arrive shortly."

There was the sound of muffled voices on the opposite side of the door and John went to it and pressed his ear against the faded wood, trying to hear. Sarah and McDermott watched him, and saw John frown in the interior gloom of the shack. Eventually,

John moved away from the door, and gestured for Sarah and McDermott to follow him to the far side of the one-room shack, where he began to whisper.

"They've posted a guard outside the door, and when I tried to open it the damn thing was locked," John said softly.

"So we're stuck here," McDermott said flatly.

"Aye, Billy boy, that we are," John replied.

"I studied the people that were watching us as we walked here," Sarah said. "They didn't look scared or like people that were being subjugated. It's possible that Tom and his people are decent folk. That all this is simply their way of being careful. You have to admit, John, they have a point. They don't know us, they have no idea if we're decent people or like Rhodes and his men."

"Ah, Sarah, don't bring up that asshole," McDermott said. "I've been doing my best to forget him and his cronies."

"Sorry, Bill, I didn't mean to upset you."

"That's all right, Sarah, I'll get over it." McDermott went to one of the two chairs in the room, where they were located next to four beds that were basically cots, and crossed one leg over the other after plopping down with a weary sigh. To his left on a small table was a candle and matches. "The way I see it, we have a roof over our heads and food and water is coming. Do we know what these people will do with us? No, of course not, but no matter what happens, it can't be worse than the shit we had to deal with back at the cave."

At mentioning the 'cave,' which was another nickname for the bunker, as massive caves were connected to the actual complex, both John and Sarah's faces grew grim.

"There is that, Billy boy," John said. "There surely is that."

Chapter 8

A knock came at the door at sunrise, waking John and the others from a fitful sleep. The person who knocked entered a moment later. It was one of the men that had been with Tom, though John didn't know his name. He thought it was Mark.

"Time to get up," the man said. "The professor's waiting for you in his laboratory."

"Laboratory?" Sarah repeated as she sat up, but the man was gone from the doorway, though he could be seen waiting outside. She shifted in her cot to face John, excitement on her face. "If they have a laboratory here, maybe they've been doing research like me and my team were doing back at the bunker."

"Aye, Sarah, and how did that work out for ya?" John asked sarcastically as he yawned.

She ignored him.

McDermott stretched on his cot and rubbed his face with the palms of his hands. "I need to use the bathroom something fierce. I had to go last night but quickly figured out there were no facilities in our little home away from home."

"I know what you mean. Maybe on the way to see this professor we can make a pit-stop, Bill," Sarah suggested as she rose, stretched and yawned. It had been a very busy day yesterday, and though she hadn't believed it, she had passed out as soon as her head hit the cot.

John put on his shoes while the others did the same—fresh clothing for the three companions had arrived last night, donated from the village, this coming after the food was delivered. The food hadn't been anything special, but it was still miles above what they had eaten in the bunker. Cold roast pork and fresh vegetables, and cool spring water was the repast. McDermott had commented that anything that wasn't fish was all right with him, especially after eating it for two weeks straight.

The three companions finished dressing, exited the shack, and followed the guard.

Unlike last night, where a few people had been lounging around lazily, it appeared that with the rising of the sun so too did the residents of the village. It was ordered chaos as men and women alike moved around the small enclave, pushing wheel barrows full of tools and other necessities that were needed to grow crops. Children were there, too, running around their parents as the elders went off to work. It was strange seeing children, and Sarah realized that she hadn't given it much thought, but deep down had wondered if there were any children even left on the planet.

Most of the villagers wore coveralls with hats or bandanas on their heads to protect them from the harsh sun. Almost all were a dark tan from exposure to the sun. There was a mix of many races, too. Sarah spotted at least a dozen different ones, from Spanish to Asian to Filipino, and Irish and Italian thrown in to keep it all interesting. But unlike the United Nations, where everyone bickered and argued constantly, these people all got along wonderfully, everyone working toward the common goal of survival. The scientist in Sarah found it all fascinating as a work study of humanity, and how given a serious enough cause, it was true that mankind could work together, despite cultural differences.

"Hey, man," John said to the guard as they walked down the dirt road. "Where's Tom?"

"He's leading a hunting party this morning. That pork you ate last night didn't come from a grocery store you know. Everything we eat here is either grown or hunted."

"Hey," McDermott called out from behind John, "how 'bout a bathroom break? I'm ready to burst."

As McDermott finished speaking, the guard stopped in front of a smaller shack than the others the companions had seen at the end of the road, the exact opposite end of where the companions had arrived the previous night, on the outskirts of the village. From the odor wafting from the open doorway, it was obvious what the building was used for. But if that wasn't enough for someone to figure it out, then the sign hanging over the door with the word OUTHOUSE would have answered any questions.

"Go in one at a time," the man said. "There's a bucket of leaves to use as toilet paper."

"Classy," John said with a sly grin.

Before anyone could ask who would go first, McDermott pushed past Sarah and John with a, "Outta the way, I need to go now."

John and Sarah chuckled, and a minute and half later, McDermott exited the building, albeit much slower than when he'd entered it. "That's better. Who's next?"

John looked to Sarah who gestured for John to go next. He did and then it was Sarah's turn.

She scrunched up her nose as she entered the building. There was only a wooden box with a hole in it to sit on and a pit dug in the ground. She figured it out immediately. When the hole was full, it would be buried and then the shack moved to another location where a fresh pit would be dug. It was simple but more than serviceable, and not much different than using a port-o'-potty. She did miss using toilet paper, however, but she made do with what was there, though the leaves were rough and scratchy in places she would rather not have scratched. When she and the others had been on the beach, she had gone off into the woods and then had washed in the ocean. For the thousandth time she envied men for being able to pee standing up. They simply had no idea how lucky they were.

Finished, she exited the outhouse to see John and McDermott smiling at her.

"What?" she asked.

"Oh, nothing," McDermott said with a chuckle. "We were just talking about our new bathroom facilities. It's not *The Ritz*, but then what is?"

"This way," the guard said, wanting to get rid of his charges so he could get on with his day.

Once more the three companions followed him and soon came upon another one-story building—none of the structures were larger than one story—this one better built than the ones they'd passed to get here. This house was made out of logs and boulders, and even some dried mud to seal cracks between logs and stones. The roof was made from the thick leaves that were found on some of the trees that thrived near the beach. It was almost a perfect square.

"Inside," the guard said flatly at the door to the well-built building. A rifle hung over his shoulder by a leather sling, but if any of the companions had wanted to jump him, the man never would have been able to brandish the weapon in time.

Sarah entered first, followed by John and McDermott, who paused to look at the man one last time. "Don't expect a tip, pal," the Irishman sniffed before entering the house.

Sarah's eyes lit up as she entered the house, her mind flashing back to the underground bunker and Dr. Logan's laboratory.

On every table were test tubes, and plant and animal specimens. The walls themselves were used as chalkboards, complex diagrams decorating every flat surface. But unlike Dr. Logan's lab which resembled a charnel house more than a place of learning and research, this lab was clean and tidy, with not so much as a drop of blood anywhere.

At the back of the room, five men and one woman, all wearing white lab coats, were huddled over a table, but when Sarah, John and McDermott entered, one of the scientists looked up and then left the group to practically run across the lab. He almost knocked over the contents of two tables on his way, but managed to grab anything that would topple before they fell. As the man moved closer, stumbling along the way, Sarah thought of the actor Jerry Lewis when he played the *Nutty Professor*; the man had the look almost perfect, right down to the thick bifocals. He appeared to be in his early to middle sixties. His skin was very pale, signifying he didn't get outside much.

"Ah, hello, hello, it's so good to finally meet you all. My name is Professor Langford. Welcome to New Eden."

"It's so nice to meet you, too," Sarah said, smiling as she took the man's proffered hand and shook it. She turned and looked John and McDermott in the eyes, her own face telling them, *I got this, we speak the same language.*

John merely shrugged and McDermott nodded. McDermott had already had his fill of science geeks to last a lifetime; he didn't want to have to deal with any more. Sarah didn't count though. He liked her and she didn't act like most eggheads. But then Fisher hadn't been that bad of a guy either. But Logan, now there was a nutjob if there ever had been one. McDermott thought back to when he'd gone into the mad doctor's lab looking for antibiotics for Miguel with Sarah after she'd amputated the man's arm. There, McDermott and Sarah had found a shop of horrors, and a tape recording of Dr. Logan babbling like a madman, or at the very least a man in danger of losing his mind completely if he already hadn't.

But it was all in the past now. Dr. Logan was dead, shot repeatedly in the chest by Captain Rhodes, who was probably dead, too.

"I hope you've all been treated well?" Professor Langford inquired with a smile. With the index finger of his right hand, he pushed his eyeglasses back up on his nose when they slid down, then not even three seconds later he did it again. It was obvious that the glasses were too big for his face and the constant gesture must have been something the man did without thinking about it; such as when a woman would brush long hair off her face.

"Sure, if you think being taken at gunpoint and then locked in a room all night is being 'treated well,' " McDermott quipped.

Sarah flashed McDermott a look that told him to shut up but McDermott acted like he didn't see her.

If the professor was offended, he gave no sign. "Yes, I'm aware of all that and may I say I am sorry if you felt disrespected. Tom is head of security around here and he takes his job very seriously—a bit overzealous sometimes to tell you the truth. But it's necessary given the state of the world. However, from what he's told me about you three, I don't think there will be any need for distrust. All he learned about you as he watched you from afar is more than enough to tell me what I need to know, that you're decent people just trying to survive, just like the people in this village. I was also so excited to hear you came in a helicopter. How wonderful."

"Don't get too excited, Doc," John said. "The whirlybird is sucking fumes, and without fuel she's nothing but a paperweight."

"Ah, yes, I see, well, no matter, there's no reason to leave this island anyway. And if there was any doubt to that than I highly doubt you three would be here now. Am I right?" He slid his glasses back up his nose once more—as automatic to him as blinking.

"You got that one right, Doc," John replied.

Sarah was looking at one of the walls, studying the diagram there. "Professor Langford, from that formula on the wall, I assume you're trying to find a cure to the dead walking, am I right?"

The professor blinked in surprise. "Why yes, I am." He gestured to the four scientists behind him, who had barely looked up at the three new arrivals. "We all are. How did you know? Are you a doctor yourself perhaps?"

"Yes, actually," she said with pride. "I have a Masters in Health Sciences. Before we came to this island, the three of us were part of a hastily formed government project that was set up to try and find a cure to the walking dead. John was the helicopter pilot, McDermott was in charge of the radio equipment, and I was one of the scientists—one of three actually."

Professor Langford was so excited he looked like he was about to start jumping up and down like a five-year-old after being told he was going to the circus. "Really? Did you have any results? What did you find out? Oh my, this is wonderful news. We must collaborate, Doctor, this is all so exciting." He took Sarah by the hand and began pulling her to the other scientists at the back of the room.

"Hey, Doc, what about us?" McDermott called out, referring to himself and John.

"Huh? Oh, yes, sorry, but this is so much more important than social etiquette. You can go to the armory and retrieve your weapons and anything else you've brought with you that Tom may have taken, then find Tom and he'll assign you a work detail. It's entirely up to him what you'll be doing. I agreed to be the leader here on the agreement that I don't have to deal with the day to day chores of running it. I leave all that to Tom. He's a good man; he'll take care of you." Then he was in the back of the room, introducing Sarah to the other scientists he worked with. John and McDermott were completely forgotten, and the word 'dismissed' came to mind as well.

The two men glanced at one another, not knowing what they should do next.

"Well, Johnny, before we find the armory, I want to find our gear," McDermott said. "My flask is in there somewhere, and I don't know about you, but I sure as hell need a bloody drink. If this place is like any other I've known, there's got be some booze around here somewhere, the trick is finding out who knows who."

John gestured with his hand for McDermott to go first. "After you, Billy boy."

Chapter 9

After all the introductions were made between Sarah and the other scientists—of which she barely remembered the names given her—Sarah and Professor Langford went off to a corner of the room to talk a little more.

"So tell me, Sarah, what's it like on the mainland?" he asked.

"Not good," she began and then told him all about the bunker and scientific team, the Army, Rhodes, and finally her, John and McDermott's eventual escape.

The professor nodded, and every now and then he asked a few questions. He was most interested in Dr. Logan's work on why the dead were walking. "I knew it had to be very bad when no more radio reports came in, and even our ham radio went quiet." He sighed. "I tell you, my dear, I truly thought we were the last humans left alive on this planet." He pushed his eyeglasses up his nose for the hundredth time since Sarah had met him.

"That assumption isn't too far from the truth, I hate to say," Sarah said. "Okay, Professor, I've answered most of your questions, now I have some of my own."

"Of course my dear, where are my manners. Please, ask away. Whatever you want to know I will endeavor to answer to the best of my ability."

"Okay, the first thing I would like to know is how you and all the people I've seen ended up here on this island?"

"Ah, my dear, that's a long story, but I will attempt to keep it short." He began a narrative of how when the first signs of the dead walking were broadcast on the news he had been very attentive of it. Later, when it was apparent it wasn't a hoax and that it truly was happening, he contacted the other people he worked with in a government sanctioned think tank. It took a little coercion on his part but eventually he was able to make almost all the others in his group come with him to the island.

As a tenured professor at a well-respected college, he'd managed to save up a hefty sum of money. Only interested in his work, he had little use for money other than to pay his bills. So he took everything he had and financed an exodus to the island, which he knew was owned by the government and was deserted at the time the dead rose.

On top of his fellow scientists, he allowed each of them to bring along their families, and of course he made sure to hire a few ex-military personnel in case things became dangerous. Tom was one such person, and so were many of the men Sarah had seen on the beach with him.

The only thing that wasn't feasible to bring were building materials, but they brought plenty of saws and tools, so they were able to make do with what the island naturally offered in way of materials.

Upon arriving, they also found piles of building materials, such as sheet metal and wood, leftovers from a former government research team that had been on the island years earlier. Prof. Langford made sure to bring everything and anything he thought he might need in the setup of his laboratory, and other than a few things that always slipped through the cracks when going on a trip, he was pretty well stocked.

The residents had been taken to the island by boat, and once close to shore, smaller boats had brought them to the beach. It had been arduous moving all the supplies like this but there had been no other choice.

All the boats that had carried them from the mainland were long gone and other than a few fishing boats they used to fish with, there was no way back to the mainland. But Professor Langford had prepared for the long haul and by everything Sarah had told him, he had been correct.

That had been almost four and a half years ago, back when the dead first began to walk.

Since then, he and his team had worked every day in the hopes of finding a cure to what made the dead walk, but so far they had found nothing they could use. There were times he thought he was close, but each time there was always something missing, that one equation that would solve the problem of humans rising after death.

"You've been searching for a cure for almost five years?" Sarah asked when the professor was done with his tale.

He nodded. "Yes, and though it seems hopeless, we won't stop until we're all dead; as ironic as that sounds." He sighed and pushed his eyeglasses back up his nose. "I know there's a scientific reason, Sarah, I just haven't found it yet."

"Well, I'd be happy to help in any way I can," she said. "Like I explained already, my colleague Dr. Logan, believed that it was the brain that allowed the dead to still function and that it had something to do with the 'R' complex of the brain, what he called the lizard part. But where he was interested in how the dead walked, my research was more about trying to reverse the process, or prevent it from even happening."

"I see," Langford said, pushing his eyeglasses up his nose yet again. "Did you have any luck before you left?"

She nodded. "Some, but like you, there was a piece of the puzzle missing, something I could never find. Maybe with us working together that can change."

"Oh, I completely agree; fresh eyes and all that." He snapped his fingers at one of the other scientists and when he had that person's attention, he pointed to a rack of white lab coats hanging in the corner. The scientist retrieved one and brought it back. Prof. Langford took the coat while mumbling gratitude, then handed it to Sarah. "Here, dear, put this on. You're one of us now, so you might as well look the part."

Sarah took the jacket and slid it on over her shirt. It was a little big but not so much that she felt she had to roll up the sleeves. She looked down at herself, seeing the coat on her and it was a weird feeling.

She hadn't believed she would ever wear one again, and had accepted with a heavy heart that the part of her life as a researcher was over. But she had to admit that it felt good to wear the coat. It felt right.

This is what Sarah had trained for, gone to school for so many years. Maybe now, here, with these people, she might find the cure to the dead walking. Maybe here she would find closure to all that had happened at the underground bunker.

"Welcome aboard, Sarah, it's good to have you on the team," Prof. Langford said with a grin. He began clapping and the other scientists quickly joined in. Sarah smiled, enjoying the feeling of being welcomed by her peers.

Maybe Tom finding them wasn't going to be so bad after all.

When the clapping died down, the professor began to show Sarah around, and once she had a decent idea of where everything was, he left her alone to get accustomed to her new environment.

Sarah, staring at the notebooks, computers powered by solar panels and a generator in the back of the building, centrifuges and beakers before her, as well as dozens of samples to test, smiled widely and with pure satisfaction.

Despite all that she'd been through, and had done, and people she'd killed and seen killed, at the end of the day she was a scientist, and here, with Prof. Langford and his team, she was home.

Chapter 10

The rest of the day went by quickly for Sarah, who happily threw herself into her research work. She only saw John and McDermott twice, once at lunch and once at dinner.

Meals were served in a communal building in the center of the village. Though the food was good, Sarah barely paid attention to it. She was excited at the prospect of doing research again. She was fulfilled, something she hadn't felt in a while, and she chatted with John and McDermott, telling them all about her day.

At dinner with them both, the Irishman had handed Sarah his .45, wanting her to have it for protection.

"Against what?" she'd asked. "There's nothing to fear here."

"Maybe so," John had said, "but just take it anyway. Keep it hidden under that shiny new lab coat you're wearing."

John had told Sarah how he and McDermott were going to be on hunting duty with Tom starting the next day.

"He figures seems we know how to handle ourselves we'd make better hunters than farmers any day," John had told her.

As night fell and it was coming on nine, Sarah rubbed her eyes with her hand and decided it was time to knock off for the night. "Good night, Professor," she called out as she left the laboratory. "I'll see you in the morning."

Prof. Langford, the only one left other than her at such a late hour, grunted something in the form of a goodbye as Sarah left.

Stepping outside, she paused and breathed in the night air. It was a beautiful night, the moon out once more, the stars twinkling overhead. As she gazed up at the night sky and stared at the stars, she wondered about what was out there. Those stars cared nothing about what was happening on her small planet. They cared little for the fight to survive as the dead overwhelmed the living. In the grand scale of the cosmos, what she did here was of little consequence.

A few people were still walking around but not many. When a person had to be up at the crack of dawn, that meant they were usually in bed as soon as the sun set.

Sarah smiled in greeting at some of the people, but most didn't respond, only walked past her without looking her way. She didn't mind. She understood completely. Sarah and her friends were new to the community, and most people distrusted outsiders at first. Hopefully in time, she, John and McDermott would be accepted.

She heard the sound of a screaming baby, then more children laughing. It came from a house to her right.

Children.

That was something she never thought she'd see again and it still filled her with happiness and amazement. Sarah thought back to her time in the bunker, and how she, John and McDermott had gone on survey missions to try and find other survivors in the helicopter. There had been none, and even when the dead came for them when they landed and called out for survivors, there were few zombie children in the horde. She had always assumed it was because children were more vulnerable and therefore were torn apart and devoured completely, so there was nothing to revive.

When she reached the small shack she called home, she stopped at the closed door and listened. She could hear McDermott snoring even with the door closed. She sighed, knowing she wasn't ready for sleep just yet. To deal with McDermott's chainsaw snoring she needed to be truly exhausted. She didn't know how John could handle it, but then there were people who could sleep through anything, while others woke if so much as a pin dropped. She was in the middle of the two, but the sound of a truck engine revving in the bed next to her wasn't going to let sleep come anytime soon.

She sat on one of the two wooden chairs that were next to the front door. With a gentle sigh, she leaned her head back against the shack, McDermott's snoring from within a stark contrast to the chirping crickets and gentle wind wafting through the nearby trees. Sarah felt good inside; she had the feeling all people have after a long day, where they feel that they've done good work. She'd forgotten how satisfying pure research was.

It was so peaceful here. Though she thought she wasn't that tired, her eyes immediately began to droop. Before she realized it, her head nodded forward and she drifted off to sleep.

Yelling caused Sarah to wake, her head snapping up, her eyes popping open. Her hand instinctively went to the .45 on her hip under the lab coat, as her eyes tried to clear the sleep-vision that made everything seem murky. She was still outside in the chair, where she'd drifted off to sleep.

Yelling people ran past her, causing adrenaline to surge through her body, banishing any remnants of sleep. She was now fully awake, and as Sarah stood up, she stepped forward and grabbed the next person to run past. "What's going on? Why's everyone running around?" she asked. It was still dark, though she had no idea what time it was.

Sarah had managed to collar a young woman in her late twenties. The woman tried to break free from Sarah's grip on her shirt, but quickly realized it would be easier to answer Sarah's questions so she could be set free. "George died a little while ago in his sleep," the woman said quickly. "Everyone thinks it was a heart attack; he was eighty-six and had a bad heart. He revived and tried to attack his wife but Ethel is a tough old woman and she fought him off. She managed to get away and get help, but by the time she returned with Tom, George was gone. He's somewhere in the village, and he's now one of the dead, so we need to find him and fast before he attacks anyone."

"What's he look like?" Sarah asked.

The woman balked, as if she didn't want to answer, then said, "Gray hair, balding on top, thick Coke bottle glasses. He's tall, a little over six feet. The skin around his neck looks like a turkey's, all flabby, if that helps."

"Yes, it does. Thank you." Sarah let the woman go and turned and went inside the shack where she found John and McDermott already up and dressing.

"What's all the noise out there?" John asked as he slid on his shoes.

"Someone died and came back," she explained. "An old man named George. Now he's in the camp somewhere and he's hungry. The village is on alert and everyone's searching for him." She quickly gave George's description to John and McDermott, almost verbatim from what the woman told her.

"Bloody hell," McDermott mumbled. "I thought we were done with dead people when we left the bunker. I've seen more in the past two days than a month inside the cave."

Sarah declined to reply, not seeing any reason to. McDermott liked to vent, that was his way.

In less than a minute both men were dressed and armed. John carried an M-16 and McDermott held a small pistol.

"You still got my .45, Sarah?" McDermott asked.

She patted her hip. "It's safe with me, Bill."

"Good, 'cause I'm gonna want that back sooner or later."

"Enough talk," John said. "We have to find that old man before he kills someone, and then that person gets back up and does the same. If it's not stopped fast, we could have a whole damn mess of them things right here on this island."

No one replied to his statement; there was no need. It was all too clear what was on the line right now. Not just for the people of the village, but for the three companions as well. Even if they wanted to leave and go back to the beach, they would never be safe if the village became filled with zombies.

Sarah was closest to the door so she led everyone outside, and once there, they decided to split up, knowing three people alone could cover more ground than if they stayed together.

"Be careful," John told Sarah.

"You too," she said before ducking around the corner of their shack to move deeper into the shadows of the night.

Chapter 11

Sarah moved between two buildings, as she tried to look in every direction at once. People calling out to one another floated on the wind, as the residents cleared parts of the village.

Sarah held the .45 before her, holding the weapon in a two-handed grip. It was another bright night with the moon high overhead, but there were still lots of areas wreathed in shadows.

She frowned as she entered a small alleyway, not liking what was before her. There were far too many places for a zombie to hide. She called out, hoping that if the dead man was in the alley, he would pop up at the sound of her voice.

Nothing.

The alley was quiet.

She began walking down it, swinging the .45 before her as she reached each section where there could be a hidden attacker. Still nothing, totally empty.

From somewhere in the village she heard a gunshot and a shout, then it went silent.

Could that gunshot mean that the zombie had been found? She didn't know, and until she did, she would act as if the dead man was still around somewhere. As if George was still searching for his first victim.

When she reached the end of the alley and took a right, she saw a figure coming at her from out of the shadows. Pointing the .45 in the figure's direction, she prepared to fire but waited until she knew for sure.

The figure moved quicker than a dead man would, and a second later the face was illuminated by a moonbeam.

"Tom," Sarah said, seeing who the figure was. "I almost shot you."

"Well, I'm glad you didn't," he said, coming up next to her, his voice low. "That's the biggest problem when something like this happens. Only a few of the people here besides me know how to stay calm in a situation like this. Most just shoot at anything that moves. I swear, we'll get more casualties from friendly fire tonight than anything George can do."

"You don't have to worry about me, John or Bill, we've dealt with this kind of situation before," she said, keeping her voice low.

"That's good to know," Tom replied. "Just watch yourself out here and make sure to make a lot of noise and call out so that anyone who sees you knows you're not George." He moved past her and down the alley. Pausing at the end, Tom peered around the corner, and satisfied it was safe, he continued moving.

Sarah mulled over his words; it all made sense. People panicked; that was a given in a situation like this. On the island, everyone was sheltered, and they hadn't had to deal with the horrors that Sarah or her friends had been dealing with on a daily basis.

As if to punctuate Tom's point, another gunshot rang out in the distance, followed by a yell and then another yell, each one from a different person.

Great, she thought. *It's bad enough worrying about getting eaten, but I need to be even more concerned with getting shot by one of the people I'm out here searching with.*

She continued onward herself. Careful when making the corner, she moved into the street and then to the next space between two buildings.

Always a problem solver, she tried to come up with a safer way of searching for anyone who was a newly risen zombie, so that no one got shot accidentally.

Ideas such as wearing lights or even colored rags tied to the searchers' arms came to mind. Really, anything could be used to differentiate the living from the dead.

Perhaps she was too concerned with what the village could do in the future instead of focusing on the present, because as she turned a corner, she didn't pause to make sure it was clear. Before she knew it, she had walked into someone in the dark.

A man if she was correct, due to the size and stature of the person.

Her first instinct was to apologize for her clumsiness, and to identify herself to the other person, but the instant she bumped into him, Sarah knew something wasn't right. For one thing, the man stunk like shit and urine, and when she bumped into him, he barely made a sound.

The second thing that told her the man wasn't quite right was when he reached out and grabbed her around the throat and began to squeeze.

The .45 in her hand was out to the side and she squeezed off two rounds as she was picked up off the ground like she was a child, her feet dangling an inch in the air.

The face before her was wreathed in darkness, due to the shack she was behind blocking the moonlight, but though it was dark, the unmistakable hiss of deflated lungs and the foul stench of death assailed her nostrils, telling her that she'd found the infamous George.

But as he prepared to tear out her throat, Sarah didn't feel so lucky to be the one to discover him.

McDermott looked up at the sound of two consecutive gunshots. They were close by, maybe even on the other side of the shack he was pressed up against, as he made his way down one of the myriad alleyways that made up the spaces between the small buildings off the main dirt road of the village. He began to run in that direction, hoping he could be of some help.

John was a little further away, but he too, ran in the direction of the gunshots. McDermott met up with Tom and a few villagers—including Ethel, George's wife—and everyone ran together as a group.

"Which way do we go?" Tom asked as the leader of the crowd.

"This way," John said as he caught up to the crowd, pointing to an alley at the end of the pathway they were on. As if to punctuate his choice of direction, another gunshot rang out.

Rounding the corner of a random, squat, one-story building, John was the first to see Sarah at the far end of the alley in the clutches of George as she fought to keep the dead man's mouth from her throat.

"Sarah!" John called out in alarm, raising his rifle but knowing to take a shot would risk hitting Sarah.

The others came up behind John and everyone stopped for a moment. It was strange actually, the way no one moved, only stared in horror as Sarah fought for her life.

Then McDermott pushed through the crowd to see what was happening. "What the hell are you all standing around for? Get the bastard," he said and ran forward, his gun in his hand, prepared to shoot George and save Sarah.

Only there was no need. Sarah, trapped in George's clutches after managing to get off three rounds that went nowhere, brought her arm up, pressed the muzzle of the gun to George's temple, and squeezed the trigger. The action was all much more difficult than it should have been due to the fact that George was strangling Sarah and trying to sink his teeth into her, and she had to use her left hand to keep the snapping jaws at bay. Her vision was blurry due to lack of oxygen and her tongue was sticking out of her mouth.

But all that ceased when she squeezed the trigger of the gun. She felt wet splatter hit her face and then she was falling to the ground. She landed in a heap and just lay there, gasping for air, while all around her she could hear footsteps and people calling out.

John's voice came through the din and she found herself being lifted to a sitting position.

"Sarah darling, are you hurt? Sarah, speak to me," John said anxiously as he held her.

Coughing and struggling to gain her breath, Sarah slowly began to breathe easier. "I'm fine. I'm okay, just give me a second." She could see past John, where George lay prone on the ground, sprawled in the dust.

People with torches arrived to illuminate the area, and as it was lighted, Sarah saw that her bullet had blown out the side of George's head, the dead man's brains seeping from the wound. His eyes had popped out of his head, due to the sudden, catastrophic overpressure that had built up inside his skull. His Coke bottle glasses were hanging askew and one lens was cracked.

Sarah couldn't believe it was she who had found George. What was it about her? Why was she a magnet for the living dead? Lately it sure felt that way, anyway.

"She killed George, she killed my husband!" Ethel screamed as she stood over her fallen husband of over fifty years. "She killed him!" she shrieked. Before anyone could stop her, Ethel pulled a small handgun from her jacket and aimed it at Sarah, who was now standing thanks to John's help.

"How could you do it? You just got here, you've only been here for a day and then you shoot my husband?" Ethel screamed, spittle flying from her mouth. Tears ran down her cheeks and she wiped them clean with the back of her free hand. "I'll kill you for this."

"Ethel, what the fuck are you doing?" Tom yelled, his gun facing the ground but ready to come up at a moment's notice. "George wasn't George anymore. He tried to attack you, kill you. You know this. We've had to deal with this kind of thing before."

"I don't know shit," Ethel spat. "All I know is this bitch just murdered my George."

Everyone other than Tom, John, Sarah and McDermott had backed away, not wanting to get involved. Most didn't care what happened to Sarah. They had known Ethel for years, but Sarah was a stranger to them. Having to pick sides, it was obvious who would be chosen to live and who would die if it came down to it.

John saw this instantly and began moving away from Sarah. No one noticed him, too caught up in the drama between Ethel and Sarah. Ethel took a step closer to Sarah, the gun shaking slightly. It was obvious the woman was suffering terribly from the loss of her husband, the grief suffusing her like a living thing.

"There's only one thing to do with a murderer around here," Ethel hissed between clenched teeth. "My George needs to be avenged." Her finger began to squeeze the trigger, and if no one had moved, she no doubt would have fired, shooting Sarah in the chest. But John managed to get behind Ethel, and just before the grief-stricken woman fired, he came up to her and pressed the muzzle of his rifle at the back of her skull.

The instant the cold metal touched her head, Ethel froze.

"You need to stop what you're doing and lower that gun right now," John said, his Jamaican accent heavy. He was sweating profusely, knowing the woman before him was mad with grief and could do anything. Emotions caused people to do things they would regret later, but if Ethel fired her gun, what happened next wouldn't be something she could take back.

"What? You think you can shoot me before I can kill her? Go 'head, I have nothing left to live for now that my George is gone. I bet I can fire my gun before you shoot yours."

"Now, now, Ethel, no one wants to shoot anyone here," Tom said calmly.

"Listen…Ethel, you're blamin' Sarah for your troubles but you know deep down this isn't her fault," John said.

"Of course it's her fault. She killed my George!"

"No, she didn't. George was already dead and then he came back," John said. "You know that, Tom knows that. Everyone here knows that. You're the one who won't accept it." He moved to the side so Ethel could see him, now the muzzle of the rifle was a few inches from her head. He hoped the fact that he'd stopped her a second ago would be the tipping point. If she'd really wanted to shoot Sarah, she would have done it, regardless of the threat to her life.

"Ethel, listen to me, woman," John pleaded. "I know you're angry but Sarah isn't the one to be angry at. Sarah did what had to be done. She didn't want to but she had no choice. If you want to be mad at someone, blame God for allowing this thing to come down on us so that even when we die we can't rest. He's the one who did this to us. Hate Him."

"I...I don't know what to say to that. I don't know anymore," Ethel said, the gun lowering slightly as doubt filled her.

Tom was waiting for just such a moment and he lunged forward, using his hand to knock Ethel's arm up so that the gun was pointed upwards. Ethel jerked the trigger out of instinct but the bullet went straight up, then shocked at what she'd done, as if horrified that she'd shot the gun, Ethel dropped it. Tom scooped it up and went to Ethel, holding her so she couldn't run.

Ethel stared at Tom, her face one of grief and horror. "Oh God, I almost shot that woman. I didn't mean to. I..." She collapsed into Tom's arms, sobbing uncontrollably.

"It's all right, Ethel, I understand. I'm just glad you didn't do it," Tom said. He looked up at the villagers surrounding them. "All right, people, show's over. I need a few men to stick around and help me here, the rest of you go back to your homes."

People began to disperse as John joined Sarah and McDermott, who were standing together. McDermott had been ready to shoot Ethel as well, but no one had seen him, all eyes having been focused on John.

"Thanks, John," Sarah said, hugging him. "I have to admit I was pretty worried there for a few seconds. I thought for sure she was going to shoot me."

Tom came over after giving Ethel to one of his men, to escort the distraught woman home. "She would have, too," Tom said. "If John hadn't talked her down."

"What are you going to do to her?" Sarah asked.

Tom shrugged. "Well, I'll have my people keep an eye on her for a while to make sure she's okay. If she is, then that will be the end of it. We don't have a jail here. We don't really have any crime here at all, and if anything does come up that's truly bad, like murder, we banish them out of the village. No one wants that so most people behave."

"What about the few that don't?" McDermott asked.

"We make them go to the mainland to scout for supplies we might need. If they come back in one piece, we welcome them back as long as they have stuff with them. That way they've done their penance and have contributed to the community."

"What if they don't come back?" John asked.

"Then we assume they're dead and that's the end of it," Tom said flatly.

"Come on, Sarah, let's get you back home," McDermott said. "You've had a hell of a time here."

"I won't argue with you, if that's what you're thinking," she said. Truth was, she felt totally drained. When the adrenaline stopped flowing it left a person weak and tired; she wanted sleep for a week.

"We're going back to our place now, Tom. If you need anything else from us come there," McDermott said and began leading Sarah away.

John nodded thanks to Tom, who replied with the same gesture. It was a male thing. Sometimes two men could say volumes with just a simple nod of the head.

"You did a good thing tonight, John," Tom said. "Ethel's a good woman; she's just broken up about losing her husband. Given time, she'll recover."

"Aye, Tom, I don't disagree with you, but if she'd tried to shoot Sarah, rest assured I would have blown her head clean off her shoulders."

Tom cocked his head to the left, as if he didn't believe what he'd heard. "You really would have done that? You would have shot down an old woman?"

John's jaw grew taut. "Aye, man, without even thinking twice about it. Good night." He turned and walked away, leaving Tom to watch his retreating back blend into the night.

Chapter 12

John caught up to Sarah and McDermott halfway back to the shack they now called home. They didn't talk much, each still on edge from the night's happenings.

When they arrived at the shack, Sarah used the small bucket of water in the room to wash up, wanting to remove the droplets of George's blood off her skin. She would have killed for a shower or even a dip in the ocean, but at the moment both were out of the question. The former because there was no shower and the latter because the ocean was too far away from the village.

John and McDermott talked softly while Sarah cleaned up. Then she changed shirts and tossed the dirty one into the corner of the room.

"I feel a million times better," she said as she plopped down onto one of the cots.

"I tell you, I could use a drink right about now," McDermott said.

"You and me both. It's times like this when the cave doesn't seem so bad, now does it," John added.

"Well, actually, I did meet someone around here who happens to have a homegrown still," McDermott said.

Sarah laughed. "Leave it to Bill to find booze on what's supposed to be a deserted island."

"Actually, I was thinking I'd go see if he's up. I figure with all the excitement tonight, I doubt if anyone's sleeping much," McDermott said.

"If you find him, make sure you bring back some for us," John said with a boyish grin.

"Well, Johnny, I won't promise anything, but I'll see what I can do. I have to warn you, though. I'm mighty thirsty." He stood up, and before leaving said, "You know, maybe this place isn't that bad after all—especially if it has booze. After all, there's always gonna be dead people walking around no matter where we go." With a wave at the door, he left Sarah and John alone. For a full minute neither said anything, the silence hanging in the air.

Sarah was first to break the silence. "Thank you again for tonight, John. I can't believe after all we've been through these past few weeks that I almost got killed by an old man named George."

"That would have been pretty ironic," he replied with a smile, but then his face grew serious. "In a morbid sort of way, of course."

"Would you really have shot that old woman to save me?"

"Sarah darling, do you really have to ask me that? Of course I would have."

"Well, I'm just glad it didn't come to that."

"Me too," he said and then it went quiet again. The awkwardness between the two of them was a palpable thing.

Sarah stared at her arm where there was a very small drop of dried blood. She rubbed it away with a finger. The silence was killing her, so she said, "So I was working all day with Professor Langford."

"Oh really now?" John said with a grin, but it was more patronizing than friendly. "So it's just like back at the cave, working all day with your test tubes and your computers, trying to figure out why the dead are walking. Is Langford the new Franken-stein?"

"No, of course not. Logan was insane, something none of us knew until the end," she said. "Prof. Langford is a rational, stable man. In fact, there's an even better chance of us finding a cure here than back at the bunker. At least here I don't have apes like Rhodes and Steel breathing down my neck, demanding this and that from me."

"So what? You think you're gonna find a cure here when you couldn't back at the cave?"

"I don't know what will happen, but I sure hope so. We've got to try, John, the alterative is too terrible to consider."

"Why, Sarah? Why is it so bad? You remember what I told you back at the cave? Sarah darling, you're never gonna figure this shit out. It's a waste of time. What's happening to the world is bigger than both of us….hell any of us. It's almost arrogant to think that you or your new Frankenstein is gonna come up with a solution to the problem. It's God's will and He's pissed. But look where we are, Sarah, we're in paradise. Let's kick back our heels and enjoy it and to hell with the rest of the world."

"You really could do that, couldn't you? You could just let the world fall apart and only worry about yourself."

"Sure, and why not? Other than you and Billy, there's no one I care about left in this world. Besides, the world has already fallen apart, you just won't accept it."

Sarah was becoming a little frustrated with John's attitude. They'd had this discussion before and it had gone nowhere. Now, here they were again, rehashing old subjects. But deep down, she agreed with John, and maybe it was just her stubborn personality that wouldn't let her accept it.

"You know, John, you're still quite a mystery to me," she said.

John had been sitting in the cot next to hers, now he stood up and walked over and sat down beside her. His shoes were off and his shirt was unbuttoned, due to the heat inside the shack. Sarah's eyes glanced at his smooth chest, then she looked away, almost as if she was a shy school girl.

"Oh am I now? Well, us Jamaican boys try to be a little mysterious, keeps the ladies guessing."

"Oh really?"

"Uh-huh. You know, we still have unfinished business from back on the beach, just before Billy came running and yelling about that fishing boat."

She rolled her eyes to the ceiling, as if she was thinking back to that moment. "Hmm, I think I might recall something on a similar subject but you might have to refresh my mind." She had butterflies in her stomach with John sitting so close to her. She could feel his body heat pressing into her and it excited her. Sarah felt like a teenager. Why was she feeling like this? She hadn't felt this way around Miguel, but then with Miguel, in many ways she had been in control of the relationship, but with John…well, he was a man who wasn't afraid to take control or relinquish it if needed. That was one of the things that had attracted her to him, the fact that he was so confident.

She was going to say something, hopefully witty, but before she could he leaned forward and kissed her. His tongue slid between her lips and she reciprocated, and as they embraced, she felt her head swooning.

John stopped kissing her lips, and slid his tongue across her cheek and to her neck, where he began to nuzzle it. She felt his goatee on her skin and it tickled her, making goosebumps appear on her arms.

Then he moved his mouth back up to hers, and once more they were kissing, their bodies pressed together, the heat of their passion consuming them both as they wrapped their arms around each other even tighter and pulled their bodies closer.

"Wait, John, not here. What if Billy comes back?" she breathed heavily, not wanting to stop but also not wanting McDermott to walk in on them in the middle of lovemaking

"Ah, Sarah darling, this is Billy we're talkin' about. Once he gets to drinking, he won't be back for a long while."

"That's a valid point," she said into his mouth as they kissed. Then, finally, Sarah let go and relaxed, living only for the moment and relishing the passion she felt for John. She let her mind go blank with the exception of simply feeling joy.

Sarah had a feeling John was an excellent lover, and as he laid her down on the cot and got on top of her, his body pressing into hers so that they became one soul, she was looking forward to finding out if her assumption was correct.

Chapter 13

The next morning wasn't as awkward with John as Sarah would have thought, and in fact it felt very natural with him. In many ways, last night had felt like a dream, albeit a wonderful one.

Sometime in the night, Sarah had gone to another cot from where they had been sleeping side by side, and sometime even later, closer to dawn, McDermott had stumbled in drunk, half falling into a cot, and began snoring like a lumberjack.

The three had risen like any other day, chatted together for a bit, and then each had gone off to their assigned tasks after having breakfast.

McDermott had been in a fuzzy daze, but the man knew how to drink and he knew how to handle a hangover. In a few hours it would be like the previous night of drinking had never happened, and John knew that McDermott would be his jolly old self again in no time.

Sarah went to Prof. Langford's lab to begin her research, and John and McDermott met up with Tom in the communal meal area after they ate, where they were informed that they would be going on a boar hunt today with Tom and two more men.

"This is Frank," Tom said, introducing the first of the two men. Frank looked like a rat, with a thin nose, pointy chin, and thin hairs that protruded from his jaw like a wire brush. He had beady eyes that made him look guilty of something, even if he was standing still and minding his own business. Frank grunted in reply to the introduction, and John and McDermott merely nodded.

"And this is Joe," Tom said, referring to the second man. Joe was short, just over five feet with a squat body and short legs. His face was plump, like a cherub's, and his brown hair was cut close to his scalp, which only accentuated his chubby face.

"Nice ta meetcha," Joe said, waving to John and McDermott who both grinned in reply. At least Joe was friendly, which was more than could be said for Frank the Rat. Frank wasn't really called this, of course but John had dubbed him the title in his head, and when he and McDermott had a second alone, John had shared it with him. McDermott had laughed out loud, but then had to lie about thinking of an old joke when Frank asked him what was so funny.

"So here's the deal," Tom said as the five men began walking out of the village and into the woods, where Tom then stopped at the beginning of a narrow path to go over a few things for the two new arrivals. "There's wild boar on this island. They're not really native to this place but when we first came here we made sure to bring some livestock, like chickens, pigs and goats. We had a bad storm one night and the stable the pigs were in was destroyed and all the little fuckers got out and escaped into the woods. Once they were in the wild, they met up with a breed of razorback wild boar that did live on the island. They all got together and began to breed like wildfire. Now the damn things are everywhere. That's a good thing though; we need the meat, but the bad is that the wild ones are ferocious as hell and the boars have tusks that will gut you like a fish if they get close enough." He held up his sniper rifle, then pointed to John and McDermott, who both carried rifles, as did Frank and Joe. John held the M-16 that was his and McDermott was given one from the island's armory, which was well-stocked. Prof. Langford had known weapons would be needed in the new world and had made sure to bring as many as he could lay his hands on. Of course, he'd had others do the work for him, finding and getting the weapons ready to be shipped to the island.

"That's why you guys have rifles," Tom continued. "If a boar gets close enough, don't worry about where you hit it, just shoot the bastard and put it down. The damn things are so big that no matter what kind of way you shoot it, there's still plenty of meat for us to take back to camp." He locked his eyes on John and McDermott. "You guys okay with this? 'Cause I need to know now if you're not. If you don't think you're up to it you can stay in the village and do something else."

"Yeah, we can always use some more cooks, or more people to dig holes for the outhouse," Frank said, snickering in a way that made John want to punch him in his rodent-like face, even though he'd just met the man.

"Billy and me can take care of ourselves, man," John said flatly. "You don't have to worry about us."

"That's good to know," Tom said. "I saw how you handled the dead fucks on that fishing boat. Next to that a few boars should be child's play." Tom began to walk down the path, Joe right behind him. As John and McDermott began to walk, Frank reached out a hand and stopped them.

"You two stay out of my way, ya here?" Frank said low so Tom wouldn't hear. "The man who bags the most meat gets extra credit in the village. I'm not gonna lose my standing as a hunter around here for two new guys who won't last a week."

John held up his hands in surrender, then forced a smile across his face. "No worries, man, we won't get in your way. Just consider us your shadows."

Frank merely grunted in response and moved down the path, shoving by John and McDermott as he went.

"He reminds me of Steel only way skinnier," McDermott said when Frank was out of ear shot. "They're both fucking assholes."

"Maybe so, Billy boy, but we know from experience that assholes can be dangerous. Just watch my back and I'll do the same for you."

"Was already planning on it, Johnny. After all, that's how we got to be standing here in the first place."

Sarah arrived at the lab to see Prof. Langford was nowhere in sight. Not that she needed to check in with him, but she wanted to talk to him about what had happened with George and how the residents of the village felt about her now.

Ethel may have lowered her gun the previous night and not shot her, but how was Sarah to know whether others weren't holding a grudge?

She simply wanted to make sure that the professor knew about everything and would make sure the entire village knew that Sarah wasn't at fault for killing George.

When Sarah inquired to the whereabouts of Prof. Langford, one of the other scientists, a small Chinese man named Ming, pointed to the back of the laboratory, where there was another door that led to a back room.

Sarah thanked Ming and walked to the back, grabbed the doorknob, and while knocking politely, opened it and stepped inside.

Sarah assumed that she was going to see Prof. Langford sitting behind a desk, perhaps scribbling into a notebook or working on one of the computers at his disposal, but what she actually saw almost made her vomit. Not so much by what the professor was doing, but taken into context the things Sarah had seen in the past at the bunker—mostly with Dr. Logan—then what Langford was doing almost made her want to faint.

The professor was standing over a waist high wooden table, his once-white lab coat now stained a dark red. Before him on the table was the corpse of George, the chest cracked open and the skull sawed in half, the skullcap resting beside the head.

On a few small side tables George's organs had been separated into individual containers; the professor held what was left of George's brain in his hands as he studied it.

The resemblance of Prof. Langford to Dr. Logan in that exact moment was uncanny.

Sarah turned away, dry heaving, then closed her eyes and thought of something, anything that wasn't about blood. It took her almost a full minute to gather herself, and when she did and looked back at the charnel house scene before her, Prof. Langford was still studying the brain. He was so preoccupied he didn't even know she was there.

"My God, Professor what are you doing to that body?" she finally managed to say, her voice almost a whisper.

He looked up. "Oh, hello, Sarah, I didn't hear you come in. Why, I'm doing an autopsy of course. We are trying to find a cure for the plague, right? A fresh specimen is always a bonus. Wish I had more of the brain to work with, however, no thanks to you."

She blinked in surprise at his statement. "Excuse me?"

"The brain, Sarah, you shot poor George in the head and destroyed his brain."

"Sorry, next time I'll let him tear out my throat so his brain stays intact," she said sarcastically.

Prof. Langford didn't even notice the quip. "Oh, no, please don't do that. That would mean you would end up on my table, which would also be a tragedy."

He was serious and Sarah blinked again at that. Obviously the man didn't get sarcasm.

"Have you…have you learned anything?"

"No," the professor sighed. "I'm afraid there's nothing new to learn here. Whatever's causing the dead to walk is still quite a mystery to me." He peered at her through his blood-spattered eyeglasses, hanging low on his nose. With his hands covered in blood he didn't want to touch his glasses it seemed. "As I'm sure it is to you also."

"Ah, well, yes, I suppose so. But now that I'm working on research again, hopefully I might find something here that wasn't available to me in my lab at the bunker I was in. You people have been collecting an entirely different amount of data. I hope once I can go through it all, maybe there might be something I've been missing."

"Hmm, yes, that does sound promising." He stared at her, then said, "So if there's nothing else…"

"Huh? Oh no, there's nothing else." What she had wanted to talk to the professor about didn't seem all that important anymore. Now she just wanted to leave the room as soon as possible. "I guess I'll get to work."

But Professor Langford wasn't paying attention to her; he was once more studying the brain, specifically where there was a large bullet hole in it.

Sarah, deciding it was time to leave, backed up to the door, turned around when the doorknob pressed into her back, opened it enough for her body to slide through sideways, and left the room, closing the door softly behind her.

"So John, tell me about this secret government bunker you were at before you got here," Tom said, as the five men walked through the woods. Tom was leading them to a watering hole where the boars were known to be.

"What's to say that I didn't tell you about already when I first got here?" John replied.

"Oh come on, John," Tom prodded. "There must be some more you left out. There always is."

John shrugged. "Nope, I told you everything that you wanted to know."

"The place was set up pretty haphazardly," McDermott said. "We were down to bare bones from day one."

"So you say," Tom said. "But I was thinking about all the guns and ammo that might still be lying around. You said the captain told you he was getting low on ammunition, but that didn't mean what was left wouldn't help us here on the island."

John shook his head and stepped up closer to Tom, taking the man by the shoulder and stopping him. "Listen, Tom, that place is nothing but a giant tomb. There's nothing there but the dead. To go there would be suicide."

Tom raised a hand in surrender. "Okay, okay, John, don't get your hackles up. I was just talking from the cuff. I didn't mean that we were gonna go there. I was just thinking out loud is all." He gestured to the path while McDermott, Frank and Joe all waited for the two men to continue. "Do you mind if we keep going? We're almost there."

"Fine, man, just hear what I say. There's nothing left in that place but death," John said.

Tom nodded and began walking again. McDermott gestured to John to slow down and Frank and Joe walked past them, Frank sneering at John as the rat-faced man passed him. When the three men were a few feet up the path and out of earshot, McDermott said, "Did I hear what I thought I heard, Johnny? Was Tom askin' about the cave?" His skin was covered in a sheen of sweat from walking in the woods. It was warm, eighty degrees at least, and along with the humidity, the trees held the heat like a wet blanket.

"Aye, Billy, the damn fool thought it might be worth goin' back to get the guns and ammo still there."

"That's a bloody fool's errand if there ever was one," McDermott said. "There's nothing on this planet that could ever get me to go back there." Without waiting for a reply, he began walking down the path.

John hesitated a fraction of a second, then followed, now the last in line. "Aye, Billy, I know what you mean."

Chapter 14

"There's one right by the water; you see him?" Tom whispered to John.

"Aye, man, he's a big bastard, too," John said softly.

"I know what I told you before, but still try to shoot the fucker in the head. I don't like lead in my meat," Tom said jokingly, then he moved closer, John right by his side.

The razorback boar snuffed and grunted at the watering hole, drinking water in big gulps. It stopped for a moment and looked up, its one good ear twitching as it tried to pick up any sound of danger. It was a big bastard, with four inch tusks and weighing in at almost five hundred pounds. The right tusk was shorter, broken two inches down from the left. There was a long scar across its back from where it had fought and won against another of its kind. Its right ear was also missing, the skin having melded into tough scar tissue. The boar was a warrior, and had lived for as long as it had because of its cunning. It was afraid of nothing...not even man

"Wait, I know that boar," Tom said when they had moved a few feet closer. Both men were hidden in the bushes on the opposite side of the small watering hole, which was fed from an underground spring. "I've been trying to kill that fucker for years, but he keeps getting away." He pointed to the boar's missing ear. "See that missing ear? I did that. Thought I had a head shot and at the last second the fucker dropped his head. I only managed to take off his ear. Then he bolted into the trees and was gone."

On the left side of the watering hole where John and Tom was, Frank, Joe and McDermott were also moving closer. The hope was that the two teams of hunters could catch the boar in the middle, and with a crossfire setup, take it down.

Tom popped up a little so that Frank could see him, and when he knew the rat-faced man had spotted him, Tom made a few hand signals, telling Frank and his team to move in.

Tom and John did the same, creeping slowly through the brush, but John wasn't as skilled at stealth as Tom, and John's right foot came down on a small twig that Tom had known not to step on. The soft *snap* filled the air the instant John's foot crushed it.

"I got you this time, you fucker," Tom hissed as he aimed his sniper rifle at the target, his eye going to the scope. He was just about to squeeze the trigger when John stepped on the twig.

The boar's head snapped up and it grunted, its nose sniffing the air. Already its haunches were trembling as it prepared to bolt back into the trees. Tom fired at the exact instant the boar's head snapped up. Instead of the round taking the pig in its head, and becoming a perfect kill shot, the bullet missed by an inch, striking a rock next to the boar's front left hoof, to then ricochet off into the trees. But the damage was done. The boar knew it was under attack.

Pawing the mud under it, the boar grunted loudly and spun around, its destination the safety of he woods. But as it turned and prepared to bolt, it found its escape route cut off by three men.

Frank, Joe and McDermott had gotten behind the boar and all three of them now stood with guns aimed at the animal.

"Take the shot, Frank, kill that bastard!" Tom screamed as he jumped up and began running through the bushes right at the boar. Maybe the hunt could be salvaged if they all acted fast.

John didn't need to be told to follow, and he popped up and began running after Tom. He wondered if there would be a scolding from Tom later for him stepping on the twig, and if there was, he would apologize. But John would also remind Tom that he and McDermott weren't hunters, nor had they claimed to be.

The boar grunted and ran at the three men, who lowered their weapons and began to fire. The boar dodged to the left and the right; like most swine it was intelligent and it had learned that guns were bad for its health.

McDermott managed to hit the boar twice in the side, but with so many folds of flesh and fat, the bullets did little to slow it down. Frank shot the boar as well, but other than making the animal squeal in pain, it didn't stop coming directly at them.

Panicking, Joe's bullets went wild, not one round touching the animal.

"Get out of the way!" Frank yelled and lunged to the right, McDermott doing the same to the left. Both men hit the ground and rolled, trying to get out of the boar's path.

But Joe stood stock-still, taken completely off guard, as the charging beast bore down on him. He had time for one quick scream and then the boar was on him, its tusks digging into Joe's stomach.

Joe's upper half folded forward, and much like a man being hit by a bull, the boar carried Joe a few feet, its tusks now embedded in Joe's stomach. Joe screamed in pain and terror as the boar began to buck like a rodeo bull, wanting to remove the screaming man from off its head.

"Jesus Christ!" Tom yelled and fired at the boar. His bullet struck it dead center on the side and the boar faltered, but then it renewed its escape. Bucking its head to the left, it tossed Joe away from it. As Joe went flying, a coil of intestine that had become caught in the boar's good tusk began to unwind, streaming out of Joe's body as the man was thrown almost ten feet to strike a tree. The body wrapped around the tree like a hand to a pole, then slid to the ground. The coil of yellowish intestine glistened in the sunlight, lying on the ground like a faded garden hose that needed to be rolled up.

The boar was still in motion, and after dislodging Joe from its tusks, it barreled into the trees to be lost from sight. The sound of it charging through the brush filled the air for a few seconds, then was gone, only the moans of a dying Joe filling the air.

Tom and John reached the others a moment later. Tom surveyed the scene. Frank and McDermott were still lying on the ground, and off to the side, Joe lay moaning, his guts hanging out of him like streamers.

"God, what a fucking mess," Tom spat as he went to help Frank up, John doing the same for McDermott. "Either of you hurt?" Tom asked the two men.

"I'm fine," Frank said, clearly angry that the boar had gotten away.

"I'll live to fight another day," McDermott added.

"That's good I guess," Tom said. "I wish the same could be said for Joe." He walked over to the fallen man, who had somehow managed to get onto his side. With Tom's help, he was lifted up so he was on his knees. Joe gasped in pain and shock, his eyes glazed over as he stared at his intestines, not understanding why they were all over the ground. They were supposed to be inside him!

John and McDermott stared in amazement. Both men knew a man could live for quite a while if gut shot, but to actually see it in person was an entirely different matter. The boar's tusks had done catastrophic damage to Joe's midsection. John thought of the fairy tale of Humpty Dumpty. No one was going to be putting Joe together any time soon. Even if there had been a helicopter waiting to evac the man to a state-of-the-art hospital, it would have been a bad bet that the man would have survived.

"You…you guys have to get me back home. I need help," Joe said through bloody froth bubbles. "I need help bad."

"Shit, Joe, I saw the whole thing," Tom said. "You just stood there and let the damn thing hit you. What were you thinking?" He shook his head sadly. "Now look at you."

"Help me Tom, please," Joe gasped, spitting blood.

"Oh I will, but not the way you want," Tom said sadly and then nodded to Frank, who had crept around Joe so that he was standing directly behind the wounded man. With a nod from Tom, the signal was given, and Frank silently raised his rifle to the back of Joe's head, and without so much as a "Sorry, pal," squeezed the trigger.

The front of Joe's face disappeared as the exiting bullet blew out more than half the contents of his skull. Joe was dead before he even knew it. The body fell forward onto the ground, a puff of dust rising up around it, the arms and legs twitching for a few seconds as the final neurons from an already destroyed brain still fired. Then the limbs went still.

John's mouth fell open in horror and he raised his rifle and aimed it at Tom. Frank saw this and swung his weapon around at John, but McDermott saw what was happening and he brought his gun to bear on Frank. It was a standoff with the four men.

"What are you doing, John?" Tom asked. "Why are you aiming your gun at me?"

"You shot Joe in cold blood, you bastard. How could you?" John asked, his eyes wide in shock. He'd just witnessed a wounded man murdered before his eyes for no good reason.

"Just say the word Tom and he's a dead man," Frank hissed, his eyes locked on John.

"And you'll be right behind him, asshole," McDermott added.

Tom raised his left arm, his hand palm out. "Now, Frank, calm down, everyone just calm the fuck down." He turned to face John. "I think I know why you're upset. It's because Frank killed Joe, right?"

"Of course it is, man! What the hell's wrong with you?" John asked, amazed at the cavalier way Tom was acting. John's forehead was covered in sweat and he desperately wanted to wipe it away, but at the moment he knew it wasn't an option.

"John, listen to me. I can explain everything," Tom said, his voice calm and soothing.

McDermott had to admit the man knew how to stay cool in a bad situation.

"How could you just kill him in cold blood like that?" John repeated.

"I didn't kill him, John, I just put Joe out of his suffering. He was already dead; he just didn't know it yet." He pointed to the coil of intestine in the dirt. "Look at that, John. His guts are all over the fucking place. So what? You think we can just wash them off and shove them back inside him, then sew him up and send him off with a few band aids and aspirin? There was no way a man lives through that, especially with the kind of medical care we can give him. So Frank did what we always do in our village if someone is mortally wounded like that. We kill them before they die and come back."

"That's barbaric," McDermott said. "The man didn't even get to say a prayer and make his peace with God."

"Oh, you think that would matter? This way he never knew it was coming. No hesitation. That's our rules around here, and if anyone doesn't like it they don't have to stay; that goes for you two as well."

"It's like putting down a horse, no different. It was a mercy killing," Frank added, spitting into the dirt.

"That's not helping, Frank," Tom said. "Best let me handle it."

John glanced at McDermott who shrugged slightly. "It sucks, Johnny, but in a twisted way it makes sense, too."

"Ah, see, John?" Tom said quickly. "He gets it. The world's changed and the way we act has to change, too. Adapt or die and all that shit."

John mulled it over for a few more seconds. Finally he nodded slowly and lowered the rifle. He didn't agree with Tom or his actions, but there wasn't a point in defending a dead man. The deed was done, risking his or McDermott's life would be stupid. "Okay, Tom, I see your point. I can't say I agree with it, but me and Billy are guests here." He sighed and added, "I'm sorry I overreacted."

"I totally understand," Tom said. "It says a lot about who you are as a man, too." He gestured to Frank to lower his gun and reluctantly Frank did, which meant McDermott lowered his. The standoff was over.

Tom clapped his hands together, as if that could end the tension. "Okay, then next we need to bury the body, it's the least we can do for poor Joe."

"Aren't we taking him back with us?" John asked.

"Fuck no. I'm not gonna carry a corpse a mile back to the camp. You can if you want to. Look, Joe has no family and not many friends so there won't be anyone to put flowers on his grave. So what's the point?"

"It's the decent thing to do," John said.

"So then you and McDermott can do just that, but me and Frank aren't helping. What we will do is dig a shallow grave for the poor sap."

McDermott walked over to John, though he never took his eyes off Tom and Frank. "The hell with it, Johnny. Joe seemed like a nice guy but we didn't know him. If his own people don't care, why should we?"

"So what's it gonna be, John?" Tom asked. "Are we burying him in the ground or are you and your friend gonna carry the body back?"

John looked at Tom and Frank, both men waiting casually for an answer, then he gazed at the body, which was already gathering flies and ants. Finally he sighed and said, "Bury him."

Chapter 15

Days passed uneventfully for a change, no one dying in the village or trying to kill Sarah, John or McDermott. They began to get a routine going, Sarah working at the lab, and John and McDermott out hunting with Tom. The wild boar that killed Joe hadn't been seen again, but Tom knew it was out there.

John suggested that maybe it was dead, that one of the bullets they'd fired into it had killed it, but Tom said the boar was too damn mean to just curl up and die somewhere. He knew he would get another chance at it sooner or later.

Sarah threw herself into her research, and with the notes of Prof. Langford, she felt she was making great strides, much more than when she was at the bunker. She was happy. She and John were doing good, and had managed to get some alone time twice since Joe had been killed—once that night, after McDermott left the shack to get drunk, and last night, when McDermott had done the same thing. If McDermott had a hobby, it was seeing how much grain liquor he could consume in one sitting.

It was just after lunch when the next crisis rocked the village.

Sarah, John and McDermott had met for lunch, which consisted of a thick stew of pork and fresh vegetables. They were hardly through the meal when a shout sounded outside. Almost everyone went to the door and piled outside, wanting to know what was the matter. Did someone else die and come back and were now wandering the village? Did more strangers arrive, either friend or foe? Was a storm coming? Or had a fire broken out?

So many things threatened the small village everyday, only the strength of its residents allowing them to overcome it all.

John pushed past a few people to get outside. He was taller than most of them and could see over their heads into the street. There was a woman there, and she was in tears. She was talking to one of the men that worked with Tom as security—John thought the man's name was Mark, the man being familiar. The two went back and forth for a few seconds and then Mark turned and faced the crowd that John, Sarah and McDermott were standing in.

"We've got a situation," Mark said. "There's trouble at the new fresh water well on the west side of town. Marcy's boy Todd and three other children were playing over there, despite knowing they're not allowed. Marcy's boy fell into the open well, which was left unattended when the workers went to lunch an hour ago. One of the other kids came and got Marcy and here we are."

Voices from the crowd sounded as everyone began talking at once. From down the street, Tom came running, another man by his side. On closer inspection, John saw it was Frank following Tom. A sour taste got into his mouth and John frowned deeply, thinking back to Frank basically executing Joe in cold blood. Sarah had been horrified when she'd been told what had occurred in the woods, but she'd agreed with John and McDermott's choice to stand down. They were new in the village, and dying for some stranger that was already dead wasn't a very rational point of view, no matter how just the reason.

Tom stopped next to Mark as he finished addressing the crowd, then he deferred to Tom's leadership.

"All right, people, let's calm down," Tom said. "Now, I don't need everyone at the well. I only need a few people to help get the boy out of there." His eyes roved over the crowd, then settled on John and McDermott. "You two come with me."

John and McDermott pushed through the crowd until they were standing beside Tom and Frank, the rat-faced man scowling at John. Tom picked two more people, a man and a woman, though the woman was built like a man and was larger than the man she'd been chosen with. She had broad shoulders and large biceps, and stood over six feet tall. Her name was Ruth and she was a truck driver before the world fell apart. She was also a lesbian, as Sarah had found out when Ruth had made a pass at her one day in the communal cafeteria. Sarah had politely declined, saying she was with someone.

"Okay, that should be good," Tom said. "Let's all get over there and…"

"Wait, Tom," Ruth said. "What if the boy's hurt? Sarah has some medical training." Ruth looked at Sarah and winked.

"Good point, Ruth. Sarah, would you join us?" Tom asked. He didn't know or care about ulterior motives by Ruth. Sarah could help, that's all that mattered.

"Of course, excuse me, please," Sarah said as she moved through the small crowd to join the others.

"Okay, let's go," Tom said. He called over his shoulder to the crowd, "Someone go tell the professor what's going on, too."

A man in the crowd said he would take on that task and ran off, the rest of the crowd now standing around, not knowing what to do. But eventually a few figured out the excitement was over and they began to disperse.

There were enough people on their way to the well to help the child; all they could do was wait for news. In such a small village, news traveled fast, and everyone would know the results minutes after it happened.

It took about five minutes of running to reach the well on the outskirts of the village. The area was mostly flat, and all the trees had been cut down so that there were stumps everywhere. Nearby were fields of crops, mostly corn and beans. The stalks waved in the gentle breeze.

There were ten people already conjugated around the well, mostly women and children. At this point the well was nothing but a hole in the ground, the wood that was supposed to be covering it off to the side. One of the women was the boy's mother, Marcy. She was in tears. Marcy was leaning over the edge of the well, almost about to fall in herself, if not for one of the other women beside Marcy holding her back. She was screaming into the well for Todd, demanding her son answer her, which so far he had not.

"What's the status?" Tom asked as he ran up. A short, stocky woman in her late thirties met him and quickly informed him of the situation. The problem was that the well became smaller the deeper it went, and the boy being tiny as well had slid into it more than an adult would, so an adult couldn't go in there and help him. No one knew how to save the boy and time was running out. Rope had been dropped down but the boy wouldn't take the end, nor would he tie it around himself. But even if the hole hadn't gotten smaller, the well diameter was no more than two-and-half feet around, a tight fit for an adult anyway.

"Can you see him?" Tom asked as he walked over to the well with John, Sarah, McDermott, and the rest right behind him. Ruth was staying close to Sarah, which made Sarah uncomfortable. Each time Sarah glanced at the woman, Ruth would smile and wink playfully.

"Yes, we can see him," the stocky woman said. "But only his head. It's moving back and forth slowly so we know he's still alive."

"That's a relief," Tom added. "Okay then, now all we have to do is figure out how to get him out of there." He went to the well and comforted Marcy, who was in tears, then leaned over into the darkness where he could barely see the boy's head as the sunlight filtered in around Tom's body. "Hold on, son, we're gonna get you out of there."

John pushed his way to Tom's side and had a look for himself. The instant he saw the boy he had an idea. "Tom, what about if we make a harness and lower it down? All we need to do is get it under the boy's arms and we can pull him out of there like he was a landed fish."

Tom considered the suggestion for only a moment, then nodded and smiled. "I like it, John, great idea." He turned to face the crowd of concerned faces. "Okay, we need to fashion a harness that we can lower down and hook the kid. Everyone get to work."

A flurry of activity was his reply as everyone went about searching for more useable rope than the one they already had.

"I can't believe this happened," Marcy said to Tom, sobbing each word. "My boy was just playing with his friends and the ball rolled near the well. He chased it and didn't realize where he was going. He fell right in; where were the workers that were supposed to be here?"

"They went to lunch and some idiot didn't put the cover back on. Don't worry, Marcy, someone's head will roll for this," Tom said, his voice cold. John had no doubt that someone was going to be in for a bad day when Tom got a hold of them.

"I don't care about blame, Tom," she said, crying harder. "I just want my boy back."

"Tom, we're done," a man said as he ran up with a hastily made harness. It had lots of loops in it so that it could wrap around the boy. The knots were set up so that if the rope was pulled, some of the loops would close. Was it perfect? Hell no, but it was the best they had at the moment.

"Okay, everyone stand back so I can get some light," Tom said, moving to the well, his feet planted on either side of the hole. "Marcy, step back and let me have some room."

"Todd, hang on a little longer, honey!" Marcy called into the hole. "We're gonna get you out of there, baby!"

Frank took Marcy by the shoulders and made her step back a few feet so Tom could kneel down and lower the harness.

"Okay, son, if you can hear me. Wrap this around your body and I'll pull you up!" Tom called down as he lowered the harness.

McDermott took John and Sarah aside so that no one could hear him. "I was thinking. Have you guys wondered if that kid's still alive down there?"

"What do you mean?" John asked.

"Well, I was just thinking out loud, but what if that kid broke his neck or something and he's dead down there. Or rather, *was* dead, and now they're gonna haul him back up."

"The mother said she could see him moving, Bill, he should be fine. The boy's probably just scared out of his wits," Sarah said, but as she spoke, what McDermott said made good sense.

"There you go, Billy, always thinkin' the worst," John added.

"I don't want that to be the case, Johnny, I was just trying to be objective here."

Sarah reconsidered her position. "Bill's right, John, maybe you should go over there and tell Tom what we think."

But as the three of them gazed over to the well, they saw that what they thought didn't matter. It was already too late. Tom had hooked the boy and was pulling him up. As the top of the boy's head appeared, everyone began to clap and cheer. Marcy ran to her son and pulled him out the rest of the way, crying, saying her boy's name in happiness over and over.

At first it looked like everything was going to be fine; a happy ending to a scary situation. Sarah was about to say that McDermott had been wrong, and thank God he was, and she began walking over to the mother and son, knowing someone should check the boy over to make sure he wasn't hurt.

She was halfway there when she saw the boy's face come up from where it had been in the crook of his mother's arm, and as the face came clear and Sarah got a good look at Todd, her stomach sank and she felt that familiar fear she knew so well when near the walking dead.

The boy had a massive dent in the side of his head, one that had obviously killed him, but had left the brain in relatively functioning order. The boy's head had been seen moving in the well, but not because he was alive, but because he'd died and reanimated, and didn't understand where he was.

He did now though, and as Marcy cradled her baby boy, thanking God for his safe return, Todd's mouth opened wide and his head snapped forward, his sharp little teeth sinking into Marcy's arm just below the elbow. Marcy didn't understand what was happening at first, but then a lightning bolt of pain filled her body and she began to scream. She shrieked louder as she gazed down at her son's face, to see his mouth pulling back with her flesh between his teeth. The flesh stretched and pulled like rubber until it reached the breaking point, then the skin snapped free, leaving a large hole in her arm that squirted blood with each pulse of her rapidly beating heart.

She stumbled and fell to the ground, her boy still on top of her, chewing away at the flesh in his mouth, and already going in for more. John was the first who saw what was happening and pulled his gun—even Tom was staring in shock, not understanding what was going on. John only accepted what he saw instantly because of McDermott's musings, which had put the bug of doubt in his ear moments ago. Now he went into action. He carried a pistol and he drew it as he ran at the screaming mother and feeding boy. "Get out of the way! Move!" John screamed, his Jamaican accent making it hard for them to understand him, he was so focused on the mother and son. It didn't matter. He barreled past them, knocking more than one bystander on their butt.

The boy was already leaning over to take a bite out of Marcy's neck when John leveled his pistol and shot the boy in the side of the head. The report of the gun sent most people running and yelling, as they panicked and tried to get away. Most were ordinary people, not hardened warriors, and had barely seen a zombie, before and after arriving on the island.

The bullet blew out the boy's head, knocking the small body off the mother, who was shrieking and shaking her head with her eyes closed. She was in total meltdown, not understanding anything, but knowing it was all bad nonetheless.

Blood spurted from her wound even harder, spraying her in the face and the surrounding ground. The boy's teeth had found a vein and it was a pumper.

As Sarah ran at the fallen, bleeding woman, her eye spotted a machete lying on the ground and she snatched it up, not even slowing down. "John, I need you!" Sarah yelled as she ran to Marcy and dropped down on top of the shrieking woman. John was at Sarah's side a moment later, looking down at Marcy, not knowing what he could do to help the poor woman, but Sarah knew and she was about to go into action. On the ground, a few feet to the left of them lay Todd. Half his head was gone, and his brains oozed out of the hole to glisten in the sun.

Marcy had only one chance, Sarah believed. It had worked with Miguel Salazar and she hoped it would work now.

"John, hold her down, we have to do like we did with Miguel; it's her only chance."

"What the fuck is she talking about?" Tom yelled as he stared at John and then Sarah, not understanding what Sarah was doing. Sarah was sitting on Marcy with a machete held high over her head in her right hand. It looked like Sarah was about to kill Marcy by driving the machete right into her forehead. Tom raised his rifle from where it had been slung across his back, aiming it at Sarah. "Get off her, Sarah, or you're fucking dead!"

McDermott came up behind Tom, his pistol aimed at Tom's back. "I can't believe we're doing this again, Tom, but if you even think of shooting my friend I'll put one in your head."

"Try it, asshole, and you're dead, too," Frank said from behind McDermott, his gun leveled at the Irishman's back.

John saw the standoff and yelled, "Will you all cut the shit! Sarah is tryin' to save this woman, not kill her. Tom, just wait a second and you'll see we're only trying to help!"

"Not from what I can see," Tom replied. "Tell me what you're going to do to her?"

"There's no time to waste talking about it," Sarah interrupted. "We have to do it now!" Before anyone could protest further, Sarah brought the machete down on Marcy's arm as hard as she could, only a few inches above the bite. The blade was razor sharp, and it bit into flesh as if it was butter. The machete almost made it entirely through the bone before stopping. But Sarah was ready for it, and she leaned on the blade, using all her body weight to push through the remaining bone and sever the arm.

Marcy went wild, screaming and shrieking, her legs kicking up and down, her butt bouncing simultaneously as the pain of getting her arm amputated without anesthesia hit her already overloaded brain. She bit her tongue, taking off the tip, blood shooting out of her mouth to glide through the air in crimson globules. They landed on the ground to be soaked up eagerly by the dry dirt.

Sarah used the machete to scrape the lower half of the arm away from the body, as dark red blood gushed out of the stump of the now-amputated arm.

"Tourniquet, we need one now!" Sarah screamed to anyone who would listen. "Hurry!" Sweat coated her face in a solid sheet, droplets dripping off her nose. Below her, Marcy's protestations had slowed as shock overtook her frail system and she fainted. But the blood shooting out of her brand new stump was going strong and Sarah knew there were only seconds before it wouldn't matter what they did as the woman bled out.

McDermott was the one who saved the day, holstering his gun and ripping off his shirt. It had been donated to him by one of the men in the village. Everyone shared when possible, and it had been known that the three new arrivals didn't have much in the way of fresh clothes. He ripped the shirt into strips, handing them to Sarah, who took them eagerly and began wrapping them around Marcy's arm.

Sarah did her best and then began to tighten the tourniquet, using the handle of the machete to twist the cloth. But even though she did her best, the blood wouldn't stop squirting out of the wound. "Damn it, I can't get a good seal on her arm!" She let up and tried again, this time moving the tourniquet up a little more, but all the while blood was gushing out of the open wound. Ants and flies had already arrived to sip at the dark pool of blood.

Sarah did her best, her vision blurred from sweat, and then she felt a hand on her shoulder and John's soothing voice in his ear. "Sarah darling, it's too late, she's gone." His other hand was pressed to Marcy's throat as he searched for a pulse with two fingers, in which he found none.

At first Sarah wouldn't quit, and she continued trying to tighten the tourniquet, but eventually she slowed and finally stopped. She let the tourniquet and machete go, and leaned back so she was sitting on the prone woman with her back straight. Sarah's bloody hands lay limp before her on Marcy's chest. She stared down at the face of the dead mother. Everyone around Sarah was silent. Tom and Frank had lowered their weapons, finally understanding what Sarah had intended. Ruth stood with her mouth hanging open in either shock, amazement or both.

"I...I don't understand. It should have worked; it worked before," Sarah whispered.

"You got lucky last time, Sarah," John said. "Cutting an arm off like that isn't the simplest thing to do. You know that." He helped her stand, and she leaned on him. "Come on, let's get you back home and get you cleaned up."

McDermott joined them, and he also helped Sarah, who was barely standing on her own.

"It should have worked," Sarah kept repeating. "It worked with Miguel."

While they stood there, no one moving, all still caught up in the horror of what had happened, Marcy's eyes suddenly snapped open as she reanimated. No one noticed her eyes open though, all still focused on Sarah and the dead boy.

Marcy moved her head slightly, seeing Sarah's legs only a foot from her face, and before anyone could stop her, Marcy reached out to grab Sarah's right leg so she could pull her body close to the limb and bite it.

But Marcy used the arm that was amputated, so instead of grabbing Sarah's leg, the arm swiped past it, the phantom limb touching nothing but air. Sarah looked down to see Marcy was awake, but one look at her eyes told her that the woman wasn't human anymore.

"Damn you," Sarah hissed. "You should have lived." She picked up the machete and began hacking at Marcy's neck, dropping to her knees a second later so she could hit the throat easier.

"You should have lived!" she screamed as the blade went up and down, severing muscle and tendons and finally the spinal cord. "Why didn't you *live*?"

"Sarah, stop it," John said into her ear. "Stop it right now." He grabbed her arm and made her drop the machete, then pulled her away from the corpse.

Sarah looked up into his face, John's visage one of compassion.

"She should have lived, John. I did it the same way," Sarah whispered.

John brushed hair from her face and wrapped her in his arms, heedless of the blood covering her. "I know, Sarah, I know."

Sarah began to cry, not so much for Marcy or the boy but for everything that had happened. Sarah was a strong woman, but she was also a human being, and though she put up a good front, keeping it all bottled inside sometimes meant that when the dam cracked, the water flowed heavily.

This was one of those times.

John began to half-carry her away. When he reached Tom, Frank, and the few other volunteers that had stuck around, he said, "I'm sorry for the loss of the mother and child. Sarah did her best to save the mother but it just wasn't to be. We're both very sorry for their deaths."

Tom stared at John and a blood-coated Sarah, still in amazement at first the amputation and then the decapitation, all in the space of minutes. He'd seen a lot in his life, and Tom wasn't a man who was afraid to look at blood, but watching Sarah basically cut off Marcy's head was something he thought he'd never see. Ruth had seen it too and after the incident had never said another word to Sarah and actually avoided Sarah at all costs.

"Yeah, it's okay. I'll tell everyone what happened," Tom said. "Well, maybe I'll leave some of it out." He turned to face the small group of people with him. "You hear that, people? Some things need to stay here with us." A murmur of ascent came from the few people still there.

"I think that's a good idea, man," John said. "Billy, let's go, we need to help Sarah; she needs to rest."

"Sure, Johnny. I'll see if I can rustle up a strong drink for her, too. And if not for her, I sure could bloody well use one."

John led Sarah away, McDermott close behind. Some of the villagers asked what had happened, as now that things had quieted down they were returning, but John ignored them. They all pointed at Sarah, seeing how she was covered in blood, whispering to one another.

"Okay, Frank, let's get going and clean this shit up. Looks like the professor'll have two more bodies to autopsy." He waved the other volunteers forward to come help.

"The Prof will be happy for that, anyway," Frank added. He walked over to the severed head, and was about to pick it up when he let out a scream that had Tom swinging around with his gun leveled to fire.

"What? What's the matter now?" Tom asked impatiently. He was on edge and was looking forward to getting this matter closed.

"It's Marcy's head, look at it," Frank said, jerking his chin at the severed head laying on the ground so that the left side of the face was touching the dirt and the right side was in full profile.

Tom calmed slightly as he glanced over at the head. He didn't know what he expected to see but what he saw sure as hell wasn't it.

On the ground, the decapitated head was still active, the mouth opening and closing, the eyes shifting back and forth like a metronome.

Chapter 16

Sarah spent most of the day after the incident with Marcy resting, but around dinner time she became restless and decided to go to the lab to do some work.

If anything, it would take her mind off things.

For a while she had thought it would be better in the village than it had been in the underground bunker, but what she was quickly figuring out was that as long as the dead walked, nowhere would be truly normal.

John and McDermott had walked back to the beach to check on the helicopter. He was considering moving it closer inland but at the moment it was still on the beach. But the second a storm began to brew he would move it, not wanting it exposed to the wind out in the open on the beach. The fuel was terribly low but there was enough to fly the chopper closer to the village, but not much.

Sarah walked down the thin paths that made up the roads of the village. A few people greeted her politely, but more of them seemed to ignore her. Sarah wondered if it was fallout from having to kill Marcy. Of course, she shouldn't have beheaded the poor woman and regretted it completely.

Sarah entered the lab, closing the door behind her. A few of the scientists looked up, but when they saw who it was, they quickly returned to their work. One was scribbling in a notebook with beakers of fluids before him, another was working on a desktop computer, and another was dissecting what looked like a human brain.

Sarah went to her own work space and sat down, then stared at her notes before her. So far she had been trying to recreate all her notes that were still at the bunker, and she'd been doing a pretty good job of it. But as she sat looking at her things, she realized she wasn't really in a working mood.

The door at the back of the lab opened and closed, the Asian scientist exiting. He was carrying something in a stainless steel specimen bowl.

Sarah watched the man go to his work station and began taking samples so they could be looked at under a microscope.

"Is Prof. Langford back there?" she asked the scientist. He nodded to her, then returned to his work. Sarah didn't mind. She knew he was a solitary soul. Standing up, she walked to the rear of the lab, and after two quick knocks on the door out of respect, she opened it and entered.

Once more she had to pause and take in the ghastly scene before her. There were now two bodies on separate tables in the room, Prof. Langford in the middle of them. On the first table was the corpse of a child, and as Sarah looked at the face, she saw it was Todd, the boy who had fallen down the well. The boy's chest had been cracked open, the organs glistening under the fluorescent lights. The skull had been cut open and the brain scooped out.

The other body was the boy's mother, Marcy. Of course, Sarah didn't know this by looking at the body because the corpse had no head, but on another, smaller table in the center of both cadavers, was the severed head of Marcy; Sarah simply put two and two together.

The head was in a strange contraption that resembled a vise, but instead of two metal pieces that would close, there were bolts on each side of the vise that could be screwed into the head to hold it upright.

The face of the decapitated head was facing Sarah, and she could see the eyes moving as the mouth opened and closed ever so slowly, as if the dead woman was trying to speak but without lungs, nothing would come out. Sarah could see the tongue flicking around inside the mouth and she felt her stomach roll.

The scalp of the head had been peeled back, the skull beneath cut so that there was a three inch hole. Prof. Langford was poking around in the hole with a surgical tool.

Though he didn't lift his head up when Sarah entered the room, his eyes did roll up so that he was looking over his thick eyeglasses.

"Ah, Sarah, good to see you. I hope you're feeling better."

"What are you doing, Professor?" she asked softly.

"Why, research of course. The boy wasn't much help due to his brain being destroyed by the bullet your friend put in him, but I must say, by decapitating Marcy here you've done me a great service. I thank you for your foresight. With her brain intact I have so much to study."

Sarah wanted to tell him that there had been no 'foresight' involved, that she had simply lost her composure and done something she wished she could take back.

"These were two of your people only hours ago, Professor. How can you carve into them like they were just meat?"

Prof. Langford stopped poking Marcy's brain and stood upright; he glared at Sarah. "My dear, I am truly saddened by their deaths, surely you must know that. But in the interest of science it's my duty to see if there's anything I can learn about them now to further my research. Or should I say, *our* research?"

"I…I don't know what to say to that," she replied, crossing her arms defensively. Marcy's eyes were staring at her and it creeped

Sarah out to no end. Images of Dr. Logan's lab of horrors flashed through her mind and none of them were pleasant.

"You don't have to. But please understand that for us to find a cure we must do all that we can. The fate of mankind is in our hands, Sarah. We *must* do anything that will help. These two sadly are dead, they can't feel pain anymore, but in death they may still help us." He placed the tool he was holding on the table.

"I hate to say it, Professor, but I've heard similar words from another scientist I knew. All I can say is that in the end it didn't work out so well for him…or any of us with him."

"Hmmph, well, I don't know anything about that, but I do know that nothing bad will happen to you here. Please trust me on that. You do, don't you? Haven't myself and my people been good to you and your friends?"

"Yes, yes, of course they have. I…I didn't mean to say anything to mean otherwise." She sighed. "I think I'll go to my station and try and get some work done. If you'll excuse me; I'm sorry I bothered you."

"No bother, Sarah, always happy to talk to you or any of my staff." He picked up a different surgical tool and began to prod the severed head's brain once more. Sarah could see she was already forgotten.

Turning, she opened the door and left the room, making a promise to herself that she would never reenter it again.

Chapter 17

The next week went by in a blur for John, Sarah and McDermott, especially once they got into a steady routine, each doing the tasks they were given to do. Nothing of importance happened either, which all three were happy about.

It seemed that they had picked a rather hectic time to arrive in the village, and the past week was what a normal time living on the island really was. Still, compared to living in the underground bunker, even those first few days seemed tame by comparison.

It was almost lunch on the seventh day when Sarah found out something that she was both excited about and at the same time concerned with. She double-checked her notes and the copies of Prof. Langford's notes that the man had given her. She then cross-checked and reread them six times before coming to the same conclusion.

"How's it coming with your research, Sarah?" Prof. Langford asked, snapping Sarah from her concentration.

"Huh? Oh, professor, I didn't hear you walk up. It's fine, I'm fine, I mean the research is going fine."

"Are you sure? I saw your face a moment ago, and it seemed like you were on to something. That's why I came over to see you."

Sarah put on her best poker face, internally willing herself to look calm. "No, nothing new here, though I wish I could find something."

"Ah, that's too bad," he said. The professor smiled proudly. "I think I may be on to something, however."

"Oh really?"

"Yes, it's thanks to poor Marcy's head. With her brain intact and still animated, I've been able to study it in great detail."

"What have you learned?" she asked, wanting to keep the subject on his work instead of hers.

"Well, I'm not at liberty to say just yet. I still need time to collate all the data, but once I'm finished, I'll be sure to include you in the staff meeting I plan to call." He winked at her behind his thick eyeglasses after pushing them up his nose. "But rest assured it should be groundbreaking. Well then, back to work." He waved and walked away, returning to the back room where he recently had been spending so much time.

"Not as groundbreaking as what I've found out," Sarah said under her breath.

That night after dinner, when Sarah, John, and McDermott were sitting outside their shack, relaxing under a sky full of stars and enjoying the cool night air, Sarah finally broached the subject that had been on her mind since before lunch.

"I wanted to talk to you guys about something important."

"Sarah darling, you look so serious. What could be so important that you look like that?" John asked with a slight grin. He felt good right now. His stomach was full and McDermott had produced a small container of organic alcohol. It burned like the dickens going down but it quickly changed to a smooth warmness.

"He's got a point, Sarah," Bill added. "You look way too serious for such a beautiful night." A few people walked past them; some greeted the three companions politely, others simply walked by, ignoring them.

"I have good reason, too," she said. "Look, you know why we were back at the bunker, right? Why we had all been put there?"

"Aye, Sarah, so you and your friends could try and find a reason for the dead walking," John said. "But like I told you before, you won't never find a reason for it. It's God's wrath. He's slapping us down for being too cocky; reminding us that He's still the boss man."

Sarah cracked a grin, one of pride. "If that's so, then how do you explain me finding a cure?"

"What?" John said, almost spitting out the sip of alcohol he had in his mouth.

"You heard me. I found a cure. Well, sort of. Look, there's no saving the ones that are already dead, it's far too late for them, but I found a cure for the rest of us. Once I synthesize the vaccine and each human being is vaccinated, if they die, they'll stay that way." John was staring at her, as was McDermott. "Don't you see? We can end this curse once and for all. It can go back to the way it was; when someone dies they stay that way."

"Sarah, that's fantastic," McDermott said happily. "I knew you could do it." Then he took it back. "Well, maybe not, but still, I had faith in you." He raised the small plastic container full of alcohol. "This calls for a drink." He did just that.

John leaned forward in his chair. "So you're sayin' you can end the dead walking. No more corpses struttin' around, tryin' to eat off our faces?" Despite himself he had a look of hope in his eyes. He knew Sarah was smart, far smarter than he could ever hope to be. If someone could find a cure, it was Sarah.

Her smile widened so that it encompassed her entire face. She nodded. "Yes, that's exactly what I'm saying."

"I can't believe it. Just think—no more dead things to deal with," John said. "No more wondering if someone will die in the night to then skulk around, looking to kill." He clapped happily. "It's a miracle!"

Sarah let him celebrate, McDermott doing the same. The three got up and hugged, laughing merrily. John took the container of grain alcohol and took another sip.

She let them be happy for as long as she thought was doable, then she pulled the plug. "But there's a catch, I'm afraid," she said, cutting into their merriment.

Both men stopped laughing and went silent, glaring at Sarah with creased eyes. Sarah wasn't smiling anymore, her visage serious again.

McDermott threw up his hands when he saw that. "Of course, there always is."

"What is it?" John asked, wanting to hear what she had to say. He was still on her side. And why not? She said she'd found a cure for the walking dead. She deserved some latitude.

"Yes, tell us, Sarah," McDermott said sarcastically. "Please tell us what the *catch* is. I can't wait to hear it."

"Billy, let her talk," John said, his tone serious.

Sarah waited until the two were done. Her stomach was doing flip-flops. She knew what she was about to say, and even she didn't like it, but there was no other way. "Well, uhm, I don't actually have the cure right now."

McDermott opened his mouth and Sarah raised her hand, palm out, to cut him off.

"I don't have it yet, Bill, and I'll tell you why but you need to let me tell it all. Okay?"

McDermott sighed and nodded, as did John.

"Okay, so as you might know if you've listened to me talk, Prof. Langford let me have access to all his notes on his research into why the dead are walking. I've been going through them, and at the same time, I've been trying to recreate my notes from back at the bunker. But though I've done my best, I can't do it all from memory alone, though I do remember a lot of it. So earlier today I'm reading the professor's notes and at the same time I'm thinking of my notes that I made back at the bunker. There was this one formula I'd been working on just before we had to leave abruptly—"

"That's the understatement of the year," McDermott said, cutting her off.

Sarah ignored him. "It took me a while, but I think—no, I know—that the formula I was working on, added to what the professor has discovered, will result in a serum to halt the reanimation of dead tissue."

"So what are you saying exactly, Sarah?" John asked, the look on his face telling her that he didn't like where she was going with this.

"What I'm telling you is that though I've figured it out, I can't fabricate the formula from memory. The missing piece is in my notes—back in my lab—in the bunker." She sighed heavily, psyching herself up for what was coming next. "We need to go back there to find the missing piece to the cure."

Chapter 18

McDermott let out a deep intake of breath, and dropped the container of alcohol he was holding. The bottle fell to the ground, the liquid seeping out to soak into the ground.

Normally, he would have picked it up immediately to begin cursing the wasted booze, but now he barely noticed. His eyes were wide, his mouth hanging open in amazement. "That's the most insane thing I've ever heard, and it's suicide. Tell her, John, tell her what she's suggesting is crazy."

"Maybe it is, Bill, but it's worth the risk," Sarah said, now standing so she was eye to eye with McDermott.

"Sarah, you can't be serious," John said, trying to keep his voice calm. He too wanted to yell like McDermott, but he figured one hothead was enough in their trio. He would be the voice of reason.

"I'm deadly serious," Sarah replied, turning to face John, though she had to look up slightly. "It could all be over, John. This could mean the end of the plague."

John took a step back, turning so she couldn't see his face. He thought about what she'd just said, how the dead could finally be put to rest. He thought about more than that though. He considered her life, McDermott's life, and his own.

McDermott was right.

To return to the bunker would be certain suicide. The corridors were filled with nothing but the walking dead.

There would be no way to get through them all. With these thoughts through his head in seconds, John weighed the cons over the pros, and when he'd made up his mind, he turned to face her. "No way, Sarah, it's not gonna happen. To hell with it."

"John, how can you say that?" she rebutted.

"You heard me, girl. To hell with the world; it's already shit anyway. Look, we're safe on this island. Why do you want to mess that up?"

"I don't, but I also began something back at the bunker and now I finally found the missing piece to the puzzle. I can't ignore it. John, I could never live with myself if I did." She spread her legs and planted her feet, while crossing her arms over her chest, her jaw growing taut. "John, Bill, you both need to listen to me. This is something I have to do. With or without you I'm going back to that bunker. I know when I tell Prof. Langford my news he'll give me all the help I need to do this."

"Damn it, Sarah, why do you have to be so stubborn?" John asked, wanting to reach out and grab her by the arms and shake some sense into her. But he knew her too well to even think that would do any good. She was a proud, willful woman and though it could be maddening, those character traits were also some of the reasons he was attracted to her.

She didn't reply to his question, there was no need. Looking into her eyes, all John saw was resolve. He knew she would do what she said. Sarah would go back to the underground bunker with or without him.

"Well, you're not going alone, even if Langford sends men with you. If you're going back then I am too," John said in surrender.

Sarah cracked a thin smile, then turned slightly so she could see McDermott's face. "What about you, Bill?"

McDermott had picked up his bottle of alcohol and he chugged the remainder, then wiped his mouth with the back of his arm. "Well, the way I see it, if you two idiots are going off on a potential suicide mission, you're gonna need me to make sure you get back in one piece." He smiled wryly, the picture of an Irish brogue. "Besides, maybe I can get to my stash of booze back in my bunk at *The Ritz*. This grain stuff is like drinking gasoline."

Sarah didn't want to wait until morning to tell Prof. Langford the good news, so leaving John and McDermott, she went to see the professor alone.

He was still in the lab, as he was most nights. He looked up to see who had entered at the sound of Sarah's footsteps. "Sarah, so good to see you. What brings you here so late this night?"

"I wanted to share some good news with you," she said, moving closer. She saw that the professor was working on a brain, the sections glistening pink under the fluorescent lights.

"Is that Marcy?" she asked.

"Why, yes it is. I'd learned all I could with it in her skull, so it was time to remove it. Even that was fascinating, I have to admit. I was able to study the head as each section was disconnected, until the eyes and mouth finally ceased to function." He picked up an already blood-soaked rag and wiped his hands, despite the fact he was wearing latex gloves. "So, my dear, what is it you want to tell me?"

Sarah began slowly, then feeling more confident, she talked faster, explaining all that she'd discovered. The professor only interrupted her a few times, and only so he could ask a quick question to better understand what she was telling him. By the time she finished, Prof. Langford was so excited he could barely stand still.

The possibilities were endless if what she said was true, and after she showed him his notes and commented on the missing piece, he had to agree with her.

"It does seem viable," he said when they were done. "But you say you need to go back to the place you left?"

"Exactly, but the complex is overrun with the dead, and though I hate to admit it, it's probably a suicide mission to even try." She sighed. "But I had to tell you about this, I couldn't just sit on my hands. And though it might be a one way mission, I have to go. I have to try and retrieve my notes. The entire world is at stake, as fantastic as that sounds."

"No, Sarah, you're right. If there's even a chance, we have to try." He held up his hand for her to wait a moment and then went to the door leading outside. Once there he called out to someone, and Sarah heard Tom's name mentioned. The professor returned to her a minute later. "I've summoned Tom. You said your two friends will accompany you on this mission?"

She nodded. She had told him that earlier.

"Good, but you'll need more than that. Weapons, too, I surmise. The only way you'll get into that bunker is with brute force and if that's the case, Tom's your man."

While they waited for Tom to arrive, they talked some more about what she'd discovered. Ten minutes later, Tom knocked and entered the lab. "You wanted to see me, Professor?" Sarah could smell alcohol on his breath but the man's eyes were clear.

"Yes I did," Prof. Langford said and quickly explained what Sarah had told him, and what Tom was needed for. "I want you to set out at first light with whatever men you think you'll need," the professor finally finished.

Tom rubbed his jaw, the feeling rough on his palm. He hadn't shaved since that morning. "I don't think we should bring that many men, Professor. A smaller party will be able to move overland quicker and less people means less food and water and gear." He looked at Sarah. "You say John and Bill are coming?"

Sarah nodded.

"Then on top of the four of us, I only want to bring four more men for a total of eight." Tom glanced at Prof. Langford. "Can I take whatever I want from the armory?"

"Yes, Tom, of course, whatever you need. This mission is of the utmost importance. If this all works out, it will be history in the making," the professor replied, then pushed his eyeglasses back up his nose.

Sarah was used to it and had barely noticed the man do it every few minutes while she was talking to him.

"That might be true, Professor," Tom said, "but before we can make history, we need to travel across fifty plus miles of infested land and at least two cities on foot, then we have to fight our way in and out of a vast underground complex with the dead nipping at our asses the whole time."

Prof. Langford patted Tom's shoulder, heedless of the blood he was leaving there. "I'm sure you and your men will do fine."

Sarah rolled her eyes, understanding immediately that Prof. Langford was more of a bureaucrat and had no concept of what the world was truly like nowadays.

Tom saw Sarah roll her eyes and he smiled at her.

She began to laugh and he joined in, the two sharing an inside joke that only they understood.

As for the professor, he thought they were laughing about the prospect of a successful mission and he quickly joined in.

The sound of laughter drifted outside to be lost in the wind.

* * *

When Sarah returned to the shack, McDermott wasn't there. John was. He was sitting up in a corner of the room in a chair, reading a book by candlelight. He was shirtless, his dark skin reflecting the light.

"Where's Bill?" Sarah asked upon entering the shack; she kicked off her shoes.

"He's out drinking, of course, but now he says there's a reason," John said, closing the book and placing it on his knee. "He figures if he's going to die soon, he might as well get as drunk as possible."

"He's being a little dramatic, don't you think?" she asked and sat on her cot.

He shrugged. "Perhaps. Or maybe he just wants to have some fun before he dies."

"Now you're being dramatic." She reached over to a small side table where there was a bottle of water. It was warm but it still tasted wonderful on her dry tongue. "I talked to Prof. Langford. He wants us to leave in the morning. Tom is coming, too, with four handpicked men."

"Why all the rush? You just found out about your notes today."

"Maybe so, but this has gone on for far too long as it is. Truth is, I should have been able to figure all this out on my own, but only Fisher was really helping me back at the bunker. Logan was off doing experiments that was nothing more than chopping up cattle. He did find out some interesting things but in the end they were meaningless."

"Aye, Frankenstein was crazy, there's no doubt about it." His accent was softer, as if he was consciously aware of it. "So we're off tomorrow, back into the big bad world like nothing's changed. Hell, Sarah, it would have been nice to have some more warning."

"It wouldn't change anything, John. It's better this way. Sometimes thinking too much isn't a good thing, sometimes action is what's needed. I learned that from Rhodes—one of the only things of value I did learn from him, too."

John made a spitting sound, though he didn't really do it. "Rhodes. Don't mention that man to me. That bastard, I hope he's burning in the bowels of Hell as we speak."

"We'll be taking a boat over," Sarah said, changing the subject to something that wasn't so distasteful to them both. "I guess there's a half dozen moored on the far side of the island. It's hidden in a small alcove, which is why we never saw it as we approached."

John put his book down and stood up, stretched, and went to join Sarah on the cot. "Enough talkin' about dead things, suicide missions and past enemies." He sat down and put his arm around her.

She leaned into him, resting her head on his shoulder. She could smell his body odor and it didn't displease her. John smelled like a cedar tree if she had to put a name to his scent.

"Haven't you noticed that we're alone?" he said. "One of the few times that I can remember. Billy should be gone all night, if I know him, and I do."

She pulled back her head and shifted so she was facing him. Her hand crept down to his thigh and rested there. He was wearing shorts and the heat of his leg was a tangible thing beneath her palm. Only a few inches away from her hand was his manhood, which was very obvious in his shorts.

"What are you suggesting, John?" she asked, her voice soft. She knew exactly what he was suggesting and she wanted it, too. Now that the ice was broken between them, so to speak, there was no reason for her not to enjoy their time together to the fullest. She was a sexual woman when the time was right, and right now, at this moment, the time was most definitely right. Besides, she needed a diversion to take her mind off the coming morning. Trepidation filled her, though she didn't want to admit it, and a distraction would be just what the doctor ordered…even if that doctor was her.

John didn't reply to her question, but instead leaned in and kissed her, his arms reaching out and pulling her close. Their kiss was slow and passionate, but it quickly changed to one of lust, as the two lovers let themselves go, John needing to forget about the world he now lived in as much as Sarah's scientific side wanted to embrace it.

They made love with complete abandon, letting their lust consume them, and after a brief rest, they joined once more, the second time more slowly, lovingly, as they were already satiated, but still wanting to bask in the other's glow.

Just before the sun rose, they drifted off to sleep, as if both had been denying their eventual slumber, knowing that when they closed their eyes, the night would be over, and the new day would be upon them and all that it would bring.

They slept dreamlessly in each other's arms.

Chapter 19

The next morning came far too quickly for Sarah, John and McDermott—especially McDermott, who had one of the worst hangovers in his life.

After a specially made breakfast for the men—and Sarah—on the expedition, they had set off to the dock at the far end of the island.

One of the fishing boats—a fifty foot schooner called the *Aurora* that was redesigned exclusively for fishing—had been loaded with their gear the previous night. Tom had only managed to sleep for a few hours, as he had been in charge of supplies.

As the schooner pulled away from its berth and the dock, John took in the nine people that were about to either commit suicide or perhaps change history. McDermott was on his left, leaning heavily against the taffrail. His skin was pale as parchment and behind the dark sunglasses he wore his eyes were bloodshot.

John watched him take a sip from his trusty flask, which made the tall Jamaican smile. McDermott saw the smile and held the flask up to John, offering it. John shook his head no.

"A bit of the hair of the dog that bit me," McDermott said. "Best cure for a hangover. Give me another hour and I'll be at top speed again."

John didn't doubt a word of it; he'd seen McDermott drink all night at the bunker and wake up ready to go the next day. The Irishman carried an M-16 rifle and wore his sidearm on his hip. He also carried a hunting blade given to him from Tom, who had taken it from the village's armory.

On John's right stood Sarah. As he watched her, he thought how beautiful she looked. She had just finished putting her hair into a pony tail so it would stop blowing in her face, due to the heavy wind. She carried McDermott's .45 still, and John guessed that it was really hers now; over her right shoulder was slung an assault rifle. He'd seen her in action and knew she could handle the weapon.

John himself carried an M-16 of his own, a pistol on his right hip and a machete on his left. The machete had been given to him from Tom, also, and though John hadn't said anything, it felt right to have one on his leg once more. He'd carried one at the bunker but for all he knew it was still laying in the same place where he'd dropped it. Perhaps he'd get a chance to retrieve it.

Tom was standing behind John, and next to him was Frank. Both men carried rifles and sidearms, as well as knives. Tom had also taken out some of the rarest items the armory contained, knowing how important the mission was after talking to Professor Langford. On a web belt across his chest were affixed nine hand grenades of different types: Three phosphorus—which were incendiary devices that burned hot and fast. Three flash bangs—used to stun, and three shrapnel—used to destroy the enemy. He also carried his sniper rifle and a Mini-Uzi that used 9mm rounds for in-close fighting.

Frank carried a Soviet-made Kalashnikov, as did the three other men Tom had picked for this mission. Across their chest the men carried spare magazines of the 7.62mm rounds the weapons took and there were backpacks also filled with spare ammunition.

John tried to remember the names of the four new men, and after a moment they came to him.

The first man was tall and skinny, with a tuft of bright red hair. He was Lou. His face had scars from a man who had battled acne as a youth and had lost miserably. The second man was John's height, with dark brown hair and skin to match. He had a Boston accent, and usually when he talked the letter 'R' was nonexistent. He was a friendly soul and John had taken a liking to him immediately. His name was Pete.

The next man was a burly fellow with the broad chest and muscular thighs of a man who worked out with weights, and looked like he could rip a man in half if he wanted to. His name was Rollo—John didn't know if it was a nickname or not and figured it didn't matter. He mostly grunted when spoken to. His jaw was square, his eyes deep set in his face, his black hair cut close to the scalp. John thought he looked like that actor Schwarzenegger. The man was no more than five foot seven but what he lacked in height he made up for with muscle. The black shirt he wore practically strained at the seams to rip.

Tom had decided to take another man with them. The last member of the team was simply called 'Schwartz.' He had German features and the crew-cut blonde hair only added to it. His dark blue eyes seemed to bore into a person when he looked at them. He was just under six feet tall and spoke softly, so that a person would have to lean in close to listen to him. It was a tactic. It said 'pay attention if you want to know something when I talk.'

Tom had told John when being introduced to the new men that each of them had some form of military or police training. John had only nodded. Training was good, but when up against a horde of walking dead, even the most prepared man might find himself cracking. Still, they all knew how to shoot, which was the one thing John knew they would all be doing.

There was one more person on the boat, and that was the captain of the vessel. He was a grizzled man in his fifties with long white hair and matching beard and mustache. His face could barely be seen under all the hair, and other than a plump nose that was almost bright red, his facial features were hidden. His eyes were a light brown and they twinkled with friendliness, but there was also something else there. John believed it was grief—a grief so strong that it would never leave him. John had commented to Sarah about it. She had stared at the old captain, while biting her lower lip in thought.

Later, when the boat was well away from the dock and nothing but water was around for miles, and the tall mast that carried both a mainsail and a spinnaker, along with the mainsheet, were flapping in the wind, Sarah had gone to speak to the captain.

John remembered the inquisitive look on her face and figured she'd decided to find out exactly why the captain had that haunted look in his eyes.

"Hi, Captain, I was wondering how much longer till we reach the mainland," Sarah said, putting on her best smile. She didn't really care about when the boat would reach land, but figured it was a good way to strike up a conversation.

"A few hours," the captain said, his eyes never leaving the sea before him. He'd been introduced to Sarah, John and McDermott when they'd first arrived, but had been busy getting ready to sail to talk much.

"That's good to know," she said, not knowing what else to say. Then she added, "So, is this your actual boat or just one that was salvaged and now you pilot it?"

"No, it's mine," he said as he gazed out over the bow at the rolling waves, then glanced up at the leading edge of the mainsail and made a few slight adjustments to keep them on course. The water was fairly smooth, with only one foot waves at most, so the boat wasn't rocking too much. More of a gentle roll back and forth, and sometimes up and down, but nothing jarring. Tom's men were pulling double-duty as the boat's crew, too. Behind the schooner, its wake was straight as a ruler.

Sarah spotted the captain's wedding band on his left hand and he saw her looking. He instinctively raised his hand up to his face so he could look directly at the ring. "She's dead, as you probably guessed."

"Who's dead?" Sarah asked.

"My wife. I saw you eyeing my wedding band a second ago. She's not on the island, she's dead. Been almost three years now, I guess."

"I'm sorry to hear that," Sarah said. "We've all lost people we love."

"Aye, girl, we have. I lost my entire family thanks to the dead walking. So when I was told you needed a boat to the mainland, I was the first to volunteer. If you can find a way to make the bastard dead stay that way, well, girl, I'm all in."

"Thanks, that's good to know," she said.

He reached into his shirt from the top and took out a small locket attached to a chain around his neck. It was more feminine than masculine, and Sarah knew automatically it probably belonged to his wife. He popped open the locket and leaned over so Sarah could see the two pictures within.

"The one on the left is my wife, Trudy, and the one on the right is my son, Robby, when he was seven." He gazed out over the water once more. "He'd be thirteen this month I reckon."

"They're both beautiful," Sarah said, studying the two small pictures barely an inch in diameter. The woman was smiling in the picture, with long hair that looked light brown. It was hard to tell due to the size and age of the photo. The picture of the boy was also faded, no doubt from exposure to the salt air for so many years. But Sarah could still see the smiling face of a good-looking boy, with chubby cheeks and wide eyes.

"Yes they were." He sighed. "I had to kill them both, you know."

Sarah looked up from the pictures, her gaze resting on the captain's profile as he stood beside her. It was hard to tell what he was thinking with his eyes hidden, and his face lost under his thick beard. She didn't say anything, sensing that if she didn't, he would reveal more on his own.

"It was two years after the dead began to walk," the captain said. He didn't look at Sarah, his eyes only on the waves before the schooner. His voice was steady but Sarah could hear a slight tremble in his voice, as if the man was about to breakdown.

"We'd been holed up in a small community for seniors on the west side of Florida. It was filled with modular homes. You know the ones, like trailer parks but a hell of a lot nicer. People used these small carts, like golf carts, to ride around in. The entire place had a hurricane fence around it, plus a gate. Later, razor-wire was added to the top of the fence. Not so much for the dead, but for human scavengers who thought they could come in and take what was ours. Of course, as time passed, people like that showed up less and less until no one that wasn't a walking corpse came near us. Trudy, my son and I were happy, but as I'm sure you know, in this new world of ours, happiness is something that doesn't last too long."

"What happened?" Sarah asked.

"Unknown to myself and the rest of the residents, the dead had been congregating near the back of the community. Now, if we'd known this we could've sent some people there to spike a few heads through the chain-link fence, but no one knew. The dead kept arriving, pushing on the ones in front until those bodies literally were pushed through the fence—well, the flesh and muscle was; the skeletons didn't go through. We'd had bad rain for more than a week, too, and the ground was very wet. Finally, the weight of all those bodies added to the soggy earth, managed to uproot one of the fence moorings and the steel post was yanked from the ground like an old tree in a storm. It was just after midnight when this happened so most of us were asleep. The dead flooded into the community, filling the streets like locusts." He sighed. "I guess you can imagine what happened next."

"Yeah, I'm afraid I can." Images of the bunker being filled with zombies came to Sarah, though she hadn't actually seen it happen—as she had been in the corral with McDermott and John—but she could easily imagine what it had been like for any humans inside.

"So let me speed the story up and say that my family and I managed to escape with our lives," he said. "I took them to the marina, hoping to find a boat I could sail. I wasn't thinking of where to go, just knew that we needed to get off the mainland. This schooner was docked there, looking as pristine as the day it'd been moored. All around the boat the other vessels had been either destroyed from past storms or had caught fire somehow—no doubt vandalism or maybe lightning. I boarded first, making sure to check if it was safe, then Trudy and my son came on. The dead had seen us and were following us, and I barely managed to get off the mooring lines and let the current drift us away from the dock. A few of the dead almost got on board but I used a mooring hook to keep them from boarding, or I managed to knock them into the water. Once we were away from the dock, I got lucky and found the keys to the engine in a small overhead compartment in the galley; the fuel tank was more than half full at the time, too."

"You got lucky," Sarah said.

"Aye, or so I thought. I anchored a quarter mile from the dock, figuring that if I didn't know where to go I should wait. Plus, it was dark out and I couldn't see a damn thing. Who knew what was in the water ahead of me? I figured I'd wait till sunrise before deciding on where to go next. The main cabin was stocked with maps so I wasn't worried about navigating. There was canned food, too. Not much but it would keep us going for a day or two." He wiped a hand across his cheek, where an errant tear had appeared. "What neither myself nor Trudy knew at the time was that my son had been bit in our escape from the community. It wasn't a bad bite, mind you, but the skin had been broken. My wife and I found out the next day when my son complained his arm hurt and that he didn't feel good. When Trudy checked his arm, she found the bite; the wound was already festering, too." He paused to adjust the boat's course, the schooner sliding through the waves.

Overhead, the sails flapped in the stiff wind. The sun was fully up in a partly cloudy sky. It was going to be a beautiful day, probably in the low to mid-eighties. A perfect beach day, Sarah thought ruefully.

Sarah didn't really need to hear the rest of the story, knowing what probably happened, but the captain was determined to tell it to the end and she wasn't going to stop him.

"She nursed him then, but not back to health. There had been some pills, valium and the like, on the boat left from the previous owner, and Trudy gave the boy these to keep him calm. Normally, I would never have allowed it, but there was nothing the pills could do to my son that the infection wasn't." He sighed. "He slowly got worse until he already looked like he was dead. His forehead protruded, or his eyes retreated into his skull, his complexion became as white as a sheet, and his eyes lost their color. I knew what was coming soon, so did Trudy, but neither of us said a word about it, as if by not speaking about it, it wouldn't happen. But of course it did, there was no way to stop it. My son was in Trudy's arms in the sleeping quarters when he died. She should have let him go and come and gotten me, but she didn't, she kept cradling him in her arms, her little boy, her baby. When he finally reanimated, the first thing he did was sink his teeth into her arm. She screamed, and that's what brought me to them. I'd been up on deck, studying the maps when I heard her call out. By the time I reached them, blood was everywhere. My son was on top of his mother on the deck, chewing on something that looked like bloody raw meat, and though I knew exactly what it was, I didn't want to think about it. Trudy's throat was shredded at the jugular, and from my first glimpse, I could already tell that she was gone; she'd bled out in less than a minute. Mercifully, her eyes were closed, though her mouth was open, as if in a silent scream.

"Before I could act, my son came at me, snarling and groaning like a wild animal. I didn't want to hurt him, despite knowing he wasn't my son anymore. I shoved him away from me and he went sprawling over my wife's body. He was up in an instant and he charged me again, but this time, though it pained me to do it, I punched him in the face. He fell back and tumbled to the deck, but a second later he was up. I could clearly see the imprint of my fist on his cheek and I felt my stomach heave inside me at what I'd done. You see, I'd never raised a hand to my son his entire life...till now.

"As my son came at me again and I tried to grab him, I didn't see that my wife's eyes were now open, and as I attempted to restrain my son, she sat up, then began to crawl towards me. I didn't know she was active until I felt her hand on my leg. Looking down, and seeing her bloody face, those blank eyes, I screamed in revulsion and kicked her away from me. My foot caught her in the face and sent her rolling away.

"Now filled with terror and revulsion, I pushed my son away from me and turned and fled to the upper deck. They came right behind me. I reached the bow and watched them coming for me, only the bucking of the deck preventing them from moving faster. As I stared at them, waiting for my family to reach me, I considered simply letting them take me. Once they killed me I would die and return as one of them. At least we would be together. But when they were only a few feet away, and I stared into their blank eyes, my resolve crumbled and my instinct for survival took over. The mooring hook I'd used before was lying on the deck, and I picked it up and used it like a club, knocking my wife and son into the water. When their bodies hit the water they didn't float, but went under immediately. I never saw them again, and to this day I wonder if they're out there somewhere, walking on the ocean floor, hand in hand. At least my son is with his mother, I suppose.

"I collapsed to the deck after knocking them into the ocean and I don't recall even to this day how long I sat there, staring at the water. Hours I suppose. When I finally came out of my fugue state due to hunger and thirst, I wiped my eyes of any residual tears and began studying the maps once more. As I did it I felt hollow inside, as if the reason I was out there no longer mattered. I'd be lying if I didn't say I didn't contemplate suicide.

"I pulled anchor and set sail, for where I didn't know. I eventually came upon the island we all live on; it was by pure luck actually. When I spotted the dock, I decided to moor for the night. Then I met Tom who had been out hunting and went to investigate when he saw my boat; he told me what they were doing and I was happy to become a part of it. Now I go out five days a week and fish with a small crew."

"You use this boat? The same one your family died on?" Sarah asked.

"Aye, I converted her into a fishing boat. I feel my family is still here, with me. I like to think that my wife and son's souls are still here, watching over me."

"A seagull!" one of the men called out and the others joined in, happy to see life amidst the endless water. If a seagull was flying then land couldn't be that far away. The coast was still hours away but at least the boat was getting closer.

Sarah reached out and touched the knuckles of the captain's scarred hand as it held the wheel. "Thank you for sharing that with me, Captain. I know how hard it was."

"Ah, think nothing of it, girl." He patted her hand with his free one. "Though it hurts to remember, it also brings me happiness to think of them again. As the years go by it gets harder to remember their faces. Thank the Lord I have this locket." He patted his chest where the locket hung around his neck, once more returned to under his shirt. He stood taller, and his face seemed to brighten. He sniffed once and forced a smile. "Why don't you go back with your friends and let me work for a bit. We'll be there soon, a couple hours at the most."

Sarah nodded, and with a forced smile of her own, she left the captain alone with his thoughts.

Chapter 20

Three hours later, the schooner was pulling into a slip in a small cove off of Florida.

The cove was a tiny anchorage, sheltered by land on both sides, much like a horseshoe. It housed a little marina with a small wharf, half a dozen wooden slips, a souvenir store, and a restaurant—the two latter now nothing but burned-out wreckage.

There were a few zombies standing on the wharf as the boat began to pull in to the slip, but they were dispatched easily by Tom using his sniper rifle. There were others nearby as well, mostly wandering around aimlessly; they had yet to see the arrival of the boat. Everyone knew the dead would have to be dealt with sooner rather than later.

Sarah and the men quickly jumped off the boat without it actually being tied to the pier, all their gear carried on their person in backpacks or duffel bags. Tom was the last one off. He waved to the captain. "We'll be at the alternate location in a few hours."

"No problem, Tom," the captain said. "I'll be anchored a quarter mile down the coast to begin with, then I'll sail in and set anchor where I can keep an eye on the dock two hours after that."

"Right, and if there's no contact after twenty-four hours, you know what that means."

The captain nodded. "Yes, I return to the island and report that your mission failed."

Tom's face took on a look of complete seriousness. "Let's hope that doesn't happen." He turned to the waiting men, and gestured for Rollo and Schwartz to come over to him. "Help me push the boat off," he said and the three men got to work. A minute later the schooner was chugging away back out to sea. The fuel in the tank was only used for maneuvering; otherwise the boat exclusively used the sails, unless there was no wind.

Tom was already jogging to the others, Rollo and Schwartz right behind him. When they reached the other five men and Sarah, he got to the front of the line and waved them on. "Frank, watch our backs," he said when he passed the rat-faced man. In single file they moved out, Tom first, John, Sarah, and McDermott next, then the other four men, and Frank last in line.

"What are we doing next?" John asked as he jogged behind Tom. "It's gonna be a hard trek if we're walking all the way there." He wasn't exaggerating. Fifty miles through zombie-infested cities and towns would be more than hard, it would be downright impossible.

"John's right," Sarah added. "Before we left the bunker we flew all over this area with our helicopter. All we found were desolate cities and towns filled with the dead. No survivors for over a hundred miles in each direction."

"I couldn't get anything on the radio, either," McDermott said, putting in his two cents. "Nothing but static."

Tom turned his head and flashed the three companions a smile. "Don't worry, we're not walking." He gestured with his chin to a warehouse at the end of the street. "We're going over there."

They were on a small street just off the wharf, with more side streets coming off the one they were on like rungs on a ladder. The street looked like most streets the companions had seen, with weeds growing through any cracks in the pavement, and houses looking uncared for with many windows shattered. A few were nothing but burned-out shells, the fires that had destroyed them long extinguished.

Bodies long dead and rotting littered the pavement, the corpses desiccated, the skin resembling dried leather, all tan and black. The soft tissue on the bodies, such as eyes and tongues, were long gone by either rot or scavengers on four legs or the winged kind.

Trash was everywhere, everything from discarded fast food containers to newspapers of the last days before society began to collapse and the news stopped flowing and the population of America started dying in droves to then reanimate and complete the cycle anew. One newspaper blew across the street and was stopped by a street lamp. The headline on the paper screamed **THE DEAD WALK!** At the time it must have sounded ludicrous but now it was as common as the sun rising and setting each day.

As the team ran past these streets, they could see people slowly moving towards them. But the people weren't alive in the normal sense and their slow, plodding gait was all the more chilling to see.

In a way, if the zombies had been able to move faster it would have made the tableau more threatening, but zombies were made up of decomposing flesh, their muscles deteriorating constantly, their bones becoming brittle. Even if a ghoul could somehow defy logic and manage to move quicker than a fast walk, no doubt its ankles would snap from the exertion.

But though they moved slowly, what they lacked in dexterity was made up a hundred fold by their sheer numbers and tenacity.

"Guys," Tom ordered Lou and Pete, "take those fuckers out." He pointed to the half dozen zombies directly in the group's path coming down the middle of the street. The dead were an eclectic bunch. One wore a mailman's uniform but was missing one shoe, another looked like a chef, two more resembled preppies; they even still wore their sweaters wrapped around sagging shoulders. The last two were women, and had the look of soccer moms. All were decaying badly, their clothes ripped and covered in dried blood and other bodily fluids. One of the soccer moms was missing an arm and the chef looked like he'd fallen into the deep fat fryer, his face a mass of red burns that bubbled in places, the fluid trapped under the dry flesh seeping out.

Standing side by side, Lou and Pete leveled their Soviet rifles at the six zombies and cut loose. Bullets riddled the torsos, making the bodies dance and jig in place, as puffs of dust erupted from each gunshot, the ghouls' clothes covered in grime. Large sections of meat were blown out the back of the bodies from the exit wounds of the 7.62mm rounds.

"Stop screwing around and shoot their fuckin' heads!" Tom yelled over the gunfire.

Lou gave Tom a slight shrug, as if saying, "Sorry, boss," then he raised his aim slightly, Pete doing the same. One second the bodies were jerking around, and then the heads were exploding like dynamite had been packed into the eye sockets and set off. One at a time, each body dropped to the ground, utterly still.

"That's better," Tom said. "Next time no games; just take them out and be done with it."

"Sorry, Tom, just havin' some fun," Lou said, looking downcast.

"Well, have fun on your own fucking time. Right now you're on my time. Got it?"

Both men nodded that they understood.

"Okay, let's keep moving, people; we're almost at the warehouse," Tom said.

While they picked up their pace, John caught up with Tom and said, "You wanna tell me what the hell that was, man?"

"What are you talking about?" Tom asked.

"That shooting gallery you just sanctioned. Every dead thing for a mile is gonna know we're here. What were you thinkin', man?"

Tom grinned, knowing something John didn't. "Relax, it'll all be fine."

"Fine? How is it gonna be fine?"

"You'll see. Trust me, I've done this before. Sometimes we need to come to the mainland to get medical supplies and other items that run low on the island. We've got a whole setup already in place."

John looked skeptical but Tom patted his arm. "You'll see in a few minutes what I mean. For now keep your eyes open for anything dead and moving."

Tom jogged ahead with Frank, and McDermott and Sarah caught up to John.

"What did he say about all that shooting?" McDermott asked.

"He told me to relax, that it's all under control," John said, his accent thicker than usual. When he was under stress it happened sometimes.

"I sure hope he does," Sarah commented. " 'Cause we're getting more company by the second." She gestured over her shoulder where more zombies had appeared, coming out of buildings, and stumbling out of alleyways, homes and storefronts. The gunshots had been a dinner bell, telling the dead that prey was nearby.

Ten more walking dead were taken down noisily before the team of nine reached the loading dock of the warehouse. None even came close to the group, and each one was taken down with a head shot. Tom's warning about screwing around had been taken to heart by his men.

The warehouse was in a relatively empty area, two blocks away from the wharf. Even parked cars and trucks seemed to be in short supply once they'd reached the immediate area of the building. There was only one vehicle near the warehouse and it was nothing but a burned-out husk. The tires were melted to the pavement from the long-ago blaze, the metal now black from fire and red-brown from rust. All the windows were shattered, and as Sarah passed by it, she saw the unmistakable shape of a skeleton in the driver's seat.

There was a pile of ragged corpses across from the loading dock door, the jumble of arms and legs told that the bodies had been tossed there with abandon. It was hard to count but there had to be over fifty bodies. Some were nothing but skeletons with rags on them, while others looked slightly fresher. When the wind shifted and blew over the pile, everyone had to cover their noses or risk gagging on the stench. Luckily, the wind shifted quickly and it wasn't so bad.

When Tom reached the loading dock, he took out a set of keys from one of his pockets, then quickly undid the padlock holding a thick metal chain that ran through welded rungs on the loading dock door.

Without so much as peeking under the door after cracking it an inch, he threw the rolling metal door up, the bright sunlight pushing back the darkness within.

"Ta da," Tom said cheerfully, the light of day exposing what lay inside.

"What's this?" John asked after seeing the contents of the loading dock.

"Our transportation to this underground bunker of yours. Like I said, we aren't walking."

"Is he serious?" McDermott asked Sarah.

She shrugged. "Yeah, I think he is."

Tom pointed to three of his men. "Schwartz, Lou and Pete, you three stay out here and take out any dead fucks that pop up. Remember, just headshots."

"Got it, Tom," Pete said. Lou and Schwartz were already moving to each side to begin taking out any zombies that came too close. So far the walking dead were still far away, the group of nine having outrun them easily. But now that everyone was in a fixed location, the zombies were catching up. At the far end of the road the warehouse was on, more and more ghouls were filling the street.

Tom pointed to Frank to get the rat-faced man's attention and tossed him a set of keys. "Make sure our transportation is up and running and ready to go on my order. We leave in ten; maybe less if it gets too crowded around here."

"Got it," Frank said and ran into the loading dock.

"Everyone else, let's load up and get ready to move."

Chapter 21

The transportation Tom was so proud of was nothing more than an RV with some metal plates bolted to the fiberglass sides and steel grates mounted over the front windshield, rear and side windows. The back end had once had a ladder but it had been removed to be one less handhold for zombies to grab on to.

Other than those slight modifications, the vehicle was the same as it had been when it rolled off the showroom floor. That is, except for the countless splotches of brown on the once white interior. John, Sarah and McDermott had seen enough dried blood to know what it was immediately.

Gunshots could be heard outside the loading dock as the three men took down approaching zombies. With each passing second, the level of gunfire rose so that in another minute if it kept up, the gunfire would be constant. That told John that the walking dead were closing in on their location and he wasn't happy about Tom's lackadaisical approach to the situation.

McDermott commented that the RV was a rolling deathtrap but Tom ignored the slight; he just waved for them to get on board and find a seat. Frank had connected the battery and he'd just started the engine when the three men standing outside shooting zombies came running back into the loading dock, then jumped on board the RV.

"There's too many now to keep shooting, Tom. I hope we're ready to go," Lou said as he climbed the three stairs into the vehicle.

"Ask Frank," Tom said, though he was being rhetorical.

"We're ready, Tom," Frank said, revving the engine a little to get out a small stutter. It roared for a moment and then the motor settled down to a smooth idle.

"Good," Tom said. "Hey, Rollo, get to the back ceiling hatch and go up it. Take out anything worth shooting, but don't get trigger happy. Bullets don't grow on trees, you know."

Rollo acknowledged his orders, picked up his weapon, and did as he was told. At the back of the RV was a small ladder. It led to a hatch in the ceiling. Rollo climbed up it and poked his upper body out, his legs straddling the ladder. Already he began firing at the first zombies that had appeared in front of the loading dock door.

"Okay, Frank, let's get moving, but take it easy," Tom said, patting Frank on the shoulder before taking the seat beside him. Both the driver and passenger seats were large Captain's chairs. "Try to avoid them whenever possible. It's a bitch getting guts out of the grille."

Frank put the RV in gear and began rolling out of the loading dock. John looked out a window to see that the door was being left open, which seemed odd.

"Why's the door to the loading bay still open?" John asked, mirroring his thoughts. "When we get back, the bay will be filled to the rafters with those things. And why the hell do you keep shooting them if they're not a danger to us? Just look at how many are out there now, man. We'll never get back to the pier to get picked up."

The RV began pushing through the throng of undead, the bodies falling like chaff to a scythe. The tires rolled over the bodies, the sound similar to driving over gravel and mud. Stomachs popped, spewing the contents onto the tires to then be splashed in the tire wells, and brains splashed as heads were flattened to mush. The odor wafted into the interior of the RV and everyone had to fight not to gag. The noise of crushed bodies filled the interior as well, until everyone had to yell to be heard.

"We don't need to get back to the pier we left from, John," Tom explained. "See we have a system in place whenever we come to the mainland. There's another cove a half mile away we use. That way we don't have to worry about any dead fucks hanging around in large numbers. We simply get to the other building where we park this rig, take out anything that's in our way, and by the time the fuckers show up in significant numbers, we're on the boat and long gone."

"So you rotate between the two," Sarah said. "That's why there was a pile of bodies outside the bay door."

"That's right," Tom said. "By the time we rotate back to where we came from, the dead fucks have spread out and wandered off. Sure, there's a few hanging around that need to be dealt with, but it's not hard to take them out. The ones we find in the open warehouse are the bodies in that pile."

Frank had pushed through the worst of the undead mob and the RV was picking up speed.

Tom leaned back in his chair and pointed at Schwartz. "Hey, go tell Rollo to get the fuck down; he's not taking target practice."

The German nodded curtly and went to the rear of the vehicle to retrieve Rollo. Seconds later, the gunfire fell silent, only the sound of the moans of the dead filling the RV.

Tom pulled out a map from a compartment in the RV and spread it across the generous dashboard. "Okay, Frank, by my calculations, stay on this street and take a right on Lexington, then follow that till you get to the highway. From there it's a straight shot to this infamous bunker, then a few side streets and we're there." He folded the map, slid it back into the compartment, and kicked back by putting his feet up. Behind him, a few of the men were smoking homemade cigarettes to get the smell of death out of the RV, and from the odor one was a joint.

Tom bent his head back so he could look at John, Sarah and McDermott, who'd been standing directly behind him, each of them struggling to stay standing as the RV bucked and rolled as it plowed over zombies. "Why don't you guys take a load off and sit down. Enjoy the scenery for a while. Because before you know it we'll be there, and from what you told me, there's no natural light in that place."

"Man, you don't know the half of it," John said. "Going down there is like going into your own grave. You'll see."

"Sounds fun," Tom said. "It's been a while since me and the boys had a good challenge. It'll be fun to take down some more dead fucks. Am I right, guys?" he called to the back of the RV. He was greeted with a cheer and a few dog woofs, the men gearing up for battle.

"There you have it," Tom said. "Trust me, John, by the time we're through with that place, it's gonna be a fucking massacre." Tom turned away and began gazing out the windshield, chatting with Frank about minor items. The action was clear; he was done with the three companions for now.

John and Sarah stepped back, McDermott, too, and they sat down at a small table that sat four relatively comfortably.

"He says it's going to be a massacre," Sarah said to John and McDermott.

"Aye, Sarah darling, that's what I'm afraid of," John said.

"What do you mean, Johnny?" McDermott asked.

"What Tom said. It's no doubt it'll be a massacre. But the question is; who's it gonna be that gets massacred? Us or those dead things waiting for us down there?"

Chapter 22

The journey to the bunker went smoothly, considering civilization had collapsed almost five years ago. Most of the problems the RV had consisted of maneuvering around stalled cars that sometimes had to be pushed out of the road so the RV could pass. One time Frank had tried to use the shoulder to go around a pile-up and he almost got stuck, and it was pure luck that the wheels finally found traction.

Twice the highway had been so choked with abandoned cars that the RV had to detour off the highway and use back roads, before returning once more to the congested blacktop of the highway. One of the times this happened, the highway had been full of cars and trucks, but the entire mess was nothing but burnt wreckage.

A fire had broken out somehow and all the vehicles had been caught up in it until there was nothing but a massive pile of fused metal. The rubber on the tires had melted onto the pavement, and the asphalt had also melted from the heat of the conflagration. Desiccated and burned corpses, now nothing but dried flesh over bones were in many of the cars, the jaws sagging in a morbid rictus of a smile.

Zombies were sporadic, and usually so spread out that to the rolling RV the walking dead were harmless. Tom let some of the men use the roof hatch and take a few shots at any zombies they passed. John and Sarah found it distasteful, but McDermott could have cared less. One less animated corpse in the world was always a good thing in his book.

Tom even got in on the fun, using his sniper rifle to shoot a few in the head. Though distasteful, John had to admit the man's marksmanship was outstanding.

"It's nice to get to practice on the real thing for a change," Tom told John and the others as he came down from his turn in the ceiling hatch. "Shooting paper targets isn't the same as shooting a man in the head, even if that man is technically dead."

One time someone had taken a shot at the RV from somewhere. The bullet had ricocheted off a steel grate but there were no more shots after that.

"Well, at least there's someone left alive out here," McDermott had said with a grin.

Hours later, after multiple detours that the RV had to make due to wreckage blocking the highway, the RV parked a quarter mile from the underground bunker so that the noise of the engine wouldn't attract any zombies—the rest of the journey would be made on foot. The sun sat high in the sky and the predicted temperature of eighty degrees had soared to over ninety, with humidity so heavy it felt like everyone was walking through pea soup.

"Make sure to stay hydrated," Sarah told everyone as she slipped on her pack. "Carrying all this gear in this heat is a quick way to get heat exhaustion."

"Okay, people, use your blades whenever possible now," Tom instructed while standing at the door to the RV. "From here on in, we're in stealth mode." He nodded to Frank to open the door, stepped outside, and with his blade in hand, took down two zombies that had been close enough to see the RV arrive. The first ghoul was taken down with a kick to the knee, followed by a leg sweep that had it falling on its ass. While that one was down, Tom went for the second one.

Lowering the knife down by his waist, he stepped up to the zombie like he wanted to give it a hug, but instead of embracing it, Tom slid the knife under its chin and up into its brain. The ghoul slumped to the ground, and Tom slid the gore-slick blade free. Before the second ghoul had settled in the dust, Tom was spinning around to deal with the first one.

The ghoul had a broken kneecap and it was trying to crawl towards Tom, who saved it the trouble. Walking over to it casually, he kicked it in the head once, then dropped down over the pale face and plunged the blade through an eye, a pinkish-whitish fluid squirting out.

The others had been disembarking the RV and caught the tail end of Tom's second kill. "See?" Tom said. "Piece of cake."

"Sure, man," John said. "It's easy when there's only two of 'em. But when there's two hundred, now, that's a different story."

"That's what we got these for," Frank said, coming out of the RV last and locking the door behind him.

"Okay, enough talk. Form up and move out," Tom ordered, while wiping his blade clean on the rags one of the zombies wore for clothes. "Frank, you take point, Pete, you cover our six."

As they began to move out, McDermott moved up close to Sarah and John so he could talk to them.

"These guys are too cocky for their own good. They have no idea what's down there," he said so only John and Sarah could hear.

John forced a grin so that anyone looking at him would assume he was talking about something positive. "Aye, Billy, that's why we three have to stick together." He leaned closer to Sarah. "You get those notes and then we all need to get the hell out of there. No screwing around. In and out. Quick."

"I don't have a problem with that, John," Sarah replied. "I wish we didn't have to go back there, but my notes are too important not to retrieve." She shuddered. "Too many bad memories."

"For you and me both, Sarah," McDermott commented as he thought back to being forced into the zombie corral with Sarah by Rhodes. He still had nightmares about it, though he hadn't told a soul. One of the reasons he drank so much was to keep the demons at bay. "I still can't believe we're actually going back to that deathtrap."

"I know, Billy, but we're here so let's focus on the job at hand," John said, his visage one of utter seriousness. "I told you before that place is nothing but a giant tombstone. Let's make sure this time it doesn't become ours as well."

"There's the hurricane fence," John said as the group of eight men and Sarah stopped at the treeline overlooking the bunker, or the field that the bunker was under. "There's the elevator, too, but it's not up."

From where they stood on a small hillock, there wasn't really anything to see that would tell anyone that there was a giant complex underground. There was a small, makeshift cemetery where the graves of fallen soldiers could be seen. It was also the final resting place of Major Cooper—before Rhodes Cooper had been in charge—the dirt still relatively fresh.

To the side of the cemetery was a collapsed tent where some of the soldiers had set up camp when on watch, the overturned buckets of marijuana the men had been growing, a small brick building, the large stone square that was used as the helicopter pad, the fuel hoses for the helicopter still lying on the ground from the last time they were used, and a rectangular hole a little bigger than a Greyhound bus—the elevator lift was still sunk into the ground. The elevator was nothing more than a hydraulic platform that was raised and lowered with the help of large pistons. Though mainly used for loading large supplies when the complex had been in service for civilian uses, when Sarah and her scientific team—and the soldiers—had taken it over, they had used it as their main form of egress in and out of the bunker.

More than half a mile from where the group stood, there was another entrance to the bunker as well. That egress was how large vehicles had been accepted into the massive storage facility. Anything from RVs to cars to motor homes, were all sitting in storage inside the complex. This was how eighteen wheelers and other forms of delivery trucks had brought in items for storage. The military had commandeered the complex at the last second years ago, to then quickly set up Sarah and her scientific team, as well as a small squad of soldiers to guard them.

Unfortunately, it had all been for naught and infighting between the scientific team and the soldiers had caused a total breakdown, and eventually one of the soldiers had gone insane due to stress, and had let the large zombie horde outside the fence into the bunker. That soldier had been Miguel Salazar, Sarah's boyfriend up until the end, when they too ended up having a falling out.

In the wide-open, grass-covered field, more than two dozen zombies stumbled around aimlessly. As John watched, he saw one of the dead wander too close to the open elevator shaft and tumble into it.

"That's where we need to go," John said to Tom, pointing to the open rectangular hole. "Luckily it's open, so we don't have to try and figure out a way inside the place from here. The only other way is an old silo a quarter mile from here. But if we went that way we'd have to go through the caves and I don't want to go in there if I don't have to."

"Why not, scared?" Frank sneered, standing behind John, the other men also gathered close to listen.

John glanced over his shoulder at the rat-faced man. "Hell yeah, I'm scared, man. You'd be scared too if you knew what's waiting for us down there."

"He means what's so bad about these caves you're talking about?" Tom asked.

"One of the doctors on the scientific team I was part of used the caves as a corral," Sarah said. "The soldiers would go topside and round up specimens for him. We kept them in the caves after building a wooden corral on the side close to the complex. See, the entire facility was dug out of the ground, then construction crews came in and poured concrete and brought in cinderblocks to build. One advantage is, being under the earth like it is, the temperature stays around sixty-eight degrees all year round, so it's great for storage."

"Nothin' down there I want," McDermott said. "Except my stash of booze."

John patted McDermott on the shoulder. "We'll see what we can do about that, Billy boy. It depends if the new occupants are agreeable or not."

"Well, enough briefing, it's time to get to work," Tom said. He pointed to Schwartz. "Get that fence cut so we can get down there and see what's going on." He pointed to Rollo. "As soon as the fence is cut, you and Schwartz move out first and take down those dead fucks. Try and stay quiet but if there's no choice, use your firearms. No unnecessary risks. Got it?"

Rollo and Schwartz nodded and said together, "Got it." The two men moved out, Schwartz pulling bolt cutters from his pack to use on the metal links on the fence. The spot the man picked to cut was hidden by brush, and as he worked, none of the zombies saw him. Rollo stood guard in case something came out of the trees.

"Okay, now it's our time to go," Tom said to Sarah and the remaining men a few minutes later when the fence was cut, and with Tom leading the way, they followed.

Schwartz had just finished cutting through the links, and after he and Rollo slipped through and began taking down zombies, Tom and the others had gotten to the breach and began entering one at a time. John, Sarah and McDermott gathered together, and Lou, Pete, Frank and Tom grouped up.

Up ahead of the seven people, Schwartz and Rollo were cutting down the zombies like they were nothing but paper mache dolls.

Tom laughed at the sight of his men taking down zombies with ease, then glanced at Sarah and John. "See? I knew this mission wasn't going to be as difficult as you said it would be."

"Aye, man, but we're not in the ground yet," John said.

Tom shrugged in reply, as if to say *it's not a big deal*, then he began jogging across the open field, Frank and the other two men right behind him.

Schwartz and Rollo had reached the opening to the bunker and were peering down into the rectangular hole when Tom and the others caught up.

When John reached the elevator shaft, he looked down into it. Even before he did, he already had an idea what he would find due to the smell. It was an odor he knew well, though he wished he didn't. A mix of sweet and sour, like the smell of brackish water that had been sitting in an abandoned, dank cellar for far too long. It was the odor of rotting flesh.

The lift itself was awash in dried blood and offal, and to John it looked as if someone had slaughtered a cow on the metal platform. But that wasn't what made him curse out loud. What made him curse aloud were the fifty or so zombies in the shaft, all of them looking up at the nine humans.

As one entity, the dead began to moan and groan, hands curling into fists to then release once more. Some tried to climb onto the backs of others, anything to reach the meat only thirty or so feet above their heads.

McDermott stood beside John, and he uttered a few choice swears as well, and when Sarah joined him a moment later, she uttered a few unlady-like explicatives that had Tom chuckling at the three companions.

"Oh my God, I was wrong, we can't go down there, it's impossible. We need to leave now," Sarah said as she stared into the shaft. Her complexion had gone white as she imagined going down into that hellhole filled with the walking dead. What had she been thinking? Had she really believed this was going to work? But now, upon standing at the entrance to what to her was basically Hell incarnate, she regretted everything she'd said and wanted to do. Now all she wanted was to return to the island and live out her days with John and McDermott, and to hell with the rest of the world.

"Relax, this isn't a problem," Tom said flatly.

"Oh no?" John asked, knowing what was in the shaft was a pretty damn good problem to him.

"No," Tom said coldly. He pulled one of the hand grenades from his web belt. "It's not."

Chapter 23

"Fire in the hole!" Tom yelled just before he dropped a shrapnel grenade into the shaft.

All together, the nine of them retreated a few feet to a safe vantage point. A few seconds after the grenade went into the hole, there was a loud explosion and the sound of what could best be described as bloody meat being thrown against a wall. Bloody pieces of body parts flew up and out of the hole to pepper the ground like red rain. Everyone was well away from the edge and didn't get touched by the spraying blood and gore.

"What the hell, man?" John yelled as he ducked from the sound of the explosion. "We're supposed to be quiet here, not setting off grenades."

Tom waved John's concerns away with his right hand. "Hey, sometimes you gotta rattle some chains to get the job done. Besides, sooner or later you knew it was gonna get loud. There's no other way around it. Now let's see what's left of those fuckers, shall we?" he said as the thunderous sound of the explosion rolled away.

He returned to the edge of the shaft, the others close behind him. Peering into the hole, Tom frowned deeply. "Shit, it barely took out ten of them."

"Grenades are for living people, Tom," John said upon joining the man at the edge. "Those dead things could care less if you blow off their arms or legs."

Below, the zombies still moaned and wailed, though a few were now nothing but a bloody mist. The air still hung thick with a crimson miasma that slowly coated all the pale faces craning up at the humans. The grenade had done some damage though, and after decimating ten bodies, ten more now had missing limbs or destroyed eyes. But they were all still moving, and though impaired, remained a real threat.

"Well then, what the fuck are we going to do?" Tom asked, pulling a different grenade off his chest this time, a phosphorus one. The explosion would rain down what resembled napalm on any of the bodies it hit, but he only had three of them and he knew without trying that three Willie Petes wouldn't be enough. Plus, wasting the precious grenades now would mean any dangers inside the bunker would be faced without the explosives, something he preferred not to do. "I only have three Willie Petes."

Sarah had been watching the zombies, and she stepped back and looked around the area surrounding the wide hole. It only took her a few seconds before her eyes settled on the refueling hoses for the helicopter. "Wait," she said. "I have an idea."

"What is it?" John asked, but when he followed her gaze, he smiled. "Sarah darling, that's a good idea; well done."

Sarah retuned his smile with one of her own.

McDermott saw them looking at each other, both grinning like children up to no good, and he didn't understand what they were talking about. He asked as much.

"Ah, Billy, boy, come with us and you'll see," John said and the three of them turned and jogged over to the fuel lines. About a dozen zombies were closing in on the area from all sides, with another dozen or so following up the first wave. But they were scattered, so it wouldn't be hard to put them down. Tom ordered Schwartz and Rollo to deal with them.

The two men jogged off in different directions, their blades out and ready to take down the walking dead. "And close that gate over there, too, so no more can get in." He was referring to the gate Miguel Salazar had opened, allowing the dead access to the wide field that led to the bunker. With the gate closed, it would stop any more of the walking dead from coming in.

"What do you two have there?" Tom asked as John and Sarah reached him, both dragging a fuel hose.

"Something to make sure your grenade works more easily," Sarah said, and after nodding to John to begin, they both squeezed the nozzles of the fuel hoses; unleaded gasoline began streaming out to spray the zombies below.

"Not too much, John," Sarah instructed. "We need just enough to burn them, but we don't want to create an inferno that will spread into the bunker."

"I hear ya, Sarah, one barbeque comin' up," John said with a grin. It felt good giving the dead a dose of their own medicine. It seemed for so long he was always running from them, always hiding. Now he was the one on top, and though he wasn't a vengeful man, it felt pretty damn good.

"Okay, that's enough," Sarah said, and she and John stopped spraying fuel; they backed away a few feet and dropped the nozzles onto the grass.

"Okay, Tom, whenever you're ready," she said.

Tom tossed the grenade to Frank. "You do the honors, my man."

Frank caught the grenade in the air, and with a wide grin on his thin lips, pulled the pin. "With pleasure." He tossed it into the shaft. "Fire in the hole!"

Once more, everyone jumped back, away from the edge. The grenade conked a zombie on the head and fell into its hands, which were down by its waist. It was pure luck that the fingers were curled enough to hold the grenade. The zombie looked at the small orb through gasoline-coated eyes and held the grenade up to its face to get a better look at it, wondering if the object could be eaten. Then the face and the body from the waist down ceased to exist when the grenade went off.

The gas and fumes ignited a fraction of a second later. There was a loud *whoosh*, and the entire shaft became a raging inferno. Like a volcano, fire and body parts shot straight up in the air twenty feet above the opening in the ground. White smoke from the grenade soared skyward as well.

Sarah had fallen to her knees, and as she peered through creased eyelids, she saw scorched heads and limbs dancing in the air, before falling back into the fire pit. The heat was a palpable thing and it reminded her of standing next to an open pizza oven, a pizzeria being one of the places she'd worked at in college.

"*Hoooly* shit!" Tom screamed as he watched the fire rage through slits in the fingers of his right hand, which were in front of his face to block the heat.

There was a loud sucking sound as air was sucked into the hole and everyone felt their eardrums pop from the change in pressure. With each passing minute, the flames subsided, consuming itself until it was extinguished, until only a thick cloud of smoke rose from the pit.

The air was filled with the foul redolence of cooking flesh and gasoline. The zombies' desiccated bodies had gone up like dry tinder.

No one moved for a few minutes, everyone waiting for the heat to die down some more. Schwartz and Rollo returned from dealing with any zombies in the area. The gate was now closed, too, so once the two men had disposed of any walking dead inside the fence, there would be no more.

But along the chain-link fence there were already more zombies arriving, having heard the first grenade. Once they reached the fence, they could easily see the humans moving around the entrance to the bunker.

John was the first to risk a look inside the shaft. Creeping as close as he dared, he peered over the lip, and when the heat wasn't too bad, he moved even closer, so he had a good view of the bottom of the shaft. Even his strong stomach roiled inside him as he gazed down at the charred and smoking bodies. A few zombies were still moving, their bodies reduced to charcoal and melted flesh. The white of teeth gleamed through the black ash, reflecting the sun shining down into the hole. Sporadic fires still burned, but without fuel they were slowly dying out.

Sarah and Tom joined John, then McDermott and the others moved up. Lou took one look and turned away to vomit, but he was the only one.

"Goddamn it, will you look at that shit? Talk about having it extra crispy," Tom said with a chuckle. He unslung the Uzi on his back and leveled it down into the hole, then sprayed half a clip at the bodies still twitching. Ash shot up from wherever a bullet struck a body, but the hole was too deep for the ash to escape.

"Okay, let's give it a few more minutes to cool off, then we drop down there and continue on our mission." He gestured with the muzzle of his Uzi to where the room below was lost from sight from a low ceiling. He could just see the bottom of what looked like a door, but he could only see a few inches of it. What he glimpsed of the door told him that the paint was scorched but the door itself seemed closed and intact. Unknown to any of the team, at some time in the past the door had been accidentally closed, which would explain why the zombies had been trapped inside the shaft.

"Over there; is that the door we want to use, Sarah?" Tom asked.

She nodded. "Yes, that'll take us into the facility, but from there we'll need to walk a good ways to the area where the labs are located."

"Maybe Rhodes' golf cart will be there in the tunnel and we can ride in style," McDermott said with a sly grin. No one acknowledged his statement.

With nothing to do but wait, everyone stood around, watching the perimeter fence in the distance, seeing the zombies pulling at the chain-links.

"Shit, how the fuck did they get here so fast?" Tom said, eyeing the dead.

"It was always like that when we were here," Sarah said. "Only there were hundreds more."

"Aye," John agreed. "Give it time, man. I'm sure more will be coming soon. It's like they can smell us out here."

"Let 'em come," Frank said then spit into the shaft. "I've got a bullet for each of them."

"Oh do ya now," John replied, walking over to Frank and staring the rat-faced man down. "You have enough bullets for a hundred of those things? A thousand? You gonna shoot them all in the head?" He shook his head and chuckled, then pointed down into the shaft and beyond. "Down there is a man who said the same thing; you know what happened to him?"

"I don't give a fuck what happened to him, and I suggest you step the fuck back," Frank hissed.

"Oh really, what you gonna do, man? You gonna shoot me, too?" John asked with a grin.

"It doesn't matter what happened to the guy," Tom broke in. "John, come help me with this rope, will you? It's about time we got moving."

John rubbed his chin like he was considering Tom's request, then he stepped away from Frank, who watched the Jamaican carefully. Both Sarah and McDermott had their hands near their weapons, just in case Frank wanted to try something.

Tom was unraveling a rope he'd gotten from one of the men's packs, and when John walked over, Tom handed him the end. "Drop it down into the hole, will you?"

"Sure, man, happy to help," John said and went to the edge and did as he was asked.

Tom had secured the other end of the rope to a protrudence in the ground near the edge of the opening. The rope had knots in it every two feet so that a person could use them for hand and footholds.

"Okay, listen up, people," Tom said, getting everyone's attention. "I'll go down first, followed by Frank, then I don't give a fuck who follows who. Rollo, you stay topside until we're all down, then you come in last. Anything in that pile of burnt bodies even twitches a finger, you take it the fuck out."

"Will do, boss," Rollo said, moving to the far side of the hole so he had a good view of the bottom.

Tom glanced at each of his men, making eye contact, then he looked at John and McDermott. With a final smile to Sarah, he dropped to his knees, wrapped his legs around the rope, and began climbing down.

His eyes began to tear up almost immediately, the odor of gasoline still filling the air, and now that he was in the pit and there was no wind to blow the fumes away, it was becoming harder to breath. Hanging with one hand halfway down, he pulled a handkerchief from his pocket and wrapped it around his nose and mouth. "The rest of you do the same, the air sucks down here," he said, his words echoing off the walls of the shaft. Tom began climbing the rest of the way down, landing heavily on the charred leg of a zombie. It was so burned it disintegrated under his boots, the ash floating in the air before settling down. He could feel the heat coming off the corpses and he began to sweat. "Okay, the rest of you get down here fast. I want out of this fucking crematorium ASAP."

Frank was next, then the other men. Sarah went after them, then McDermott, and John was last. Rollo shot a few bullets into what he thought was a moving zombie but whether it was really an animated corpse or simply bodies settling was unknown. The report of the rifle was loud in the shaft.

Tom walked over to the bunker door. As he moved through the charred corpses, kicking some aside to clear a path for the others, a blackened hand shot out of a pile and wrapped around his ankle.

Cursing at being taken off guard, Tom pulled his knife and stabbed the arm, then began to hack at it with the ten inch Bowie. The fingers never released their grip, despite the blade slicing into its arm, and only when all the tendons had been severed did the fingers finally let go, the arm retreating into the pile of charcoal-like bodies.

Tom wanted to kill the zombie that had grabbed him, but it was buried under half a dozen bodies, so he left it alone. The char-broiled ghoul wasn't going to be crawling out any time soon, if ever, and only its arm had been free to grasp him.

"Shit, I fucking hate this," Tom hissed under his breath so the others wouldn't hear him, and with the mask on his lower face, no one saw his lips move.

Rollo dropped down heavily, his boots crushing the skull of a zombie, the landing echoing off the walls.

Everyone now wore something over the lower part of their face, so only eyes could be seen. They looked like a bunch of desperados about to rob a bank in the Old West.

They all gathered around the steel door leading into the bunker, the low ceiling making everyone feel like the weight of the world was over their heads.

The sun was blocked out here, and with all the fluorescents in the room destroyed in the blaze, flashlights were pulled out so everyone could see. Shadows were everywhere, and the few small fires still burning only added to it.

Rollo was last, the large man standing relatively alone between two piles of corpses. Because of this, no one saw a zombie rise from within the mound of bodies behind him.

The ghoul was almost as large as Rollo, and as it rose, bodies fell from its shoulders and head as if they were dry leaves. The bits of charcoal that were once human bodies rolled down the piles to create ash and let off trapped heat. The sound it made resembled a hissing tea pot, only much, much softer.

Rollo glanced over his shoulder at the sound, more out of instinct than because he felt any conscious threat of danger, and when he turned, he found himself face to face with a vision straight out of the bowels of Hell.

The burned zombie was something only seen in nightmares. Its clothes had all burned off, as well as its outer flesh. The charred skin sloughed off the body like melted wax, leaving behind a glistening skeleton of muscle and tissue.

The soft tissue in the face was shrunken and cracked from the heat, and the only reason the ghoul had eyes was because some instinct had made it close them when the blast had surged over the dead.

The tongue was there, but the mouth had been open at the time of the firestorm. It had shriveled up so it now resembled a dead snake left in the sun to bake and dry out. But its teeth were the most unusual thing. They were pure white, as if the ghoul had just flossed and brushed before deciding to pop up out of a funeral pyre of corpses.

Most men, or really any human being who had nights as a child when bad dreams threatened their slumber, would have been taken aback at the sight of the monstrosity before him, if even for only a few seconds.

In that time, the zombie would have easily been able to lunge at the hapless victim and tear out his throat. But Rollo didn't so much as flinch at the sight of the monster before him.

As the ghoul let out a whisper that attempted to be a low moan, Rollo spun his rifle around and took a step closer to the crimson figure, and with one thrust of the butt of the rifle, he smashed in the face so that brains seeped out around the weapon.

Yanking the butt of the weapon back out, there was a squelching sound as the suction let go.

The ghoul slumped over, its brains seeping from the open wound where its face had once been. As for Rollo, he wiped the butt clean with the side of his hand, and after shaking the hand to clean off most of the gore, he wiped it on the side of his leg.

The entire altercation had taken less then five seconds and had occurred in almost total silence.

Tom looked past the faces of the other men and Sarah to see Rollo looking up from wiping his hand. "You okay back there, Rollo?"

Rollo nodded. "Fine, how's the door?"

"It's not locked," Tom said, "but something's blocking it from opening." He gestured for Lou and Pete to give him a hand, and together the three men pushed the door with their shoulders.

"Wait, Tom," Sarah said quickly upon seeing that the man was about to open the door without a care for what might be on the other side. "You don't know what's on the other side of that..." But she didn't get to finish.

The door opened more than six inches, whatever was blocking it giving way, and five pale hands—some missing fingers—shot through the opening and grabbed the arms and faces of the three men who suddenly found themselves under attack.

Chapter 24

Everyone began yelling and screaming at once as pale hands grasped body parts of Tom and the others.

Lou and Pete screamed to be let loose, while Tom yelled for the two men to control themselves and pull the door back from opening more than it was.

Frank and Schwartz yelled for everyone else to get out of the way so they could shoot the hands, and Tom yelled at them to hold their fire, not wanting to get shot.

The only ones not yelling or screaming were Sarah, John, McDermott and Rollo. John found it odd that there were five arms and not six coming through the door opening, that is until he saw that there was a one-armed zombie in the mix. The other two zombies were pressed up against the door, their arms thrust through, their shoulders stopping them from coming inside. The classic *Three Stooges* bit came to mind, though there was nothing funny about the present situation.

One pale hand grasped Lou by his red hair and he fought to escape.

He finally yanked his head free, but now there was a tuft of red hair in the hand and a small bloody spot where the scalp had been pulled off Lou's head; it was bleeding rather profusely as head wounds often did.

"Jesus Christ, calm the fuck down, you two!" Tom yelled as he pulled his Bowie knife and began hacking at the hand that held Pete. "Rollo, get over here and help me!"

Rollo did as he was told, and after pulling a ten inch blade of his own, he began hacking at the arms. One at a time, hands rained down to the floor, where twitching fingers continued their dance until finally stopping. With nothing but stumps now waving in the door, it was easy for Tom to swing his Uzi around and shoot half a clip into the doorway. He wasn't aiming for heads, just bodies, and just as he'd hoped, the impacts of the 9mm rounds pushed the zombies clear of the door. Before anyone could move, Tom pulled a stun grenade, tossed it through the doorway, then slammed it closed. An instant later there was a loud *thump* from the opposite side of the door and everyone's ears popped.

Tom shoved Lou and Pete to the side. "Rollo, Frank and Schwartz, on me," he said, telling the three men to follow him as Tom kicked open the door and charged inside the bunker with his Uzi blazing a path of fire and destruction. Rollo, Frank and Schwartz were right behind him, their Kalashnikovs spraying bullets in all directions. The four men lined up side by side, and as the smoke began to clear from the grenade, they saw that there were more than a dozen zombies before them.

Perhaps to a single, unarmed person the zombies would have been threatening, but to the four well-armed men, the dead were no more than target practice. The stun grenade didn't do much damage to the zombies, and Tom knew this would happen, but it did make a lot of noise, blinding light and smoke. The small distraction was all he needed to gain an edge on the dead.

The four men fired for a full ten seconds, the reports of their weapons loud in what was basically a large cavern. The zombies danced a jig as bullets peppered them continually. One was blown backwards from the force of the impacts, while others had their limbs blown off.

When the men were done having fun, their aim shifted higher. Bullets tracked up the ghouls until necks and heads were hit. Faces imploded from the powerful 7.62mm rounds, the backs of skulls disintegrating. Bone and brain matter painted the cavern walls behind the dead, and one at a time the bodies dropped to the ground to lay still.

"Clear!" Tom yelled as the echoes of gunshots still reverberated off the walls.

"Clear," Rollo repeated, as did Frank and Schwartz.

Tom took a step back to the door and called back, "Come on in, guys, the coast is clear." He looked off into the shadows to see more zombies approaching. "For now." He shifted his gaze to Rollo. "Secure the area and shoot any dead fuck on sight."

Rollo moved off a few feet, already lining up the first ghoul in his sights; he was just waiting for it to stumble closer. In the shadows, he could see the RVs, campers and cars that were being stored in the complex. He spotted a classic car, mid 1950's in the back, and he wished he could have gone over and checked it out. But the thought only flashed through his mind for a moment. He was here to do a job and that was what he'd do.

John, Sarah, McDermott, Lou and Pete stepped into the bunker, the first three looking on the familiar surroundings with something that resembled a fondness. After all, they had called the bunker home for a while, and though it had been filled with danger, at the end of the day the place had been a safe haven to sleep at night. Or had been.

Now it was filled with rotting corpses. John saw past the zombies just gunned down to see others that had been lying there for far longer. "It looks like Rhodes' men gave as good as they got,"

John said. His eyes scanned the dead to see if he recognized any of them, but none of the corpses wore Army uniforms.

"Maybe some of them got away after all," McDermott said.

John shrugged. "I doubt it, Billy boy. I'd bet money on it that they all died down here."

"Come on, we need to keep moving," Tom said. "There's more coming from down there." He pointed in the direction that led into the part of the bunker carved out of rock, where the zombie corral was located. As if to state his point, behind him, Rollo opened fire on a trio of ghouls, taking them down. More were right behind the fallen zombies.

"I'm not surprised," John said. "The way you and your men are blowing this place up, I'd think every dead thing in the cave will be heading right for us."

"Then I guess we need to get a move on, don't we," Tom replied. He glanced at Sarah, who was also looking around, her eyes wide as she took in her former home. "Which way to the labs?"

She pulled her focus from looking into the cavern to Tom. "That way." She pointed down a long hallway that was wide enough to drive a semi through. It was the same one Capt. Rhodes had driven his golf cart down when running from the dead so many weeks ago. "If we go down a ways, there's a door that will bring us to the labs and living quarters."

Rollo was shooting constantly as more and more of the dead came forward. None of the zombies cared when the ones by their side were taken down. The dead had a one track mind and wouldn't stop until they were destroyed.

"It's getting kinda crowded over here, boss," Rollo said as he popped out a spent magazine and slid in a fresh one, to begin firing again.

"Fall back, Rollo, we're moving on," Tom said. He looked at Sarah. "Lead on, we're right behind you."

Rollo shot one last zombie in a clown costume. He'd picked that one on purpose. He hated clowns, and had for his entire life. The clown had been standing near the rock wall of the cavern where a sign was located.

Seminole Storage Facility
Office ----------------------->
Boats ● Campers------------>
Trailers------------------->
Maximum Security <---------

The sign was splattered with the clown's rotting brains, the body falling against the sign to leave a bloody smudge before collapsing to the ground.

Sarah and the eight men began to jog down the wide corridor, their gear bouncing on their backs. Only a few zombies were in the corridor and it was child's play to take them out.

Minutes later, after a good run by all, they reached the closed door leading into the complex. The door was dented at head height, as if someone had pounded on it with a fist repeatedly. The locking mechanism for the door had been on the doorknob facing into the complex, but none of that mattered now. The entire section around the doorknob had been destroyed by gunfire, the bullets tearing the metal and making it sharp to the touch. No one knew what lay behind the door. There could be a massive horde that would spill out the instant it was opened, or it could have been an empty hallway.

"We need to go in here," Sarah said, standing before the door. "This is the living quarters and labs. It's not as big in there either, a lot like an office building. A lot of corners, too."

"Right, everyone stay sharp," Tom said. "We've made it this far without a problem; we can make it the rest of the way, too."

"Aye, that's true," John said. "The dead have spread out throughout the cave after being here for so long, but with all this shootin' goin' on, they'll be coming to get us soon."

Tom patted his Uzi. "And we'll be ready for 'em." He nodded to Frank to get the door, then said to everyone, "Line up side by side and don't get in each other's way. If there's too many to take down we'll need to retreat, but only if I say so."

Frank did as instructed, and after taking the dented doorknob in his hand, he pulled the door open, then jumped out of the way in expectation of a swarm of bodies spilling forth.

Nine guns were aimed at the doorway but nothing came out.

Five heartbeats went by before Tom slowly lowered his Uzi. With his hand in the air to tell the others to hold their fire, he crept up to the doorway and poked his head inside, craning his neck so he could see around the doorframe. A second later he pulled it back. "It's empty. Some bodies on the floor but nothing walking."

"Then what are we waiting for?" Sarah asked and walked into the corridor.

"Sarah wait," John said quickly, and seeing that she was doing nothing of the kind, he ran after her, McDermott falling close on his heels.

Tom watched them go and then looked at his men, who were waiting for orders. "Well, what are you dumb fucks standing there for? Go after them! We're here to protect them, not the other fucking way around!"

As one group, the men moved towards the door. Tom watched them and for a moment he thought there was going to be yet another *Three Stooges* moment as all five men attempted to get through the doorway simultaneously.

Tom swore to himself if that happened he would shoot each of them in the eye before they knew what had happened. But before they collided, Frank stopped and pulled Pete and Lou aside so that

Rollo went first followed by Schwartz. Frank glanced at Tom and rolled his eyes, as if the two men had been thinking the same thing, then he shoved Pete first then Lou before him, and after their passage, Frank was right behind them.

Tom sighed, glad that at least Frank was on the ball, which was why he'd taken the man on the mission in the first place. Of course he wouldn't have shot the men for screwing up, but that still didn't mean he wouldn't have been tempted.

He glanced down the wide, long tunnel behind him, his eyes picking up the forms of more zombies as they began the long walk from the cavern to where Tom now stood.

Unslinging his sniper rifle, he popped the cap off the scope and lined up the first ghoul in the crowd of fifty or more. Slowing his breathing, he let his mind calm, and as he breathed in and out, in and out, he didn't even think about it when he squeezed the trigger, it was done so naturally.

The rifle coughed as it fired, and hundreds of feet down the corridor, a head snapped back and a puff of pink mist erupted from the scalp before the zombie dropped down like a sack of potatoes.

The shot had been perfect, right between the eyes. He shifted aim and shot another, then another, but there were too many to keep shooting like this so he stopped.

Lowering the sniper rifle, he put the cap back on the scope, took one last look at the plodding ghouls, then entered the complex, closing the door behind him, for all the good it would do; there was no way to lock or secure it.

Chapter 25

"Sarah, wait up," John called out as he raced to catch up to her.

"We're almost there, John. The labs are so close," Sarah replied as she fast-walked down the corridor. She ignored her surroundings. They looked very different from the last time she'd been here, however.

One side of the corridor was made up of concrete cinder blocks painted white, while the opposite side was the natural stone the complex had been cut out of.

The once white cement walls were now covered in dried blood spatter and multiple bullet holes pockmarked the once pristine facade. The floor that was a white tile was also different from before.

Now it was covered in dried pools of blood and bits of organs.

No bodies however, not so much as one corpse littered the floor.

John finally caught up to Sarah and he grabbed her shoulder to stop her. Behind John, McDermott was rushing to keep up, his smaller legs not as swift, unless he wanted to full-out run. The rest of the men were thirty feet behind him.

"Sarah, slow down and let the rest of us catch up," John said. "We don't know what's here. Just wait a second."

They had stopped just before taking a corner. The corridor was bright, the fluorescent lights humming away thanks to the self-contained nuke generator deep underground.

"There's no time, John," Sarah said. "We need to get my notes and leave this place before it's too late. We've been lucky so far, but that luck can run out just as easily."

"I didn't say I disagree with you," he said. "But let me join you."

She sighed. "Fine, but try and keep up." She turned and began walking before John could reply, and as she turned the corner, she stopped cold. John, who had started to run after her the instant she walked off, now bumped into her back, not expecting her to stop so suddenly.

McDermott did the same thing to John, not understanding what the hold up was. He slowly leaned to the side so he could see around John's body, and when he did, his mouth dropped open in amazement at the sight before them. Now he understood why Sarah and John had stopped dead center of the corridor.

Footsteps from behind told of Tom and his four men arriving. McDermott took a step back so he was back around the corner again. He held up a hand to stop them, and said, "Wait a second, there's something in the next hallway you gotta see for yourself."

"What is it? More dead fucks?" Tom asked as he passed his men, who had stopped and were waiting with weapons aimed in every direction in case of an attack.

"Sort of," McDermott replied. "But no one shoot, there isn't any danger."

"What the fuck are you talking about, McDermott?" Frank asked, his face one of annoyance.

McDermott stepped to the side so Tom and the others could walk. The men shuffled forward around the corner and all stood stock still, not quite understanding what they were seeing.

"What the fuck is that?" Tom asked, as he stared at Sarah and John's backs, which were slightly blocking the view of what had McDermott so flustered.

"That, my good men," McDermott said, "is the illustrious Captain Rhodes."

Sarah was still standing in shocked horror at what was in the corridor as she turned into it. She had believed she would never see that face again, with the exception of her nightmares, and now here he was, albeit dead, but still here before her.

The term *half a man* came to mind as she looked down at the upper part of Captain Rhodes. The lower half was gone from the waist down, and as the *thing* moved, it used its hands to propel it forward. Ropes of intestine dragged behind it, leaving a bloody snail trail of gore.

Rhodes growled and hobbled over to her, hissing and snarling like a wild animal, wanting to attack her, but with no legs he was pretty ineffectual. When he was two feet away, Sarah pulled her .45 and pressed the muzzle against his forehead, the pressure keeping Rhodes from advancing. With only his arms for locomotion, all he could do was jerk his head from side to side as he feebly tried to reach her. In between his growls and moans there was something else. To Sarah's ears it sounded like he was saying, "F…F…F…F…" but there was nothing else but that one sound so she dismissed it as nonsensical noises.

"I don't believe it," John said, aghast. "Rhodes."

"He looked better the last time we saw him," McDermott quipped, always comical no matter what the situation.

Sarah's hand holding the .45 was trembling.

John could see she was about to squeeze the trigger and blow Rhode's brains all over the floor. Slowly, so as not to surprise her, he reached out and touched her arm, then slid his hand down it until his palm was resting on the gun. "Wait, Sarah, don't kill him. Leave him be."

She turned to look into John's eyes, her blue ones watering. Images of Fisher came to mind once more, how Rhodes had shot the scientist in the head without a care in the world. "Why?" was all she could manage to whisper.

Rhodes still fought to reach Sarah, his eyes flicking back and forth from her to John. Sarah didn't let him move, keeping the pressure of the muzzle of the .45 constant.

"Because he doesn't deserve the mercy of a bullet, that's why," John explained. "It's still not as bad a fate as he deserves for what he did to all of us, but it's a start." Using his rifle, John pressed the muzzle into Rhodes' chest and shoved. The half-zombie toppled over to land on his back, where he began waving his arms as he tried to get up.

"He's no danger to us now, and the thought of him haunting this place for eternity seems like the best justice we can hope for," John said, almost whispering in Sarah's ear.

Floundering like a turtle on its back, Rhodes snarled and hissed. "F...F...F..." slid through his gritted teeth.

Tom could see there was some history between the three companions and the half-zombie on the floor, but he knew their time was limited, so after waiting for what he felt was long enough, he stepped up to Sarah and John and said, "Look, we need to keep moving. There's more dead fucks coming and there was no way to bar the door, so either shoot this fucker or leave him alone, but decide now or I'll decide for you."

Sarah stared at Rhodes as he pathetically tried to right himself. The pale face was still filled with what to her look liked anger and rage. Even in death the man was a bastard. In the end, she figured that if there was even a tiny part of the man still inside his rotting brain, then letting him suffer like this was the way to go. She sighed and nodded, the gesture clear to all.

"Good," Tom said, so if we're done with this little reunion, "let's keep moving."

From the far end of the corridor, in the direction they were moving, a trio of zombies appeared, attracted to the talking of the humans. They moaned and groaned, their feet sliding across the white tile as they moved closer to the nine humans. It seemed silly to John to see the three ghouls coming forward.

Nine against three, and those nine with guns, had to be the worst odds any attacker could have. But zombies didn't think, only acted, so the three rotting corpses shambled onward, ignorant of their coming fate.

Tom glanced to his side to see Pete standing at attention. He nodded to the man to be the shooter to take down the approaching ghouls. Pete took a step forward, then to the side of Rhodes, as he didn't want to get too close, and leveled his rifle. In three quick bursts, he took down the zombies, neck and heads shots for each one.

The bodies dropped to the floor in a tangle of arms and limbs, the tiles already covered with dried blood and gore getting a fresh coat.

Without another word, Tom moved out, his men following. "I'd keep up if I were you," Tom said over his shoulder as he passed the three companions.

"He's right, Sarah, we need to go," John said.

Sarah hadn't stopped staring at Rhodes as he floundered on the floor. He kept trying to roll over but wasn't having much luck.

"If you ask me," McDermott interjected. "It gives me a fuzzy warm feeling knowing that prick is down here like that."

John very gently gave Sarah a shove forward. "Come on, Sarah darling, we have a world to save," he said softly.

She let herself be moved; she and John stepped to the side and past Rhodes, who growled and snarled at them. He tried to grab their feet but wasn't close enough.

McDermott took one final look at Rhodes and then kicked the half-zombie in the head out of spite, then he followed his friends.

Seconds later, the three companions had reached the next corner and were gone from sight, as they went deeper into the complex.

With a low moan, Rhodes managed to finally roll over enough to use his hands to get onto his stomach. With his head craned up, he watched the retracting backs of Sarah, John, McDermott, and the other six men.

Just before Sarah had turned the corner, Rhodes' eyes locked on her like a magnet, and he began to utter, "B...B...B…" This went on for many minutes until finally, as if something popped open in his mind, Rhodes spit out the word, "*Bitch.*" To anyone hearing it, the word would have sounded more like a guttural growl, and would have been all but unintelligible, but to Rhodes it was the beginning of something that with practice would come easier.

Getting back up and balancing on his hands, he turned and wandered off the opposite way the humans had gone, all the while uttering, "*Bitch,*" over and over under his breath.

Chapter 26

Tom got ahead of Sarah, John and McDermott, and with his men they began clearing all the rooms of zombies.

The steady staccato of their weapons filled the corridor and flowed through the bunker.

Dozens upon dozens of ghouls were shot down as the men went from room to room, mercilessly killing the enemy.

When the area was clear, and everyone was standing in an intersection where three corridors met, Tom called out, "Okay, Sarah, that should be all of them. But stay on your guard in case we missed one. Now go find those notes so we can get the fuck out of here." Sarah was about to do just that when Tom called after her, "Wait, take Lou with you to watch your back."

"I don't need anyone to go with me," she said proudly.

"Uh, yeah, you do. Just do as I say." Tom had the look of a man who wouldn't take no for an answer.

"Let him go with you, Sarah, it's a good idea," John said. "That way Billy and I can go check out some other rooms; see if we can find some medicine the people back home can use." He thought it was odd that he was standing in what was his former home talking about the village, that he now considered his home.

She threw up her hands in surrender. "Fine, whatever, just stay out of my way," she told Lou.

"You won't even know I'm there," Lou said. He now had a bandage on his head from where the scalp had been torn, Pete having dressed the wound.

With Sarah in the lead, the couple set off down the corridor. At the end they took a right and were gone from sight.

John turned to Tom and said, "Billy and I are gonna go see what we can find to take back with us. When we left here we didn't get to take anything with us. Like I told you, we left pretty abruptly."

"Okay, but stay within earshot," Tom said. "If we need to bug out I won't send my men to come find you. You'll be on your own."

John grinned and rubbed his chin. "Billy and I have been on our own for a long time, man. That's not a problem." He patted McDermott on the back. "Come on, Billy, let's see what we can find."

The two men set off, and at the end of the corridor where Sarah had taken a right, they took a left.

Tom surveyed his remaining men: Frank, Schwartz, Rollo and Pete. "You guys do the same. Now that this area's secured, go back into all the rooms and see if there's anything of value we can take with us. Medicine and weapons are the most important. Find where they've been storing their guns and ammo and take all you can carry."

"Right," Rollo said, the others answering in kind. With Rollo in the lead, the men stomped off, their boots echoing off the stone walls.

Tom watched them go, then he turned and went back the way they'd all come, wanting to check on the status of the zombies he'd seen before at the far end of the tunnel.

* * *

It only took Sarah a few minutes to reach her lab. Lou went in first to make sure it was clear, and when it was, he allowed her inside. Lou stood guard in the corridor.

The instant she entered the room she felt a sense of déjà vu. As she looked at the familiar walls, she couldn't help but think back to all the countless hours she'd spent working to find a cure to why the dead rose. Looking back, if someone had told her the journey she would undertake, and the results of it, she would have told that person they were mad, that the prediction was insane.

Yet here she was doing that exact thing.

There was a calendar on the far wall with each of the days crossed out. She idly thought that the month was wrong, that it wasn't October but November, and she almost crossed the room to change it, then stopped, realizing how silly it would be.

The room itself was a mess, with splotches of blood everywhere. Zombies had been there, only to leave when they found nothing to eat. But before they'd gone they'd destroyed the room. The files that had once been neatly stacked a foot high on the corner of her desk were all over the floor, and as she crouched down and picked up a few, she saw they were hopelessly out of order, almost all of them having come out of the manila folders they'd been in.

Sarah knew it was going to take a while, sorting through everything to find those few important notes, for out of the large mound of files, there were only a few sheets of paper that had what she needed. The rest was nothing but kindling. With a weary sigh, she dropped to her knees and got to work.

Rhodes waddled all the way back to the shot up metal door that led into the tunnel and finally the main storage facility. Here, he came upon the slowly moving horde that had been traveling down the tunnel. There were hundreds of zombies, all of them having become trapped inside the bunker. All had been attracted to the shooting and were now on their way to find the humans. But being basically stupid, they were wandering aimlessly and had pretty much lost the trail of the humans upon reaching the closed metal door. Though not locked, such a concept as opening doors was beyond them, so they merely stood in the tunnel, crushed tightly together, not knowing what to do.

Rhodes pushed open the door with his head and waddled out into the tunnel, then used his head again to close the door behind him. He began to grunt and growl, but not like an animal. He was trying to talk though he still couldn't do it. Other than the slurred words 'fuck' and 'bitch' intermingled with other animalistic sounds, no language was actually used.

But the zombies perked up at this and soon they were listening raptly as Rhodes continued his tirade. Rhodes went to a tall zombie, well over six feet, and tugged on its pant leg to get its attention. When the zombie looked down, Rhodes set his torso on the ground and raised his hands like a child wanting to be picked up by his mother. He also slurred an order, telling the large zombie to pick him up. The zombie seemed to understand, barely, and it leaned over and picked Rhodes up, placing the half-zombie on its left shoulder. Rhodes intestines draped over the tall zombie like garland but the giant ghoul could have cared less.

He used the larger zombie like he was the rider and it was his steed, using his hands to tell it which way to go. The zombie capitulated easily, too stupid not too listen to a higher functioning mind.

Deep in Rhodes' dead mind was Sarah's face. He wanted vengeance, blaming her for all his troubles. He wanted to feed on her guts, tear out her insides as she watched, to scream in agony and fear. Then he would do the same to John and McDermott, feeding on their still beating hearts after he pulled them from their chests. He would have his revenge, and it would be measured in buckets of blood.

He began to get other zombies to follow him as he directed the large zombie he rode to open the steel door leading back into the complex.

Slowly, one at a time, the living dead began to file into the corridor, filling it from wall to wall, with Rhodes at the front like a warrior king going into battle.

The time of reckoning was coming, and Rhodes managed to actually smile as he roared for his horde to move onward, though to anyone who saw it, the smile looked more like a scowl and the roar sounded more like a moan.

Chapter 27

John and McDermott were off searching by themselves. John had found a small black duffel bag and he was using it to carry anything he thought was of use to the village. So far he'd found rubbing alcohol, bandages and an assortment of office supplies that he knew would come in handy.

In the village, money wasn't used as currency, but instead there was a form of trade, so all the items he found would mean he, Sarah and McDermott would be well off upon their return.

So far they'd only found half a dozen zombies in different rooms, and each man had shot the ghouls in the head before ransacking the rooms for goods.

Later, when they'd turned a corner, they found more than ten zombies standing in the corridor. They were in what was basically a dead end, the fire door closed. Once there, they didn't know what to do, so they'd simply stood in place, staring at the walls or each other.

Both John and McDermott had leveled their rifles at the dead and sprayed the entire group from side to side. The zombies shook and fell back as the rounds tore their bodies apart, finally ending in a head shot that put them down for good.

When the two men stopped firing, the only sound was the residual clinking of spent shells and the drip-drip of congealed blood from within the corpses.

Satisfied at their marksmanship, they turned and continued their search of nearby rooms.

When they ended up outside the late Dr. Logan's main lab—next to it was the same room where the zombie nicknamed Bub had been chained as Dr. Logan tried to teach the zombie to use household objects—it seemed a good idea to see if the mad doctor had hidden anything of use somewhere.

"I'd bet a million bucks the crazy bastard has a bottle of booze or two squirreled away somewhere," McDermott said as the two men stood outside the door.

"Then let's go check," John replied and they entered the room. The door was ajar as they entered and they stepped inside with weapons ready to fire.

The room was devoid of animated corpses, but it was still a horror house made of nightmares. All around the room were vials and test tubes, as well as containers filled with formaldehyde that kept bodies fresh, back-lighted as well for easy viewing.

McDermott remembered the last time he'd been in the lab; he'd been with Sarah. They were looking for antibiotics for Sarah's then ex-boyfriend Miguel after she'd amputated his arm. But once in the lab, they'd been sidetracked at seeing Dr. Logan in the next room, talking to Bub like the ghoul was a friend. Then Rhodes had arrived, discovered that Logan had been feeding Bub human remains taken from Rhodes' fallen soldiers, and the shit had really hit the fan.

McDermott's eyes went to a small table once used to hold scalpels. It had a spherical object on it covered with a white towel. The towel was moving gently, almost undulating. He knew what was under the towel before he even took a peek. It was the severed head of one of Rhodes' men, still lying where it had been found the first time McDermott was in the lab. Though the head looked paler and the skin was more withered and dried, the mouth still opened and closed slowly, the eyes shifting back and forth in recessed sockets. Disgusted, he let go of the towel and it fell back onto the abomination of nature.

John was in the far corner of the lab, looking through some file cabinets.

"Find anything, Johnny?"

"Nah, Billy boy, nothing but files."

"There's got to be something in here we can use," McDermott said.

"Hey, I found some antibiotics," John said and began taking the pills out of the drawer and shoving them into the duffel bag.

"Any booze?"

"Not yet, Billy, sorry."

"Don't be sorry, find me some liquor. I didn't come all the way here for the fun of it, you know."

In the opposite corner of the room where John was standing there was a walk-in cooler. It was the same one where John, Sarah and McDermott had witnessed Rhodes shoot Dr. Logan after Rhodes had found out that his men were being cut up and fed in pieces to Bub as a reward for good behavior.

As McDermott moved closer to it while he was checking through the desk, he thought he heard a sound from within the cooler. It was faint but it resembled banging.

"Hey, Johnny, I think I hear something coming from in here," McDermott said as he stepped up to the cooler and placed his ear to the stainless steel door. It felt cool to the touch against his cheek.

"Wasn't that door open the last time we were here?" John asked, remembering when he, McDermott and Sarah were led away after Rhodes had shot Logan as the mad doctor stood before the open cooler. John had seen Logan go down, the doctor's chest riddled with bullets. The man had surely been killed.

"Maybe someone closed it after we left here," McDermott suggested. "I know it's crazy, but I want to see inside."

"It can't be good, whatever it is," John said as he eyed the cooler warily.

"Oh come on, John, whatever's in there can't be a match for our guns. And if we don't look now, there'll never be another chance."

"Don't open it, Billy, there's no reason to," John said.

But McDermott was a curious soul and he needed to know what could be in the cooler that was making noise. "Cover me, Johnny," he said and pulled on the door handle, opening the door and taking a step back as well, just in case there was a zombie inside.

McDermott's rifle was already coming up to shoot if there was a ghoul inside, but as the door swung open and the mist created from the outside air mixing with the cooler air within parted, the figure that stepped forward was such a surprise that McDermott hesitated, his mouth falling open, his eyes popping out of his head in amazement.

In the blink of an eye he took in the zombie before him. But like most ghouls he came upon, he'd never known the dead person in life, but the one before him was none other than Dr. Logan.

The very dead doctor's face was as pale as could be, the eyes staring blankly, devoid of color. His gray hair was a tangled mess, standing up in places, and his eyeglasses were hanging half off his face, only his left ear holding them up. His once white lab coat was stained with blood, but where he normally wore a lab coat stained with the blood of his 'specimens' now the blood was mostly his after being riddled with bullets from an angry Captain Rhodes. His green scrub shirt was a patchwork of bullet holes, and as Dr. Logan stepped out of the cooler, McDermott saw that not one bullet hole marred the dead man's face. When Rhodes had shot Logan, he hadn't shot the man in the head and so eventually Logan had reanimated to be stuck within the cooler. Whether Rhodes had done this intentionally or not would never be known, but the result was the same.

Dr. Logan lived again…so to speak.

The dead doctor stepped out of the cooler and looked at John and McDermott as if for the first time. McDermott was still transfixed at seeing someone he knew now one of the walking dead, his rifle useless in his hands.

John wasn't of the same dilemma, and he wanted to fire but couldn't; McDermott was standing directly in front of Dr. Logan.

"Billy, get out of the way, man! I don't have a clear shot at him," John said anxiously as he began to run towards his friend.

McDermott heard none of it, his eyes locked on Dr. Logan. But slowly, McDermott began to snap out of it and he began to squeeze the trigger on his rifle. But Logan was faster. With a slight burst of speed that belayed the dead man's appearance, Logan lunged at McDermott, who was completely caught off guard. McDermott was tackled, his finger pulling the trigger of his rifle, and a spray of bullets flew off in all directions. A few specimen jars holding withered zombies were shattered, the contents spilling onto the floor. The room took on the odor of formaldehyde.

John had no choice but to drop to the floor and roll behind a desk as bullets zipped past his head like angry bees, despite the fact that he wanted to get to his friend. The bullets ceased after a moment and then there was only the sound of Dr. Logan grunting and McDermott's protests to get the dead man off him.

The zombie and Irishman had gone down in a heap of limbs. McDermott had to let go of the rifle in order to keep Logan's snapping teeth at bay. The fighting pair began to roll around the floor as McDermott struggled to keep his flesh intact. Logan was a larger man than him in life, and this didn't help McDermott battle the dead man in death, Logan seeming to have renewed strength thanks to becoming one of the walking dead.

John had gotten to his feet to find McDermott fighting for his life on the floor. John raised his M-16 to shoot Logan, but with the two rolling around on the floor, the shot would still be risky and he might end up hitting McDermott instead of the intended target. John spun his rifle around and was prepared to race over and use the butt end to club Logan in the head, and hopefully save his friend, when suddenly, McDermott cried out as if in pain, but John couldn't see why.

Then McDermott reached out to his side on the floor with his free hand as the other one kept Logan off him, and his hand fell on a fallen tool knocked off a desk as human and zombie battled.

McDermott raised the object he'd grabbed and jabbed the dead doctor in the side of the head, right in the ear, with a surgical drill. It was the same surgical drill Dr. Logan had used on a prone zombie strapped to a gurney after it had broken free of its straps and sat up, its guts sliding out to hit the floor. Sarah had witnessed it and had almost vomited at the sight.

For all the zombies Logan had slaughtered in the name of science, there was a certain amount of poetic justice coming to the doctor now that he was one of the living dead.

As McDermott pressed the drill bit to Logan's ear, his finger found the power button and he pressed it. The drill surged to life and began to bore into Logan's head all the way up to the shaft, piercing the brain and churning the section it penetrated into red paste.

When the spinning drill bit was removed, blood seeped slowly out of the ear.

The blood was like molasses, the low temperature in the cooler making it thick and syrupy.

Logan twitched a few moments, his face curling up into a look of what seemed like happiness, his eyes rolling up into his head, then the face went slack and the head slumped forward, the body going limp on top of McDermott.

John had reached them and was about to use the butt of his M-16 when he saw that McDermott had taken care of the matter. John lowered the rifle.

"If it's not too much trouble, Johnny, would you mind getting this goddamn body off me?" McDermott asked, his voice muffled from the weight of Dr. Logan.

Leaning over and pulling Logan off McDermott, John stepped away as the body rolled off the Irishman to lay belly up on the floor. The dead doctor's eyeglasses were gone, lost somewhere in the scuffle, and his hair was even more of a mess, if that was possible. But other than syrupy blood seeping out of his ear, he seemed the same as when he'd stepped out of the cooler.

"Are you all right, Billy? I heard you yell. Are you hurt?" John asked quickly.

"I'm fine. I just panicked is all. The crazy bastard never touched me," McDermott said, then he focused on John and glared at his friend. "No thanks to you. Why the fuck didn't you shoot him before he jumped me?"

"I wanted to, but you were standing in the way. You stood there like a statue."

"Then shoot around me, for Christ's sake. Jesus, Mary and Joseph, he almost killed me!"

John was about to reply when faint gunshots were heard coming from outside the corridor a ways. Normally that wouldn't have been a cause for alarm, as Tom and his men took out any zombies they found, but when the sounds of people screaming and yelling was added to the gunshots, the two men knew something wasn't right.

John lent McDermott a hand and helped his friend up.

"Sounds like trouble," John said. "We need to find Sarah and make sure she's all right."

"Agreed. But we're not done with this conversation, Johnny," McDermott said. "But we'll talk about it over a glass of Scotch back on the island."

"Sounds good to me, Billy," John said, and after gathering his duffle bag and tossing it over his shoulder so his hands were free, and McDermott grabbed his fallen rifle, the two men left the lab to investigate the noise.

Chapter 28

Sarah shifted another section of papers to her right and began digging through yet another pile. So much research and up until now it had all been for naught. But thanks to Professor Langford, she knew the final piece of the puzzle. She just needed to find it amidst a mound of paper.

Lou had checked in on her twice. A little while ago, he'd opened the door to the lab to tell her he was going to walk around some, check things out. She'd barely heard him talk and had waved just so she could make him leave. He was a distraction, and that was something she didn't need right now.

Leaning back, she rubbed her eyes and sighed. She was tired, both physically and emotionally. Coming back to the bunker had taken more out of her than she ever would have imagined; when she'd seen Rhodes, well, that had been the icing on the cake. She'd assumed the man was long dead before returning, and he was, dead that is, but to see him still moving around as one of the walking dead was somehow worse than if she'd seen his corpse lying somewhere in the cave.

She regretted listening to John now about leaving Rhodes alone, and simply wished she'd put a bullet in his head and been done with it. She swore if she came across the half-zombie abomination again before leaving the bunker she would do just that, and to hell with what John said about it.

She closed her eyes and calmed her mind, pushing everything down. Now all that mattered was finding her notes.

It was as she opened her eyes and looked down and to the right, that she spotted the manila folder with the right markings just sticking out from under a pile of papers. Less than an inch of the folder was showing, and it was only the tab on the right side that she'd written on. Praying that what she wanted was still inside the folder, she reached over and pulled it out, then with yet another prayer, opened it.

The notes were there. She'd done it. She quickly glanced through them, refreshing her memory. Yes, this was it all right. With these notes and Professor Langford, it should be easy to synthesize a vaccine to stop people from rising from the dead after they passed on. She thought of Fisher then, wishing he was still alive so she could share the good news with him. But he was dead, like so many other people she'd known.

Standing up, she placed the notes on her desk and began to gather her gear, which she'd taken off to be more comfortable. Now she slid on her backpack and picked up her assault rifle, sliding it over her shoulder.

She was about to pick up the notes and secure them inside her shirt, where there would be no way they could get lost, when a steady staccato of gunshots, followed by a piercing scream, came from the corridor outside her door.

The voice was Lou's, and by the sound of it, he was in trouble and needed her help. Before she left, she grabbed her notes and quickly folded them in half and slid them into the back pocket of her pants.

The notes were sticking out of her back pocket, and as she ran for the door, they already began to shift slightly. The more she moved her body the more they might work their way out. It wasn't the best place to put them given their importance, but she was too distracted to think about it. Her focus was on the man screaming in the hallway.

Charging out the door, her assault rifle leading the way, she found Lou on the floor with four zombies ripping into him. Another half dozen ghouls were dead on the floor a few feet away, their bodies riddled with bullets. Lou had taken out the six on the floor, but then the other four had reached and swarmed over him, taking him down and tearing into his flesh.

Lou was in a bad way. Half his throat was torn out and one arm was hanging by a thread of gristle as the zombies leaned over and fed on him. One of his cheeks was torn away as well, the lower jaw peering through like a medical skull with take away parts. Sarah was just able to see the man's face through the bodies on top of him, and for just a second, Lou's eyes met hers. "Kill me," he gargled as blood shot out of his mouth. "Please kill me."

She didn't need to be told twice, having already assessed the man's chances of survival even if she managed to save him. Knowing she didn't need to be careful with her aim, she fired her assault rifle on full auto at the backs and sides of the zombies. The steel-jacketed rounds struck the ghouls and sliced through them to hit the wall behind them. Bullets blew large chunks of meat from the bodies as each round destroyed one more section of the bodies.

One bullet struck Lou in the right eye, exploding the orb on impact before burrowing into his head and blowing out the back of his cranium.

Blood, brains, skull fragments and matted hair splattered across the floor.

As Lou's body went limp in death, Sarah continued firing until the four zombies were also down for good, then she stopped and surveyed the scene.

Her ears were ringing for a few seconds from the report of her rifle, but as the ringing faded, she realized she could still hear gunshots and people yelling. It was coming from the same route she'd used after leaving Tom and the others.

"Shit, what now?" she muttered under her breath, turned, and raced down the hallway, while behind her, the dark pool of bright red blood under Lou slowly continued to spread across the white tile.

Tom walked down the corridor that would bring him to the steel door that led to the long tunnel and the storage facility part of the complex.

His Uzi was in his hands and he was whistling a tune, and as he rounded the last corner that would be the home stretch to the door, he stopped cold as he came face to face with a horde of zombies.

"Holy shit," he whispered at seeing so many zombies only a few feet away from him and closing fast. Backpedaling, he began to shoot indiscriminately at the horde.

His bullets had no direction and they merely stitched across torsos, only a few finding heads.

The zombies came forward, heedless of his onslaught, and Tom fired one more time, then seeing it had absolutely no effect, he turned and ran as fast as he could.

He needed to reach his men and form a skirmish line, only then might there be a chance of stopping the horde. He pulled a grenade and tossed it over his shoulder as he ran.

He didn't see what he'd grabbed and a few seconds later heard the flash bang go off.

That wouldn't do much of anything, but it did fill the hallway with smoke.

Picking up his pace, he ran as fast as his legs would carry him, while calling out for his men.

By the time Tom reached the area where everyone had split up earlier, Tom was yelling so loud that his voice cracked a little.

Frank, Pete, Rollo and Schwartz came running, their weapons held in their hands across their chests.

"What's the matter?" Frank asked when he reached Tom. "What's all the yelling about?"

Tom quickly filled Frank and the rest of the men in, then ordered them to form up side by side and follow him back down the corridor.

"Where's Lou and Sarah, and John and McDermott?" Tom asked quickly. "We need as many guns as we can gather."

Frank shrugged. "I don't know where John and his buddy are, but Sarah and Lou are probably still at her lab."

"Forget it then, there's no time to get them," Tom said quickly. Each second he delayed the horde was moving closer. "We'll have to handle this ourselves. On me, move out."

With Tom in a slight lead, they ran off, their boots echoing off the walls. They had to jump over fallen bodies and be careful not to slip in spilt blood. Tom had run so haphazardly that he'd fallen twice on the run back. Now though, he knew where to be careful and watched his step.

When they reached a place in the corridor where the zombies were in sight, all the men stopped short. For a fraction of a second, no one spoke, all staring at the horde coming right for them. Even Rollo, who was afraid of nothing, looked shaken.

"Fire at will!" Tom yelled and began firing his Uzi, spraying back and forth, without care. There were so many bodies it was impossible to miss.

Hearing their leader start shooting, the other four men began shooting as well.

Bodies in the front of the horde fell down, but the ones behind them simply stepped over their fallen brethren. The five soldiers continued to fire, sending a barrage of death at the undead crowd. More bodies fell to the floor only to be trampled as the horde moved ever forward.

"Shit!" Tom yelled. "This isn't working, there's too fucking many of them!"

"We need to fallback, Tom!" Pete screamed in panic as he sprayed body after body with bullets! "Don't be an idiot, we need to retreat."

"No, we don't. We need to lay down decent covering fire. All you assholes stop shooting their chests and start hitting their fucking heads!"

"Why?" Pete stammered in reply. "For every one we shoot there's five more to replace it. We need to go, Tom, right now! Don't be an idiot!"

"You know what, Pete? You're right. We do need to fall back, but before we do, we need something to slow those dead fucks down."

"What are you talking about?" Pete asked, and upon turning to face Tom, he found the muzzle of the Uzi aimed directly at him. "Wait, Tom, don't do it I…"

Tom didn't hear the rest as he fired at almost point-blank range into Pete's chest. The black man was thrown backwards to bounce off the concrete wall, then he slid to the floor, leaving a trail of bright red in his wake on the white stone. His mouth was open but nothing came out but bloody froth. He clawed at his chest, feeling the blood pumping through the wounds, blinking in amazement.

"Okay, everyone on me, fall back!" Tom yelled over the firing. "Pete will slow them down enough for us to gather the others and find another way out of here!"

The men regrouped and began to walk backwards as they fired. Each man glanced at Pete, but only for an instant. They had each heard Pete disobey Tom. Before the mission, when he'd been choosing men, Tom had been painfully clear on the chain of command. He was to be followed without question. If any of the men didn't like it, then they didn't have to come. If they disobeyed him in the field, they might just receive a bullet for their trouble. All had agreed, but like many circumstances that can happen in the heat of battle, Pete had lost his cool. Tom didn't have time to help the man regain it, instead Pete was going to be used as bait.

Pete raised a bloody hand in a wait gesture as the four men began running back down the corridor, then the hand dropped back into his lap. For some reason the hand was too heavy to hold up anymore. He felt tired and wanted to sleep. He felt cold, too, but he didn't understand why. His pants were wet and he wondered if he'd peed himself. If he did it seemed an odd thing to do at the moment. He was foggy, blood loss making his reasoning skills hard to maintain. Shock had taken over, his body now numb.

"I'll just sit here for a second and then I'll get up. Tom'll want me to keep moving," he said to himself, the words coming out in a jangle of nonsensical gibberish.

Then there were figures standing over him. *Good, Tom's come back for me*, went through his head, but a second later he felt his arms grabbed roughly, followed by his legs. Another set of hands wrapped around his head, holding it by pressing palms over his ears so that everything became muffled.

Then the pain began; mind-blowing, ear-shattering rib-splitting agony that filled him from the tips of his toes to the hair on his head. How does a person describe what it feels like to be pulled apart from all angles, to be basically drawn and quartered? Tom's delaying tactic had worked well. Not a single zombie would move past the fallen Pete, each wanting to get a taste of the man's flesh.

Pete found himself floating off the floor a few inches as each limb was pulled in a different direction. He screamed as loud as he could, until a hand slid into his mouth, grabbed his tongue with cold fingers, and ripped the flailing muscle out like pulling the cap off a can of Pringles.

Blood poured into Pete's mouth from the missing tongue, threatening to drown him. Suddenly, getting shot by Tom, and feeling the bullets enter his body, seemed like nothing more than bee stings compared to the agony he now felt.

The zombies were still pulling on him, each wanting a piece of Pete for themselves. Pete could feel himself ready to blackout, and he consciously tried to force his mind to take the fall into oblivion faster. Anything to end the suffering.

But there would be no reprieve for Pete this day. He felt his left arm go first. One second there was that unending tension as the muscles and tendons in his shoulder were stretched to the breaking point, then a split-second later there was a feeling of coldness as the limb was torn free of its socket and yanked from his body. The flesh tore like taffy, then snapped as the last bit was pulled free. Pete felt his body drop to the floor on that side but it wasn't for long as his left leg gave way. Like a chicken leg pulled from a roast, the skin tore and peeled, then snapped as the limb came free. Blood was spurting out of the severed limbs in a wave, splashing the faces of the dead as they fought to get at their victim. Pete saw so much blood, he couldn't believe it was all coming from his body.

He began to feel tension on his neck. It felt like he was a wine cork and someone was doing their damndest to pull him from the bottle. His head began to twist, like someone holding him decided he was a cap on a bottle. His head went to the left and kept going, far beyond what it should be allowed to. The snap of his neck cracking was the last thing he heard as he fell into the darkness that waited for all men. His head was twisted again and again until the flesh and tendons gave way. The spine cracked like a wishbone and the head was pulled from the now very dead man's shoulders. The tongue-less mouth sagged open as the head disappeared into the crowd of feeding zombies. The last two limbs on Pete's body were eventually torn free of the torso and dragged into the horde to be fought over. More zombies dove onto the torso, ripping open the chest cavity, and multiple hands began scooping out organs and going lower and pulling out intestines, foot by bloody, greasy foot they were unwound to be pulled into the hungry crowd.

The feeding went on for more than ten minutes, until every scrap that was Pete was devoured, leaving behind only bloody bones and clothes.

Rhodes stood by and watched, knowing there was nothing he could do until the feeding frenzy was complete. He didn't try to get at any of the tasty flesh. His hunger was for others, and when he feasted on their flesh it would be oh so satisfying.

When the last scrap was gone, Rhodes grunted and growled, making his army begin moving again. Satiated for the moment, they did as he commanded and began moving down the long corridor once more.

The horde was on the move again and this time it wouldn't stop until all the humans were within their grasp.

Chapter 29

Sarah raced down the corridor, as the sounds of more gunfire echoed through the complex. It sounded like the commotion was coming from far away, and with the amount of firepower being used, it couldn't have been for a good reason.

She reached the intersection where she had first left Tom and the others. Tom was there, with Frank and one of his men, the big one called Rollo. The blonde German—Schwartz—was missing. Sarah didn't remember his name and didn't care. She didn't see John or McDermott either, which was a call for concern for her.

The second Tom saw Sarah, he went to her. "There you are. Where's Lou?" he asked, not seeing the redheaded man.

Sarah could see Tom was flustered, though despite it he was still in control of his emotions. Still, whatever was going on had to be bad.

Sarah shook her head at the question. "He's dead, torn apart."

"Fuck, that's all I need; another man gone."

"Why? Who else is dead?" Her heart began to beat faster, thinking it could be John or McDermott that had been killed.

"Pete's dead," was all Tom said.

Sarah tried to remember who Pete was, what the man looked like, but other than him being black nothing came to her. Unlike John, the names of the men who'd come as soldiers on the mission weren't relevant to her. They reminded her too much of Rhodes' men when she'd been living in the bunker under the captain's rule. Of course, that rule had been cut short before it began.

When Major Cooper had died, Rhodes had been the next in rank to take command. The man wasn't ready for it, quite frankly. From day one the pressure of being responsible for other men weighed heavily on him. Then, to add to his pressure, he'd been running low on ammunition and the bunker was woefully under stocked with basic items needed to get the job done. And his men kept dying thanks to Dr. Logan making them capture zombies for specimens, and to top it all off the only woman in the bunker gave him no respect. Rhodes was an older type, more of a male chauvinist actually. He believed women had their place. All this piled together to make a man who wasn't ready for command even more unstable.

Perhaps if he'd talked to Sarah privately, or she had gone to him, and explained in a rational voice what each of them was so concerned about, it might have worked out, and finally the scientific and military teams could have worked together.

But Rhodes' ego was far too large to allow him to do that and Sarah was far too proud to kowtow to Rhodes, who she considered a pompous ass. So instead of talking it out, he'd yelled and screamed and cursed, which made the people he was talking to reciprocate, until all anyone did was yell and swear and argue. The human condition at its worst had been within the bunker, a microcosm of opposing personalities where none would give so much as an inch.

In the end, their total lack of cooperation had caused the deaths of everyone but Sarah, John and McDermott.

Schwartz came running down the corridor, his rifle held before him. "They're coming; minutes away at most," he said as he came up beside Tom.

"Who's coming? What are you talking about?" Sarah asked, her heart beating even faster.

Tom quickly filled her in on the zombie horde, and as he did, her eyes went wide.

"Then we need to get out of here," she said, her face flush with worry. "I found my notes; we can leave. But we need to find John and McDermott first."

"Fuck them," Tom said, almost spitting the words. "I told them I wouldn't go chasing after them if they wandered away to explore." He glared at Sarah. "Now tell me how to get my men out of this fucking maze."

"No," she snapped back. "I'm not going anywhere without my friends."

Tom spun on her, jamming the muzzle of the Uzi under her chin. "Maybe you're not hearing me, lady. I said tell me how to get out of this fucking place or you're dead."

She blinked in surprise but held her ground. The muzzle of the Uzi was warm under her skin; it had been fired recently. In as calm a voice as she could muster given the circumstances she said, "I won't leave without my friends. If you kill me you're on your own, and good luck finding another way out of here, and you'll have to explain to Prof. Langford that I'm dead."

"Langford will know what I tell him and only that," Tom snapped in reply. "Maybe you don't realize it but I'm the real leader of New Eden. I let Langford be the figurehead 'cause he's a better politician than me. He thinks he's in charge but anyone who matters knows it's me."

"Then why did you come on this mission if you didn't have to?" she asked, the muzzle still pressed into her chin.

"Because I wanted to see what was here. Guns, ammo, who knew what might still be here, rotting away, just waiting for me to come and take it. But this place is a joke."

"Tom, there's no time for this," Frank said, stepping up next to Tom. Already, Rollo and Schwartz had begun firing at the approaching horde as the zombies came down the corridor like a wave of rotting flesh.

Tom spun on Frank, the muzzle of the Uzi coming away from Sarah's chin. "I'll tell you what we have time for and what we don't!" he screamed. "You do as I fucking tell you!"

Sarah could see that Tom had cracked, the man was losing it and what he might do next was totally unpredictable. She knew she needed to get way from him and fast. But before she could run, the horde reached the end of the corridor and began to turn onto the one where Sarah and the others were. Rollo and Schwartz had been backing up as they fired, each man covering for the other one when they needed to switch magazines. They were burning through bullets lightning fast and still the tide of dead flesh kept coming.

The sound of hundreds of voices moaning and wailing filled the corridor along with the steady beat of gunfire.

"Oh my God," Sarah whispered as she took a step backwards. She looked at all the dead, pale faces—most covered in blood— and she felt her stomach drop into her legs. There were so many. Hundreds of them, all packed tightly in the corridor. For as far back as she could see there was nothing but a sea of bobbing heads.

Then she spotted one face she recognized in the sea of nameless visages towering over the others near the back.

Rhodes.

The half-zombie was on the shoulders of a tall zombie, and Rhodes was riding the ghoul like it was his horse. The top of Rhodes' head was almost brushing the ceiling.

Rhodes spotted Sarah as well and he raised his hand, his gold West Point ring with a red jewel flashing in the fluorescent lights of the ceiling. His mouth opened wide and he let out a yowl that sounded a lot to Sarah like, *"Bitch, get her!"*

But Sarah knew she had to be mistaken, that with so much noise commingling—such as gunfire, wailing, moaning and footsteps slapping the tiles—she'd heard something that hadn't truly occurred.

The zombies surged forward in an all out blitz and Tom, Rollo, Frank and Schwartz, like the fools that they were in Sarah's eyes, stood their ground and fought. She knew it was hopeless. Like death itself, the walking dead could never be stopped.

Upon seeing that no one was watching her, Sarah began back-pedaling, and when she reached the corner in the corridor, she ducked away and began running.

Tom saw her just as she turned the corner and he spun around and fired at her, the 9mm rounds chewing up the plaster and cement of the wall. "Sarah, get the fuck back here!" he screamed. "If I find you you're fucking dead! Do you hear me! Dead!" But then he had to focus on the threat before him, not behind.

With no choice, he began to fire from the hip with his Uzi, taking down body after body as the never-ending wave of animated corpses threw themselves at the four armed men.

Chapter 30

Sarah ran for a minute until she knew she was clear of Tom. Behind her, the corridor twisting and turning like a maze, were the sounds of gunfire and yelling as Tom and his men fought the horde.

Leaning against the wall, she tried to think of what to do next. She should leave, but she couldn't without John and McDermott. But she didn't know where they were? They had said something about checking out the other rooms for anything of value. She was in the same area they went to, but without knowing exactly where they were it would be hopeless. She could call out but that would attract any of the dead in the area, which wouldn't help her dilemma.

Suddenly footsteps could be heard coming from in front of her. Sarah raised her assault rifle, ready to shoot anything that appeared.

Her knuckles were white on the gun and it was amazing to her that her fingers weren't leaving indents in the polished metal, she gripped it so tightly.

Her breathing came in shallow gasps as she waited for the arrival of the owner of the footsteps.

Her finger was on the trigger and a quarter ounce of pressure would be all it took to unleash a barrage of death.

Shadows crossed the far wall at the adjoining corridor from whence the footsteps were coming.

It would be only seconds now.

Then two figures appeared, and Sarah was about to fire, when John raised his hands in a gesture for her to stop. "Wait, it's us! Don't shoot!" he yelled, seeing her aiming the assault rifle in his direction. He figured she was jumpy, and he didn't blame her. He was jumpy too.

Every damn corner in the bunker was the chance of a hundred zombies popping up at him.

He'd never given it much thought until now, and not when he'd lived in the complex—or outside it in the storage facility in a camper he and John had called home—but the damn place was a warren of twisting, turning hallways.

Like rats in a maze he and his fellow survivors had lived in the bunker and gone about the maze on a daily basis, only instead of cheese, they had been searching for something else. Something they never found.

Sarah was a hairsbreadth away from shooting them, but at the last microsecond she held off. "John! Bill! Thank God it's you guys." She ran to them and they did the same, still moving forward. When John and Sarah met, he crushed her to his chest, the two having a brief moment together. But it was only for a moment and then he gently pushed her back so he could look into her face.

"We heard shooting and yelling, Sarah. Do you know what's going on? Where's Tom, where's the rest of his men?" John asked.

"The dead, they're coming. Rhodes is with them," she began and then quickly filled him and McDermott in on what she'd seen and Tom trying to kill her.

"That bastard," John said, referring to Tom. "I knew there was something off about that guy." He'd tried to kill Sarah and John wanted to return the favor if he saw the man again.

McDermott grunted in anger. "Well, people, it seems it's time we left this place for yet the second time. The Promised Land awaits our return."

"Aye, Billy," John said. "It's time to go. Sarah, did you find what you wanted?"

Sarah nodded, patting the notes sticking out of her back pocket. "Yes, I have them right here. We found what we came for."

"Good," John said. "Then should we get out of here. What do you think?"

She grinned. "I think that's a great idea."

"Okay. It's time to say goodbye to this place, this time forever," John said before the three companions began to race down a side corridor to what they hoped would lead to an exit they could use.

Tom realized too late that he and his remaining men needed to retreat. Not that it would have mattered if they had. The dead were everywhere.

Even if they had fallen back to some storage room or lab, and had managed to barricade the door, eventually they would have run out of food and water and died of starvation.

Sarah had been the key. She was supposed to lead Tom and his team out of the warren of corridors at completion of the mission. But she'd cut and run, leaving Tom and his men to fight the dead by themselves. Tom swore to God if he saw her again he would put a bullet in her head.

"Fall back to the next hallway, fall back!" Tom yelled to his men. He saw that Schwartz was getting too close to the front line of zombies and he yelled that the man had to fall back, but Schwartz heard nothing. The German was in a berserker rage, firing as fast as he could reload his rifle. But then he ran out of fresh magazines, his hand reaching into the utility belt at his hip and coming up empty. Tom watched Schwartz pull his sidearm and started firing at almost point-blank range as the dead swarmed over him. The man began to scream as he was enveloped with rotting bodies. The German fought like a warrior, punching and kicking, and somewhere in the tangle of limbs he drew his hunting knife and began hacking and slashing at anything that came too close. Fingers were sliced off, throats were severed from ear to ear, and bodies were punctured, but none of it so much as slowed the hungry dead as they reached out and tore the knife from the German's powerful hand.

Then the dying started.

Fingers curled into claws, with fingernails longer than normal from death and shrinkage of skin, tore into Schwartz, tearing off his clothes and sinking into his flesh.

Schwartz had a powerful physique, his abdomen like a washboard, but nothing stopped the dead as they tore through the tight muscles and began to rip away tendons. Schwartz fought silently at first, his teeth locked in a perpetual grimace, but as more and more hands tore at his flesh, no man, no matter how resolute, could resist screaming. Nor would he be called a coward for doing so.

When Schwartz finally let loose a wail of agony, it was like the floodgates had been released, and the man began to scream and shriek in agony as his body was torn asunder.

Tom watched Schwartz die in unbelievable pain, and it made his blood run cold. Though a warrior and a soldier, Tom cringed inside. Was that his fate as well and he was just delaying it? He knew he didn't want to die like that, like a pig to the slaughter.

"Frank, Rollo, on me, we need to find a better position to fight them off!" Tom yelled over the gunfire, moans of the dead, and the fading screams of Schwartz.

The two men joined Tom and they began running down the corridor, but they didn't get far. Upon reaching a three-way intersection, one of many in the complex, they found that both of the alternate directions were already blocked with more zombies, the groups of ghouls moving up the corridors slowly but purposefully.

"What the fuck!" Tom screamed and sprayed his Uzi into one of the new corridors, taking down a half dozen bodies in the barrage. The dead fell to the floor and were promptly walked over or stepped on by the crowd behind them.

Unknown to Tom, Rhodes had directed half of the dead to circle around through the storage facility and then back into the complex, thus flanking the humans.

Trapped in the intersection of three corridors, the zombies came at the trio of warriors from all sides.

Rollo fired from the hip, his Russian rifle becoming so hot the muzzle glowed bright red. Still he continued firing, until finally the barrel was so hot that a round cooked off in the weapon. Metal shrapnel flew off in all directions, some of it hitting Rollo in the face. The man dropped the ruined weapon and raised his hands to his face, screaming as a hot piece of metal burned through his right eye and into his skull.

He was in the same exact position when the dead reached him and swarmed over him, pulling at his clothes and tearing at the flesh beneath.

Rollo stopped screaming about his eye when he was attacked and began fighting off his attackers, but for every one he knocked down, five more took its place. More than a dozen zombies were on him, like a dog pile gone horribly wrong, and Tom watched in horror as yet another of his men was killed.

But then the pile of bodies began to move and shift, until they were raised into the air and thrown across the corridor to bounce off the wall. In the center of the cyclone stood Rollo. Blinded in one eye, he roared in rage at the dead attacking him.

But there was always more there to replace the ones he'd tossed off him, and once more another wave of bodies piled on as zombie after zombie tried to get a piece of Rollo's flesh. With a loud roar, Rollo threw them off him again and once more he was piled on. Five times this happened in the span of two minutes, but after the fifth time, Rollo's indomitable strength was failing, and as the dead covered him for the sixth time, and Tom waited to see the powerful man throw them off, it didn't happen.

Only screaming happened as Rollo, too tired to fight off the waves of rotting human flesh covering him, succumbed to the living dead as all eventually do.

With so many bodies on top of him, his dying shrieks were muffled until they were lost amongst the moans of the dead as they fed on fresh meat.

Only Tom and Frank were left, and the two men stood back to back and kept the hordes from coming at them from all sides.

Minutes went by with only the sounds of the dead and the reports of Tom and Frank's weapons, then Frank called out, "My rifles out, switching to my sidearm!"

The sheer amount of bodies in the corridor was something to behold, and the foul odor of reeking death was enough to make anyone gag. Rats scurried amongst the feet of the dead, feeding on the rotting meat. When the elevator shaft had been left open, it was the perfect entrance for the rats to come into the bunker.

The blood covering the floor could be measured in inches and the corpses were piled so high that they became a firewall that the two men could use to shoot from behind. But there were always more. Hundreds of zombies had ended up inside the bunker when it had been overrun. With the elevator shaft left open, many more had fallen into the shaft over the past weeks to then explore the bunker. Only the perimeter fence gate finally being closed had stopped the torrential onslaught.

Tom's Uzi finally clicked dry on his last magazine. He dropped the Uzi to the floor and unslung his sniper rife. Shooting from the hip, he began firing at more bodies. The powerful rounds blew out fist-sized chunks from torsos, and if he struck a head, then that head disappeared in a blast of pink mist. But there was no way to continue forever, and as he fought and screamed at the dead to fuck off, he knew his and Frank's lives could be measured in minutes—or less.

The sniper rifle clicked dry and there was no time to reload, so he dropped it and pulled his sidearm, once more shooting into the mob of dead faces. The dead had to climb over the pile of bodies and fall to the floor, where they then had to get to their feet. It was simple for Tom and Frank to shoot them as they did this but still, that only mattered as long as the two men had ammunition.

"I'm out," Frank said, dropping his sidearm and pulling his knife, the last defense he had.

"Right, stay close to me," Tom replied as he shot a fat female zombie wearing what looked like a muumuu, though the material was so encrusted with blood and pus to be unrecognizable.

Frank pushed even closer to Tom and began slashing at anything that came near him. It was truly amazing that the two men were still alive; only their determination to remain that way and the amount of ammunition had made it so. But now the latter had dried up and no matter how powerful their desire to live, the dead had other ideas.

Tom swung left and right, lining up faces in his gun sights and taking them down. His clip went dry and he popped it out, ignoring it as it fell to the floor. Before the clip had landed in the pool of blood at his feet, he'd already popped in a new one and was firing again.

He was in his own world, his mind focused on only one thing, shooting. He took down one target after another, until he became like a machine. Aim, shoot, shift, aim, shoot, shift, aim, shoot, then return to first position and begin again.

Something pushed him from behind and he thought Frank had miss-stepped and bumped into him. He risked a glance over his shoulder but the rat-faced man was nowhere to be found. A zombie stood there though, so Tom spun around at the waist and brought the pistol under the zombie's chin and fired. The bullet went up through the mouth, into the nasal cavity and into the frontal lobe, taking the zombie down. As the top of the head of the ghoul blew off and matted hair and bits of skull danced in the air, Tom was already facing forward and shooting again.

But then a face got in his sights that he recognized, and he froze for one spilt second as he stared at the thin face of Frank. It didn't make any sense. How did Frank get in front of him? And why did his head seem like it was floating without a body? But then Tom pulled back from his tunnel vision and he saw that Frank's head wasn't floating. It had been ripped clean of his body. Bits of muscle and tendons hung down below the neck, where it had been pulled off his shoulders. The mouth hung slack, the eyes glazed over in death, the entire head covered in blood.

Angry that his friend was gone and he hadn't even heard one iota of his death knell, Tom shot Frank's face in the forehead. The bullet left a neat hole in the forehead, just above where the eyebrows met. The exit wound was larger. The bullet traveled through the head and out the back of the skull, fragmenting slightly, but there was still enough kinetic energy in it so that the round slammed into the eye of the zombie holding Frank's severed head, killing it instantly. Tom couldn't save Frank from death but at least he had avenged his friend by taking down the ghoul that had killed him...or at least another of the ghouls.

As if fate was intervening once more, that was the last bullet in Tom's sidearm and he had no more clips. Throwing the pistol at a zombie, he pulled his Bowie knife as the dead swarmed over him from three sides.

He knew the only way to keep living was to be a moving target, so he chose a direction and ran that way, shoving bodies out of his way. It worked briefly, the ghouls not able to grab him as he barreled by them, but then he reached the firewall of corpses, and the only way past it was to climb over it. So he began climbing, but it caused enough of a delay that more ghouls could grab him. Plus, more were coming over the corpse-wall with every second, and they also grabbed for him. Tom was enveloped in seconds and forced to the floor. The first thing he felt was the coldness on his back from the tiles as the blood on the floor soaked into his shirt and pants. The second thing he felt were the countless hands clawing at him.

The feeling of claustrophobia was overwhelming, and it was all he could do not to go mad right there. How could one person explain to another what it would feel like to truly be trapped on the floor, while hundreds of dead people stood over him, or knelt beside him and clawed and tore at his body. How terrifying would that actually be? Or was it a terror that no amount of description could fully allow for the experience, for the visualization of absolute and pure horror it truly was?

Tom tried to stay strong, but he was only human, and the first thing that happened was his bladder let go. The inside of his legs felt warm as his pants absorbed the urine.

He screamed once. It was quick, barely even a scream, but it was there, let loose into the world for all to hear. But there was no one alive to hear his screams and the dead didn't care.

Well, if one scream was okay, why not two? Tom's mind rationalized as he felt his flesh being torn asunder. He then let loose with a tirade of screams, and added in some choice curses as well. He'd made a promise to himself earlier, that he wouldn't die like Schwartz, torn apart like a deer cornered by hyenas in the wild.

With one last ounce of willpower, he got his body under control enough to make his right hand reach down to his chest, and to the web belt.

His hand wrapped around a grenade; what kind it was he didn't know, and he pulled the pin, letting the pin drop to his chest as well. He opened his mouth and yelled, "See you fuckers in Hell!" An instant later the grenade went off. It had been a shrapnel grenade, and as it exploded, it ignited the few remaining grenades on his web belt, including the Willie Petes, creating an explosion five times greater than the original.

Tom's body was vaporized at ground zero of the eruption, and more than fifty zombies were torn limb from limb in the secondary blasts as white smoke and fire filled the corridor.

Ceiling tiles were blown off their foundations, fluorescent lights shattered, and the walls and ceiling outside the main blast zone were coated in blood and gore. Droplets of bloody flesh dripped from the ceiling rafters and slid down the walls slowly, like snails without their shells.

Bodies burned out of control, the incendiary grenades adding to the maelstrom.

The explosion reverberated throughout the bunker, shaking the very walls of the complex.

It was a death that any warrior would have welcomed when the time had come.

Chapter 31

John, Sarah and McDermott stopped moving through the corridor they were in, as the entire complex shook slightly, and a rumbling thump could be heard.

"What was that?" McDermott asked, looking up at the ceiling, as if he expected it to come down on him at any moment.

"One of Tom's grenades?" John suggested.

"That was a pretty big explosion for a grenade," McDermott replied.

"It doesn't matter," Sarah said. "All that does is getting out of here and returning to the island."

But as they rounded one of the corners in the myriad of corridors inside the complex, they all halted as if they'd hit a wall.

At the far end of the corridor was a crowd of people, and even though they were a good distance away, it was obvious that the people were of the dead persuasion.

"Shit, can't go that way," John said, pulling on Sarah's shirt so she would follow him. "Take it slow. Just walk backwards; they haven't seen us yet."

They slowly began to walk backwards, careful not to a make any sudden movements that might call attention to them. But no sooner did the words leave John's mouth than one of the ghouls spotted the three humans at the far end of the corridor. It elicited a low moan that got the others' attention, and they all turned to see what the first zombie had spotted.

"Shit, they've seen us," McDermott said under his breath. He looked to John. "Time to run?"

"Definitely," John replied, and side by side, all three of them turned and began running back the way they'd come.

The three companions didn't get far before coming to another roadblock. The entire hallway was wall to wall bodies, the zombies slowly walking down it, almost meandering. As soon as the three humans were noticed, the zombies began to pick up their pace.

With John in the lead, the three survivors were off again, desperately trying to figure a way out of the complex. But from where they were at the moment, so far all the exits were blocked.

"Come on, this way; there's one more way we can try," Sarah said, leading them off in yet another direction. Behind them, the zombies followed, albeit not as fast.

With Sarah now in the lead, they weaved their way through corridor after corridor. Sarah's idea was to go by the assembly room where she and the other scientists had once taken their meals and had meetings with Major Cooper, and after he died, with Rhodes, updating them on the progress the scientists were making.

If she was right, it was possible to circle past that room to another exit that would lead them to the main storage facility. From there they could go through the caves and then to the silo, the same one that she, John and McDermott had used to escape the bunker last time.

They had just passed the assembly room door and rounded another corner, when once more they had to stop.

"Holy shit," John whispered. "Is that Rhodes?"

No one replied, all three sets of eyes simply staring at the horde of ghouls coming down the hallway. In the middle, his head towering over the others on the shoulders of another zombie, Captain Rhodes could be seen.

"Back, we go back," John said as he began to back up, the others with him. But as they began to run in the opposite direction, back the way they'd come, the three companions didn't get far before they saw the other zombie mobs that had cut them off.

"Shit, they've blocked us off," McDermott said.

"That's impossible," John snapped. "How can they be doing this?"

"It's Rhodes," Sarah said flatly, as if that was all the explanation needed.

But there wasn't time to discuss it. McDermott leveled his rifle, about to start shooting but John stopped him.

"Don't bother, Billy. There's too many of them. It's a waste of time." John's Jamaican accent was thick now that he was under stress.

Sarah was searching the corridor, as she tried to come up with an idea that would get them out of their predicament. Unfortunately, nothing came to mind. Then her gaze fell on the door to the assembly room. Though the room was a dead end, there were really no other options.

"John, Bill, this way," she said and was off. John watched her go, not knowing where she thought she was going, but following her anyway. He didn't have any other suggestions and didn't want to let her out of his sight.

She ran straight for the door that led into the large room. The door itself was nothing more than wood, the upper half made of glass. It certainly wasn't a security door, but was there more for sound control. There was a shade on the door to use for privacy, and after she and the two men had entered, she closed the door and pulled down the shade

Sarah glanced around the large room, but there was nothing there to use to blockade the door but a few card tables and file cabinets. None of it would be enough to hold back the amount of bodies in the corridor. Sure they could try, but each of them had been through enough already to know when it was a hopeless situation. Better to spend the time together than working towards a pointless goal. On the far wall was an electric clock with a metal grate over it, still ticking along happily, oblivious to anything that had happened in the bunker over the past few weeks.

"You know that's not going to stop them for long, right," John said, pointing to the door with the muzzle of his M-16.

"Don't you think I know that?" she replied. "Look, if you have a better idea of what to do I'm all ears."

He smiled at her, his face taking on a calmness that seemed inappropriate given the circumstances, but John had always been a practical man. "Sarah darling, I wish I did."

She leaned into him, that reassurance and calmness rubbing off on her. "Me too."

"Well, we could always grab a meal while we're here," McDermott said, gesturing to the box of MRE's on one of the card tables. "It looks like it'll be our last meal, too."

The horde arrived at the door, the shadows of countless bodies silhouetted against the shade. It took only a few seconds before an arm came through the glass, only the shade preventing glass shards from hitting the three survivors. They backed away, not wanting to stand by the door.

"Well, let's not go down without a fight," John said. "Billy, Sarah, help me turn over these card tables. We'll get behind them and take out as many as we can when they enter. They can only come in one at a time. Maybe we can choke the doorway with so many dead that they can't get in." The tables had been setup in an 'L' shape for meetings between the scientists and military. They were quickly separated and flipped on their sides.

"This gonna be our last stand, Johnny?" McDermott said with a sly smile.

"Yeah, I'm afraid so," John replied.

"Ah, the heroes once more trapped by the walking dead. Will they survive to see the sunrise? Or will they die terribly."

"Not helping, Bill," Sarah said as she flipped a card table onto its side. Trash went flying, food stuffs and old MRE's mostly. Behind her, trash cans were piled high with garbage of bygone meals. The soldiers were supposed to take care of cleaning the bunker, but Major Cooper hadn't cared much for cleanliness.

"Sorry, I know I can be morbid sometimes," McDermott said. Across the room on the wall were multiple posters. One was of the state of Florida. That one had been used when John and McDermott had briefed Rhodes on how far they'd gone in the helicopter searching for other survivors. They'd never found any, all the times they'd gone out. The other poster was of the entire United States. An American flag was in the other corner.

Back at the door, five hands covered in blood were waving in the opening where the glass had been. So far none of the zombies had figured out how to turn the doorknob and the door was holding from the pressure of the bodies pushing on it.

That wouldn't last for long.

Sarah and the men crouched down behind the card tables, placing their rifles on the edges of the tables after laying out their spare ammo next to them on the floor.

John's fingers caressed the hilt of the machete on his hip, knowing he was going to be using it soon when the bullets ran out. He repositioned the duffel bag on his shoulder so he could move more easily.

The door began to crack as more pressure was applied to it. Splinters appeared in the facade, and without warning, the door burst open and three bodies spilled into the room to fall flat on their faces.

No one had to give the order to fire, it was implied the instant the door was breached. The three zombies on the floor, as they were trying to get up, were each shot in the top of the head as they crouched on all fours, the tops of their craniums the only thing the companions could see given their position.

More bodies began to pour into the room, one at a time, but an endless wave that would never cease. Sarah chose her shots carefully, but more often than not her bullet went wide and didn't kill like she wanted to. A head shot on a moving target wasn't as easy as in the movies, not unless the shooter was a trained marksman, which Sarah was not.

But with such close range she and the men were able to mow down the zombies with ease as, one at a time, the horde tried to get through the door.

Some did manage to get inside the room and almost to the card tables, but they were taken down before they could get close enough to be a threat. The bodies began piling up between the three shooters and the door, but there were always more ghouls to replace those that had fallen.

A zombie got past the barrage of bullets by the three companions and it stumbled into the room. Sarah saw a bloody St. Christopher medal hanging from its teeth, the chain lodged there. The blood was long dried, but she recognized the medal instantly. It was identical to the one Miguel had worn and kissed constantly.

Seeing the medal told her something she hadn't wanted to admit to herself, but knew it to be true. Miguel was definitely dead, and if a ghoul had his medal in its teeth, then he hadn't died easily.

The zombie was almost upon her before John shifted his aim and shot the ghoul in the face. It dropped only two feet from the turned-over card tables.

"Sarah, what's the matter with you?" John yelled. "Get your head in the game."

She snapped out of it. "Sorry, I'm okay. I… I'm okay." She wanted to tell John about the St. Christopher medal but decided not to. It wasn't the time and it didn't really matter anyway. She and the men would probably be dead soon anyway.

"Johnny, I'm out of ammo!" McDermott called out.

John tossed him a magazine. The Irishman caught it, popped it in, and began shooting once more.

It had been over five minutes since the door crashed in and the zombies still kept pouring into the room. Heedless of their destruction, they climbed over the bodies of the fallen. But there were more bodies than the companions had bullets, and once more McDermott called out that he was out of ammunition, even his sidearm was empty. Half a minute later Sarah said the same thing after shooting her last round in her .45, and finally, John fired the last bullet in his last magazine. He pulled his pistol and began firing, but after fourteen bullets and ten zombies dead thanks to some bad shots, he too, was out of ammunition.

The living dead came into the room but now there was nothing to stop them. More and more flooded the large space until the door was lost from sight. But instead of attacking, they stopped a few feet from the card tables, as if something was controlling them.

"What's going on?" McDermott asked. "Not that I'm complaining, but why aren't they coming at us?"

"I don't know but it can't be good," Sarah said as she stood up. There was no point crouching behind the table any longer. John and McDermott stood up as well and moved next to her. John put his arm around Sarah and she fell into his embrace, wanting to feel his protection, even if it was false.

The large room had over a hundred zombies in it with more still coming. The zombies that had formed a line before the card tables began to shift forward to make room for the ones still entering the room. John, Sarah and McDermott began to back up out of instinct. They kept going until their backs were up against the wall way at the far end of the room.

One thing was painfully clear. There was no escape; they were doomed to suffer very painful deaths.

Finally, when the room could hold no more bodies, and even the card tables had been knocked over as the dead shuffled forward to surround the three companions, but not getting closer than ten feet, the influx stopped and the room actually became relatively quiet.

Of course with so many zombies in one place it was never completely quiet. The buzzing of flies, the squealing rats running around the floor, the rustling of clothes, and terrible odor of rotting flesh, was an ever present reminder that the massive crowd before the three humans consisted of animated corpses.

"What the fuck are they waiting for?" McDermott asked, holding a hunting knife in his hand. John held his machete as well. But he wasn't going to use it on the zombies, oh no. The second they surged forward, he was going to turn on Sarah and cut her down and thus save her from being eaten alive. John hoped he had the time to turn the blade on himself, too, slicing his throat and bleeding out before suffering too much.

As if in answer to McDermott's question, the zombies by the door began to part and a tall zombie stepped into the room. Once inside the doorway, the ghoul raised what it had been carrying and placed the object on its shoulders.

"Rhodes," John hissed. "You son of a bitch."

The half-zombie sat on the shoulder of the tall zombie, more than two feet above the tallest head around him. The zombies began to move out of the way so that the tall ghoul carrying Rhodes could move deeper into the room. The three companions could only watch in amazement as Rhodes was carried all the way up to the front of the horde, where he then looked down on Sarah, John and McDermott with what sure seemed like hatred and contempt, a look of genuine emotion that none of the three friends had ever seen on a zombie before—except for Bub.

It was still painfully silent. It was so quiet that John could hear the air coming into the room as it rattled the vent grating a few feet over his head. Even with death suffusing the complex, utilities like the lights and circulated air still continued to function, and would do so even if another human never set foot within its walls.

"Rhodes, you son of a bitch," John spit. "If you can understand me, I should have killed you weeks ago when I had the chance." He waved the machete at the half-zombie to punctuate his words. "And if not then, I should have done it earlier the second I spotted you."

Rhodes didn't reply, not that he could if he wanted to. He smiled slightly, barely a grimace really, but to the three trapped humans it spoke volumes.

He raised his hand in the air, the red jewel in his West Point ring once more catching the lights of the overhead fluorescent lights, and he let out a howl that had every zombie in the large room moaning and groaning, their hoarse voices bouncing off the cold stone walls.

It took all of John's willpower not to wet his pants at the sound. It was unbearably horrible to behold. He gripped the machete tighter, knowing he was going to use it in a matter of seconds.

He glanced sideways at Sarah and his heart broke, knowing she was going to die. The side of her slim neck was right there, and he decided that was where he would strike her. The machete would slice in so fast that she would be dead before she hit the floor. He cursed coming back to the bunker again. He knew it was a fool's errand and now that belief had become a gruesome reality.

As John stared at Rhodes, the half-zombie's hand still raised, he knew that the second it dropped, the horde would attack.

Then the dying would begin.

Chapter 32

"It's been nice knowin' you both, Johnny, Sarah," McDermott said as Rhodes hand began to descend. John turned to the side slightly, the machete already going up and back to slice into Sarah's neck and kill her.

McDermott wanted a drink badly. In fact, he couldn't remember ever wanting a drink as bad as this one moment in his entire life.

Time seemed to slow for Sarah as she watched Rhodes begin to lower his hand. She knew what it meant, too, and she felt her bowels weakening. She wanted to cry, not so much for herself, but what her death would mean to the world. The cure would be lost forever and mankind would no doubt fade away over time.

With all eyes on Rhodes, none of the three companions were looking over at the doorway, so they didn't see it when another zombie appeared and stood framed in the opening. The zombie looked like every other zombie they'd seen, with two exceptions. The denim jacket it wore was very recognizable and even more so, the pistol it held in its left hand had once belonged to Rhodes himself.

Bub raised the pistol and aimed the gun sight on Rhodes' head. It was easy to do as the half-zombie was so much taller than all the other living dead in the room. He stuck out like a sore thumb, a target so easy a child could hit him.

Bub fired once, the bullet finding its home like it was meant to be there. Just before Rhodes' hand came down, his head rocked to the side and slumped forward, a large chunk of his skull blowing out along with his brains. He slid off the tall ghoul he was perched on and dropped to the floor, his remaining brains seeping out of the exit wound in the side of his head.

Bub lowered the pistol and saluted with his right hand, and his job done, he turned and walked away, back to wherever he'd been hiding.

Sarah, John and McDermott all stood in shocked amazement as Rhodes toppled to the floor. Released from whatever hold Rhodes had over them, the zombies also stood immobile, their minds totally blank.

John was the first to realize there was now an infinitely short window for escape. The air vent rattled over his head and he spun around and looked up at it, an idea taking hold. He grabbed Sarah roughly in his excitement and pulled her to him, then spun her around so she was facing the wall, then picked her up by the waist and said, "The grate, Sarah, pull it off. We can use it to get away."

She understood the instant she was raised, and she stuck her hands between the square metal openings and pulled as hard as she could. The metal dug into her fingers but she ignored the pain, knowing this was their only chance to get away before being torn apart and eaten. She yanked as hard as she could, and on the third try the grate popped off and fell to the floor with a dull clang. Air whistled out of the vent, blowing her hair around her face and neck. It cooled her sweat-covered forehead as the air washed over her.

The loud noise of the falling grate was also a catalyst to break the zombies out of their fugue state. Suddenly they were looking around, not sure where they were. Sarah was already scurrying into the open air vent as the zombies' heads all turned as one to the remaining two humans standing only a few feet before them. McDermott swallowed the lump in his throat as he looked at John, who pointed to the vent for McDermott to go next.

The Irishman opened his mouth to protest but John shook his head no, his jaw set tight; the look told McDermott there would be no discussion. McDermott was shorter and if he was last, then there would be no way for him to jump up and reach the edge of the vent. John had to be last.

John lowered his hands and cupped them together, weaving his fingers tightly, to make a step for McDermott, who placed his right foot in the proffered step and a second later was slithering into the vent.

John was next, but before he could jump up, the zombies began to surge forward. With machete in hand, John took the initiative and went to them, hacking and slashing with wild abandon. But he knew what he was doing, and he took down the four ghouls that were right before him, then kicked their bodies into the rest of the crowd and hopefully, slowing them down for a few tension-filled seconds. Conscious of the weight of the heavy duffel bag on his shoulder, he pulled it off and tossed it at another zombie, the weight of the bag knocking it onto its back.

That was all he needed to make his escape. He spun around and ran for the vent, dropping his machete as he jumped up, his fingers catching the metal lip. He pulled himself up, but though the zombies had been slowed, it wasn't enough to prevent them reaching him.

As his waist became even with the edge of the vent, and he prepared to fall flat and crawl inside, he felt himself being inevitably drawn backwards and out of the vent, thanks to the hands holding his feet, grabbing him, pulling him backwards.

The zombies could only reach up, and just barely managed to get a hold of his ankles as John's feet hung down from the vent. If he hadn't been caught, the dead never would have been able to reach the vent themselves.

The other zombies that were holding John reached their hands high over their heads, all wanting to grab the human, wanting to feed on his warm flesh.

John reached out with his hands to stay his reverse momentum, but there was nothing to grab hold of. The interior of the vent was nothing but smooth, stainless-steel metal, the seams welded to a flat finish.

His hands slapping the sides of the vent, they squealed as the flesh of his palms pressed against the metal, but it wasn't enough. His eyes wide in panic, he could do nothing as he began to be pulled backwards inch by agonizing inch.

He let out a yell when his waist hit the edge of the vent, knowing there was nothing that could stop his fall. Believing it was all over, he closed his eyes as he was yanked back one last time.

Chapter 33

John opened his mouth to scream as he felt himself being pulled out of the vent, but just before his waist went past the edge of no return, a hand grabbed his left wrist and stayed his fall.

Not understanding what had happened, John opened his eyes to see McDermott's smiling face only three feet from his own, the light from the assembly room filtering into the vent easily past John's shoulders.

"You can't leave us yet, Johnny, there's still too much to do," McDermott said as he began to pull John back into the vent. Sarah was holding McDermott's legs so that the weight of the two people was enough leverage to yank John free of the zombies and back inside. Once John's feet were free, however, it was simple for him to crawl into the vent and McDermott let him go.

"How, Billy?" was all John could say. His heart was beating a mile a minute, his body flushed with adrenaline. He was so wired his hands were shaking, even as he crawled.

Sarah was pulling McDermott as the man crawled backwards, so John was looking right at the man, face to face as he crawled. But the deeper they went the more the light began to fade.

"Luckily, there's a junction twenty feet down, John," McDermott explained. "When I didn't see you behind me when I reached it, I spun around and came back for you."

"I'm glad you did," John said with a wide grin. "I thought I was done for."

At the junction, McDermott spun around so he was facing forward, and with Sarah in the lead, they began crawling through the ductwork. As they passed gratings that opened into rooms, Sarah would peer down to see if it was a good place to get out, but each time she did, all she saw was the living dead. They were everywhere once more.

So they continued crawling, yard after yard, until finally Sarah came to a room that was empty. She didn't recognize it as a room she'd ever been in before, and she told the others as much.

"No, Sarah, keep going a little more," John said. "The further we can get away from where we were the better. We can always come back if nothing promising comes along." They began moving once more, the light from the gratings as they passed each one seeping into the duct and giving them a dull gloom to see by.

John noticed that McDermott was slowing down and he was making soft grunting noises as he moved, as if it was an exertion just to move his body. "Billy, what's wrong with you?" he inquired with genuine concern for his friend. "You're dragging ass, man. Are you all right?"

"I'm fine, John," McDermott said, his voice flat and humorless, nothing like the way he usually was. "Just tired."

John didn't believe him. "Billy boy, we've been through a lot together. If something's wrong, you need to tell me."

"Damn it, John, I'm fine, now stop asking. Besides, we have more important things to worry about."

John wished he could see McDermott's face instead of talking to the bottom of the Irishman's shoes, but inside the vent there was nothing to be done for it.

"All right, Billy, but this isn't over," John said.

"Yes it is," McDermott replied, and then scooted forward a little so that John wasn't directly behind him. They crawled for another twenty minutes until Sarah stopped again before a grate and peered out of it.

"Guys, I think this is as good a place as any," she said, her face pressed up against the metal mesh. "We've been going for a while; we have to be on the outskirts of the complex." She shifted onto her side so she could look down her body at McDermott, and just barely see John with what light filtered into the grating from the room. "It looks empty. It's an office of some sort.

"Go 'head, Sarah, I've had about enough crawling around like a rat," McDermott said, making sure John agreed as he looked down his body to see John's dark face staring back at him.

"Aye, Sarah, go for it," John said.

There was enough room for Sarah to move sideways and press the bottom of her boots up against the gate. Then she kicked out, sending the grating flying across the room. It landed on a desk, and bounced on the floor once before going still.

They all waited for over five minutes inside the duct to see if anyone—or anything—was going to arrive, and when none did, Sarah slid out first to be followed by the two men.

"Wow, it's good to be out of there," Sarah said while stretching, and rubbing her neck with her hand.

"Billy, check the hallway, see if there's anyone out there," John said, going to a file cabinet and searching it. "Sarah, check that desk for anything we can use. Mostly a weapon."

"Right," she said and went to the desk while McDermott moved to the only door and opened it slowly after peering out from behind the drawn shade. The door was wood with a glass window exactly like the one in the assembly room. The doors were used throughout the complex for office spaces, living quarters and the labs.

The office appeared unused, the papers on the desk still there from when it had been in use by some unknown personnel. There was almost no dust, as the air was filtered and circulated constantly.

Upon opening the last drawer on the desk, Sarah let out a soft cry of success and held up a small handgun. It was an old Lorcin .25. The petite gun had been designed for women to carry in their purses. It held six rounds of .25 caliber bullets, with a snub two-inch barrel. The gun had a satin chrome finish and a smooth white stock. Sarah checked to see if it was loaded and found that it had five bullets.

"Go ahead, John, you take it," she said and handed it to him. John also checked the rounds. The small gun seemed to be in good condition and smelled of gun oil. Whoever had put it in the drawer would never be known, but he thought a silent thank you to him or her, wherever they might be.

The door closed silently and McDermott joined John and Sarah at the desk. They were all whispering, not wanting to take any chances on being discovered.

"The hallway's clear. Clean too," McDermott said. "Not a spot of blood or a bullet hole anywhere I could see. I think we're in a part of the bunker that wasn't in use when we were here."

That made sense to all of them. When the bunker had been commandeered by the government, and Sarah and her team had been assigned there, she had been told that they were only going to use a small portion for labs, offices and living quarters.

"We probably are in an unused section," Sarah said, "but to get out we need to backtrack to the corral and from there we can go through the caves until we reach the silo."

"Why not, we did it before," John said with a shrug. "But before we go, we need some more weapons." He scanned the room, his gaze resting on a wooden chair next to the desk. "There, that'll work nicely." He went to the chair and laid it on its side, then used his foot to break off two of the legs, then flipped the chair over once and broke one more leg. He handed one leg each to Sarah and McDermott, keeping the last one for himself.

McDermott took the makeshift wooden club and shrugged. "Any port in a storm…"

John saw that McDermott looked paler than normal and the man was sweating profusely. He was going to ask but decided it should wait. They were still far from free of the complex, and until they were, nothing else mattered.

With John in the lead, as he carried the only firearm, they exited the room and gathered in the corridor. Sarah and McDermott still had their knives also, but to use them they would have to get far too close and personal to the zombies to use them; the clubs were safer.

About twenty feet down from the office door, there was a map on the wall under plexiglass. The maps were scattered throughput the bunker so personnel wouldn't get lost.

Sarah traced her finger over the red spot that said where they were and then followed it to where she knew the corral was located.

Weaving their way through the corridors, they managed to make it to a fire door that opened out in the storage facility without coming across a single zombie. But though they didn't come in contact with one, the presence of the dead was everywhere they looked. Moans and groans could be heard as well, echoing through the corridors, but it wasn't close by, which was fortunate for the three weary survivors.

Darting through the storage facility, using the cars and RVs as shelter, they reached the corral easily. But as they peered around a large pile of metal barrels, they saw that the corral wasn't empty. On the side closest to them there were a dozen zombies, just hanging around with nowhere to go. The fence had a central section where there was a transitioning pit for zombies to be grabbed with a neck noose and then dragged into the square hole in the fence. Once inside, a wooden gate would drop drown, trapping the ghoul within its small prison.

When the soldiers were ready, they would open the gate on the side of the complex and then the zombie would be taken out and brought to Dr. Logan's lab.

Once there, it would be chained to a wall to await the mad doctor's experiments. By having it setup like that, the soldiers only had to deal with one ghoul at a time.

As the three companions studied the wooden fence, they saw that a zombie had somehow become trapped inside the small transitioning pit. It held a piece of wood and was whacking the sides of its prison over and over.

John wondered if the banging had been going on for weeks, ever since the bunker had become filled with the dead. The only problem he saw was that once they climbed onto the platform, they had to be careful that the trapped zombie didn't grab their legs.

John pointed to the fence. "We can run right past them, jump onto the platform, and jump down on the other side. Just be careful of the one trapped behind the gate. Then we run for it and follow the red lights to the silo like last time. There can't be many of those dead things in the corral anymore. We killed most of them the last time we were in there."

"Sounds like a plan, Johnny. I say we go for it," McDermott said.

Footsteps in the gravel and dirt, and moans from behind the companions, decided their next move for them. Turning together, they saw a score of zombies coming right for them.

"Shit, we've been spotted," McDermott said.

"Then let's move." John readied the gun in his right hand and the club in his left. Sarah and McDermott raised their clubs, too. John hoped he didn't have to shoot, not wanting to waste a bullet.

John went first, followed by Sarah and McDermott, who was moving much slower than the other two. The second the three humans appeared, the dead turned and began shuffling for them. John bent over slightly and used his shoulder, checking a zombie to the side like a hockey player. He didn't have to kill the ghoul, only get it out of the way for the few seconds the others needed to get past it. Once they were on the platform and over the fence, it wouldn't matter how many zombies were left.

John whacked another zombie in the face with the club, sending it sprawling. It flailed on the ground for a few seconds, rolled over, and began to slowly get up.

The others were past it a second later.

John climbed the ladder, and when he was on top of the platform, he glanced over his shoulder to make sure the others were still with him, then dropped down onto the other side of the gate. There were six zombies close by and they began coming towards him. He raised the Lorcin and waited for the others, hoping they would be fast so all three of them could run for it.

Sarah dropped down beside John a moment later. John looked up and over his shoulder to see where the hell McDermott was.

As McDermott ran onto the platform and prepared to jump down, he miscalculated how close he was, and the trapped zombie reached out and grabbed his ankle.

"Down boy," McDermott said and whacked the zombie on the top of the head. The skull caved in like a rotten cantaloupe, and the zombie slumped to the ground, its other hand dropping the piece of wood it had been pounding its prison with. At least there wouldn't be any more banging in the corral area. He had to pause for a few seconds on the platform as a wave of dizziness overcame him. Shaking his head to clear it, he dropped down next to John, went to his knees from the exertion, and then stood up.

"Where the hell have you been, Billy?" John asked.

"Sorry, I'm here now, so let's go," McDermott replied.

"Right, you two go left and I'll go right. We'll circle around these six and keep going," John explained as he gestured with the club at the approaching zombies. "Just get them out of the way; we don't have to kill them."

The companions split up, doing what John told them. John had to club one ghoul out of his way and another he body checked. McDermott used the club to whack a ghoul in the knee, the kneecap disintegrating into pulp. The ghoul fell onto its face and began to crawl. McDermott moved past it.

Sarah simply darted left and then went right, avoiding the reaching arms of the ghoul trying to grab her. The next one she simply ran wide around it, and caught up to John, and with McDermott joining them, huffing and puffing like he'd run the mile in two minutes flat, the three survivors continued deeper into the caves, retracing footsteps they'd taken weeks before.

Chapter 34

With John leading the way once more, the three companions moved through the large cavern-like tunnels adjacent to the bunker. Perhaps at one time the plan had been to expand the storage facility, but with civilization in ruins, that would now never come to pass.

As the companions made their way cautiously, they passed the prone bodies of zombies that had been put down the last time they were here. McDermott came upon one that had its head taken off by a shovel right at the nose. The half head, with brain still intact, was exactly where McDermott had flipped it. The eyes still moved back and forth, but they did so much slower now as the half-head slowly rotted into the ground.

When they finally reached the entrance to the silo, John slipped in first before waving the others to follow. There was one lone corpse on the floor. It had been shot by McDermott to save John as he'd climbed the ladder, only to have his foot grabbed, the ghoul trying to sink its teeth into his ankle.

John would have shot the zombie himself but the revolver he'd been using—taken from Rhodes—had been out of bullets. The revolver was still lying in the corner of the circular room where John had dropped it, having left it behind the last time he'd left the bunker. This time things were different, so he picked up the silver revolver and slid it into his belt. There were bullets for the gun back on New Eden.

Moaning could be heard from out past the entrance to the silo. The zombies inside the caves were following them and would be there soon. It was time to begin the long and arduous climb to the surface.

"Okay, Sarah," John said. "Up we go."

"I feel like we've been here before," she said with a smile. It was still hard to believe they were actually alive, that they'd beaten the odds yet again and were escaping the bunker in one piece. She hugged him quickly and kissed him on the cheek, before beginning the long climb to the surface.

"Okay, Billy boy, you're next," John said, but McDermott didn't move to the ladder, and in fact, he took a step backwards.

"Billy, what's the matter? Come on, man, we need to go. Can't you hear them? They'll be here soon."

"I'm not going with you, Johnny," McDermott said, his voice cracking slightly.

John blinked, not believing what he'd just heard. He must have been mistaken. "Billy, stop screwing around, come on, we're running out of time."

"I know, so I need to make this quick," McDermott said and slowly rolled up the sleeve of his right arm to show John a bite mark, the clear indent of a pair of teeth in the tanned skin. The skin had been broken and the wound looked infected. Yellow pus seeped from the sore and blue lines could be seen going up and down his arm. There was a smell in the room now that the wound was exposed to the air, a sickly sweet-sour aroma.

"I...I don't understand," John said, his voice almost a whisper.

Above, Sarah had stopped climbing, seeing that there was something wrong. "John, Bill, what are you waiting for?" she called down.

John didn't reply to her, only stared at his friend. "Billy..." was all he could manage to get out.

"It happened when I was wrestling with Logan," McDermott said. "The bastard got a piece of me after all. I found out after we left the room when we heard gunshots."

"Okay, then fine, we can deal with this, Billy. Sarah can amputate your arm, like she did to Salazar. She can save you."

McDermott managed a smile. "Ah, Johnny, always the optimist. It's too late for that. Maybe if it was just after it happened, but it's been hours. The infection or whatever is inside me. I can feel it, Johnny. My joints hurt and my vision is a little fuzzy. I admit that at first I thought I was gonna be all right, I'd hoped that maybe it wasn't as bad as I thought, but then I began feelin' sick."

"But Sarah has a cure now, she can save you."

"No, John, it'll take time to make something up. This isn't the movies; it won't take five minutes to make. And we still would have to get all the way back to the island by boat. Besides, the cure is so after you die you stay that way. There's no way of knowing if she could cure someone who's already been bit."

"Why didn't you say something before, Billy?" John asked softly. He was getting choked up, knowing deep down that no matter what he said to try and convince McDermott, his friend wouldn't be leaving the bunker.

"When John? We've been on the run for hours; there's been no time. If you and Sarah had stopped to deal with me, even if there'd been a chance in hell of it working, it would have been the death of us all."

A zombie appeared in the entrance to the silo and McDermott spun around and whacked it on the head with his club. It collapsed to the floor with a cracked skull. Brain matter seeped from the jagged line in its scalp.

McDermott turned around to face John again. "Go, John, they're here. I'll be fine," he said, trying to do his best to keep his voice strong. "You take care of Sarah for me. Tell her goodbye for me too, all right? Tell her…tell her I'm sorry about all of this."

John had tears in his eyes as he stared at the cocky old Irishman that he called his best friend. He couldn't imagine life without him. "What are you going to do?"

McDermott shrugged. "Well, for starters, I'm gonna go back to *The Ritz* and get my booze. I could use a drink like you wouldn't believe. Then I guess I'll find a nice place to hole up and enjoy the time I have left, however little that is."

"But you could come with us. At least then you'd be with friends at the end."

"And have that Langford guy lay me on a slab when I turned to see how I tick? Sarah told me what he was doing to cadavers he gets a hold of. That guy's almost as crazy as Logan was. No way, that's not gonna happen to me."

John frowned. "I would never let that happen, you know that, Billy. When you finally did turn, I'd put you down myself and bury you in a peaceful place."

"No, Johnny, I don't want you to have to do that, or see me like that. Go now, I'll be fine." He smiled, and the gesture was one of peace and tranquility. McDermott had made his peace with his mortality.

More dragging footsteps could be heard just outside the room. Seconds were all that was left one way or the other.

John's jaw went taut as it always did when he'd made a decision. He tossed McDermott the Lorcin, the Irishman catching the small gun easily.

"Then take this, you'll need it," John said. "And when you get that drink, have one for me, too. In fact, make it a double."

"I will, Johnny, count on it." McDermott turned to go and then paused and looked back at John, who had placed his hands and one foot on the ladder to begin climbing. "Hey, John, we really were heroes, weren't we?"

John's voice shook with sorrow and he nodded his head. "Aye, Billy boy, the grandest of them all."

Without another word, McDermott slipped out of the room, leaving John to stare at the space he'd vacated. A moment later, John heard the sound of wood meeting the bone of a cranium and then the sound of a gunshot. A zombie appeared in the doorway and he began climbing, the club he'd had now on the floor of the bunker. As he climbed, the zombie moaned at the bottom of the ladder but didn't have the dexterity to follow. More ghouls shuffled into the room seconds later. John heard two more gunshots before he was too high to hear anything but the wails of the dead.

Sarah, upon seeing John climbing alone asked, "Where's Bill?"

"He's not coming, Sarah," he replied, tears running heavily down his cheeks. A man never to proud to shy away from emotion, and had no problem showing it now.

Sarah saw his tears as she looked down, and she opened her mouth to say more, but John took his left hand off the ladder and gestured for her to stop. "Later, Sarah, I'll explain it all later. We have a long climb ahead of us. Just give me a minute and I'll tell you everything."

"But Bill?" she said, despite his request.

"He's doing what he wanted. It was his choice. Now go, please."

She nodded, understanding that John needed a minute to regain his composure, though she was dying to know what was going on. Why wasn't McDermott with them? What choice did he make and why? What had happened that would make him go back into the caves?

It took almost an hour to climb to the top of the silo, and by the time they reached the surface, both John and Sarah's arms and legs were shaking from the exertion. Both were starving, not having had anything to eat since the beginning of the day, before they'd left New Eden. There were rations on the RV, and once they returned to it their hunger could be satiated.

As Sarah and then John climbed out of the silo and set foot on solid ground, they both collapsed to the grass and sighed with relief. The day was fading and a beautiful sunset of red and orange filled the sky.

Sarah's cheeks were wet from when she'd been crying over McDermott, after John filled her in while they climbed. At first she had accepted it as stoically as was normal for her character, but as she continued to climb, and was alone with her thoughts, the loss had crept in on her until she began to sob. John had wished he could have held her, comforted her, but on the ladder there was no way. All he could do was say a few comforting words to try and lessen her grief, which was hard because he felt it too.

The area around them was quiet, not a soul—living or dead—in sight. They stayed there for a full ten minutes, resting, gathering their spirits for the trek back to the RV and then the drive to the pier where the boat captain would pick them up. The maps in the RV would tell John what pier to go to for the alternate pickup point. And if it came to the worst case scenario, the RV had a ham radio stashed away in a compartment that could be used to contact New Eden.

It was as Sarah was standing up that she reached to her back pocket to retrieve her notes, wanting to put them somewhere safer, that she found that the pocket was empty. A look of abject terror crossed her face and John, seeing this, went to her, not understanding why she looked so upset.

"What is it, Sarah, what's wrong?"

She turned to look at him, her lower lip trembling. "My notes, John, they're gone."

"What are you talking about?" he asked, not understanding. "You said you had them."

"I did. They were in my back pocket. I put them there before the dead attacked us. But I never moved them to someplace else. There wasn't time to think of it, we were all so busy just trying to stay alive."

John didn't know what to say so he said nothing.

"They must have fallen out of my pocket somewhere while we were running and fighting. John, they could be anywhere. Anywhere!" she screamed. Tears were flowing down her face once more. It wasn't just the notes, it was everything. McDermott was gone, all the others that had come on the mission, now they were all dead. She may not have known them personally, but they were still people and she felt human life was sacred.

She fell to her knees, her face in her hands as she sobbed. Her shoulders shook as she let it out. John knelt beside her, rubbing her back. Sarah took her hands away from her face and wrapped her arms around John, pressing her face into his chest. His arms wrapped around her and they hugged, two people in the middle of nowhere, in a world ruled by the dead. But despite all of it, there was still love.

"It was all for nothing, John. Bill's dead and it was for nothing. Tom and his men, all gone, dead. And for what?" She was yelling now, her sadness turning to anger. "For what? It was all a waste? It was all for nothing? How can a god, any god, let this kind of thing keep going on?"

John let her rave for as long as she wanted, and when she was out of fuel, exhausted both mentally and physically, he stood her up and put her at arm's length from him. Her eyes were closed and tears rolled done her cheeks, only now they were tears of rage.

"Sarah, look at me," John said softly.

She ignored him, her eyes closed, her head hanging low.

"Sarah, look at me, damn it," he repeated. This time his voice was more forceful.

Slowly, she opened her eyes, sniffed, and looked up at him.

He smiled at her, his hands coming up to cup her face, his thumbs gently caressing her cheeks to wipe away the tears. "Sarah darling, it wasn't for nothing. We tried…and as long as there are people who'll put their lives on the line for the greater good, maybe there's still hope for humanity."

She laughed slightly, forcing it to come out with a trembling voice. "That's an awfully positive thing to say considering the speech you gave me before, right after I'd amputated Miguel's arm."

He shrugged. "People change, Sarah," he replied almost casually. "Maybe being with you has changed me a little, too."

She hugged him again, and he placed a hand under her chin and tilted her face up to his. They kissed. Softly at first, then more passionately as each reveled in the fact they were still alive.

"Come, on, let's get going, we still have a ways to get back to the pier, but first we need to get to the RV," he said.

They began walking, and soon reached the perimeter fence where the hole had been cut. John slid in after Sarah, then closed the hole behind him, simply by wrapping some of the cut links around unbroken ones.

The RV was still where it had been parked, and it was a simple task for John to hot wire the engine after getting inside by forcing the door. The keys were no doubt somewhere in the bunker, still in Frank's pocket.

John drove the RV close to the perimeter fence so that he and Sarah had a quick view of the field and the open elevator shaft that led to the bunker. As zombies pounded on the side of the RV, he and Sarah gazed out the windshield at the place they had called home for so long, and was now the final resting place for so many of their friends, and even more of their enemies.

Finally, John put the RV into gear and began to drive off, the zombies either getting shoved out of the way or crushed under the wheels of the RV.

The sunset splashing across the sky more than any other was a sunset of the dead—not the living—but John still had hope that there could be a better future. Sarah had re-read some of her notes upon finding them, and before putting them in her back pocket and losing them, it was highly possible that with time, she and Prof. Langford could still create a vaccine for the walking dead.

In a world where the dead walked, anything was possible.

You just had to have hope.

Epilogue

An unknown time later, deep within the corridors of the bunker, the moans and wails of the dead echoed off the walls with a chilling finality.

In many places there were zombies huddled in groups, each of them feeding on the remains of the slaughtered men who had foolishly arrived in their domain. Even where Tom had died in a blazing explosion of blood and gore, the dead gathered, peeling gobbets of flesh from the walls and floor to greedily shove them into their mouths.

In one desolate corridor, a few pieces of paper blew slightly in an errant wind, due to fire doors being open somewhere in the complex. On the papers were numbers and formulas, and on the top of each was the name *Dr. Sarah…* With the last name scribbled so that the name was unreadable. One of the overhead lights was flickering, thanks to a stray bullet that had hit one of the long fluorescent bulbs that hung on the ceiling in pairs, leaving the other one struggling to stay on.

A zombie slowly walked down the corridor, taking its time as there was nowhere to go. One of its shoes stepped on some of the papers, then the other shoe did the same. The bottom of the ghoul's shoes were sticky with blood and the papers immediately stuck to the soles to be dragged away deeper into the bunker.

Security cameras were in each corridor, though they hadn't worked since a few months after the dead began to walk.

But if the one in this corridor had still functioned, it would have panned up from the bloody shoes, up the short body coated in blood, until it rested on the pale and bloody face of Bill McDermott.

There was a large chunk of flesh torn from his neck, and from the blood coating the front of his clothes, it was painfully clear the man had bled out. The blank eyes were sunken into his head, and his hair, usually a mess anyway, was even more tangled with dried blood.

In his right hand he held a bottle of brandy, though the bottle itself was long empty. Acting out of instinct, from some long forgotten memory, he tipped the bottle to his cracked lips and mimed drinking. After a full minute, he lowered it to his side, turned around, and started walking away, the empty bottle swinging lazily by his side.

He was now one of the walking dead, and would forever stalk the halls of the underground bunker.

VICTORY OF THE DEAD
ANTHONY GIANGREGORIO

CLAN OF THE BIGFOOT
BY ANTHONY GIANGREGORIO
LIVING DEAD PRESS.COM

UNDEAD PRESS

UNDEADPRESS.COM

ZOMBIE FICTION AT ITS BEST!

www.ingramcontent.com/pod-product-compliance
Lightning Source LLC
Chambersburg PA
CBHW070436120726
47910CB00003B/802